MEKANISMO

Journal

II

ARGO NAVIS

A NOVEL IN TIME

Copyrights

No part of this book may be reproduced or transmitted in any form or by any means, electronic or mechanical, including photocopying, recording, or by any information storage and retrieval system, without permission in writing from the copyright owner.

The right of **Bill Allerton** to be identified as the author of this work has been asserted by him in accordance with the Copyright, Designs and Patents Act, 1988.

This book is dedicated to
my long-suffering partner
and Muse

Bryony Doran

CONTENTS

The Mechanism

Around Easter 1900, Captain Dimitrios Kondos and his crew of sponge divers from Symi stopped at the Greek island of Antikythera to wait for favourable winds. During the layover, they began diving off the island's coast wearing the standard diving dress of the time – canvas suits and copper helmets.

Diver Elias Stadiatis descended to 45 meters (148 ft) depth, then quickly signalled to be pulled to the surface.

He described a heap of rotting corpses and horses strewn among the rocks on the seafloor.

Thinking the diver was drunk from nitrogen in his breathing mix at that depth, Kondos donned diving gear and descended to the site. He returned to the surface with the arm of a bronze statue.

Shortly thereafter the men departed as planned to fish for sponges but, at the end of the season, they returned to Antikythera and retrieved several artefacts from the wreck.

Kondos reported the finds to the authorities in Athens, and Hellenic Navy vessels were quickly sent to support the salvage effort from November 1900 through 1901.

Together with the Greek Education Ministry and the Royal Hellenic Navy, the sponge divers salvaged numerous artefacts. By the middle of 1901, divers had recovered bronze statues, one named "The Philosopher", the Youth of Antikythera (Ephebe) of c. 340 BC, and thirty-six marble sculptures including Hercules, Ulysses, Diomedes, Hermes, Apollo, three marble statues of horses (a fourth was dropped during recovery and was lost on the sea floor), a bronze lyre, and several pieces of glasswork. Many other artefacts were found and the entire ensemble was taken to the National Archaeological Museum in Athens.

The death of diver Giorgos Kritikos and the paralysis of two others due to decompression sickness put an end to work at the site during the summer of 1901.

On 17 May 1902, archaeologist Valerios Stais made the most celebrated find while studying the artefacts at the National Archaeological Museum in Athens. He noticed that a severely corroded piece of bronze had a gear wheel embedded in it and legible inscriptions in Koine Greek. The object would come to be known as the Antikythera Mechanism.

Originally thought to be one of the first forms of a mechanised clock or astrolabe, it is now referred to as the world's oldest known analogue computer.

Under the direction of Dr. Lazaros Kolonas, a new team recovered nearly 300 artefacts and human remains of the crew and passengers.

A five-year comprehensive survey program which began in 2021 recovered additional artefacts, including the head of a marble statue, possibly the missing head of a statue of Hercules, recovered from the same site in 1902.

Although the retrieval of artefacts from the shipwreck was highly successful and accomplished within two years, dating the site took much longer. It was speculated that the ship was carrying part of the loot of General Lucius Cornelius Sulla Felix (138BC to 78BC)(latterly also named *Epaphroditos, Favoured of Venus)* from the successful Roman siege of Athens in 86BC and was on its way to Italy.

A reference by the rhetorician Lucian of Samosata to one of Sulla's ships sinking in the Antikythera region gives credence to this theory and coins discovered on the wreck in the 1970s were found to have been early Roman.

In 1974, Professor Derek de Solla Price from Yale University published his interpretation of the Antikythera mechanism.

He argued that the object was indeed an analogue calendar computer. From gear settings and inscriptions on the mechanism's faces, he concluded that the mechanism was made prior to 87 b.c. and lost shortly afterward.

CHRONICLE

VIII

VISIONS

1999

AUGUST 16th.
MONDAY

6:31 P.M.

'Fabrienne… *Fabrienne…*'

Raoul snatches the finished device from her. She moves a hand towards it but he pushes her away. 'I can't let you hold it again until I know why it has this effect on you.'

He puts the device in the empty clock-case at the end of the bench, locking the door against the fine bronze gears and gleaming dials.

'What happened to you? Where did you go?'

'I didn't go anywhere.' She knows the lie will register through the touch of her fingers on his skin… and hopes that he will allow her this small deception.

The vision of a high sun over ochre dust and small rocks had been too complete… there had been other people… other voices… she pushes her fingers through her long blonde hair, shaking it out.

Raoul leans back against the bench. 'When I touch it, the whole mechanism seems to spin at random and I can make no sense of it. Wherever it is your mind decides to take you, it seems you must go alone.'

'That's because…'

The rest of the statement eludes her. It has disappeared along with the voices and the visions when Raoul took away the device.

In the place the mechanism had taken her to, she felt she

had already owned the answer. The key to that must be somewhere between now… and there.

'Raoul… I need to hold it again.'

'You know that I can't let you.'

'You are my brother… not my keeper.'

'I am both.'

In her vision, she had experienced a sensation of hands pushing through hair, again and again, displacing a weight and lustre unlike her own.

She stares at her fingers in the poor workshop light.

There is a fine ochre dust in the webs between.

'I may not be alone, Raoul.'

'I will always be here.'

'Of course you will.'

Her smile masks an earlier vision, also shown her by the device, of a bullet carving a slow path through the air. It is copper-coloured and the airstream through which it flows draws a cloak of silence behind it.

With the part of her brain still connected to the device, she wonders why the bullet is not rotating.

AUGUST 17th
TUESDAY

5:32 A.M.

Fabrienne has woken early and dressed in silence. The device had called her again from her childhood room in Maman's.

She has made her way quietly to Rue Coste Chaude where Raoul is still sound asleep in Artus' old bed in the house that cradles the workshop.

She takes the device from among the rafters where Raoul has hidden it, but for now it remains silent in her hands. She replaces it in its hiding place.

She sweeps through sawdust and filings on the bench, clearing a familiar patch. Under her fingers a faded black stain describes the rough shape of a cross. She presses until her arm aches. This stain and her memories are all she has left of Artus… but his blood soaked into the bench has always seemed to be the real bond.

He had shown it to her many years before, trying to explain in the way a child might understand that while it remained, so would a part of him.

She stares upwards in an appeal to the dust of time layered on the rafters and shelves but the whole workshop is silent tonight. The drawers are lipped shut, the window tight and impenetrable.

'Artus… I need another pair of shoes… I have been shown a journey. One I must make without you or Raoul.'

She opens her eyes again, searching for the sign she knows has been left.

In his time, Auguste Godenot had left the drawings. She has always wondered if he could have known… but no… that seems impossible.

Hanging from a nail behind the door is a sheet of oak-tanned leather. Cut from it were the soles of the shoes that Artus had repaired for her when she first visited Oriel. He had wanted to use it for other things but she had asked him not to… the holes being reminders of the emptiness created by her silent years. She takes it down, noticing two larger shapes drawn on the leather. Dropping it to the floor she places her bare feet inside the patterns. They fit exactly. She looks up, and begins to read aloud the carved sampler the leather has been hiding.

I saw in his hand a long spear of gold, and at the iron's point there seemed to be a little fire…

She knows exactly where the key to the Chapel padlock hangs… she has stolen it many times.

AUGUST 17th
TUESDAY

6:48 A.M.

The candle is so vast that decades have accumulated in frozen waves of wax around its base. Fabrienne lights it with one of Raoul's boiler matches. The plaster saints are more than real in this shifting light... bat-wings of emotion flickering their painted eyes as she moves around.

Behind the altar is another statue, much smaller than the others.

Inscribed at its base are the words:

THE ECSTASY OF SANTA TERESA DE ÀVILA
AFTER THE STYLE OF GIAN LORENZO BERNINI

AUGUSTE GODENOT
1939

She sets the statue on the altar where the candle sheds its glow.

There is something about the face of Santa Teresa that seems familiar to Fabrienne. The painted eyes of grey-blue... the gold-leaf of her hair... but her expression is what now seeks all of Fabrienne's attention.

The Angel inflicting her pain is tall, handsome and remorseless. The strength of his arm so assured... the spear in his hand so informed by the way the Saint offers her heart for piercing that he has little need for aim.

Fabrienne blows the dust from it.

The tip of the spear is bright red... the only relief from the dusty wood and the verdigris of the brass. She scrapes at it with a fingernail. It is hard and polished under the dust.

She holds a match to it and sealing wax flows like blood across the Saint's breast.

Beside the Angel's fingers are two small wings, she grips them and the spear slides easily from his hand. Held in the light it is fluted unevenly along its length. The tip she has uncovered is hollow and smooth with a bevelled edge… the way she has suspected that it must be.

The wings fit inside her own fingers like the head of a key.

Raoul will take this from her if he finds it… but now, not even for his sake… could she wish to be rid of it.

7:20 A.M.

Raoul has never been good at secrets. Fabrienne has always known where he has hidden the device. It has called out to her so often across the early hours, dragging her from sleep to read again the old magazine article Auguste had stashed away along with his notes and drawings.

Taking it down now, she inserts the key she has found fully home, prodding the wheels into alignment as it passes.

As it reaches the farthest point the light above her is extinguished.

Fabrienne stares upwards to find nothing but an echo of the bulb behind her eyes… but in that nothing there seems to be everything… the pain that Raoul had to embrace… his taking of another life to save hers and that of Maman… and somehow that pain is sweet and she recognises the desperation and goodness contained within his gift… and the selfishness of silence which was all she'd had to offer by way of return.

She turns the key.

'Fabrienne… *No!*'

Culled from sleep by a sudden compulsion of voices, Raoul prises the device from her fingers.

'You promised me. What kind of a sister breaks her promise to…'

'Raoul there is something here… but I don't know what it is.'

'It is a nothing, Fabrienne. And if it is anything it is called danger. A thing you have always failed to recognise.'

'But I have never shied away from.'

'I know you are not safe alone with this. I will look after

it while you accept the archeology place you were offered at Uni. Perhaps the roots of this future you think you see are buried somewhere in the past.'

L'UNIVERSITÉ DE NÎMES
LANGUEDOC-ROUSSILLON
FRANCE

2006

MAY 23rd.
TUESDAY

9:30 A.M.

'Professeur Henri, I *have* to leave…'

'But Fabrienne, your graduation… and the dig on Antikythera you requested with André Barnard… I have a letter only this morning. He has agreed and the papers are due back from the Cretan Authorities in one week.'

'I can be back by then.'

Henri's reply carries the concern she has lately come to expect. Since she had asked him to clarify a date for her, he has become attentive in a way she finds uncomfortable.

'He has taken on a new assistant already this week. Do not let this opportunity slip away.'

'I had a phone call today. My brother, Raoul… he has been…'

She hesitates for the words she doesn't want to speak, scanning the length of the path and the oaks that line either side where they cast light and shade, but finds no further inspiration. These years away from Maman and Raoul have seemed an eternal winter.

Henri Lefevre intrudes into her thoughts.

'There has been an accident?'

'No… a fire in his workshop.'

'Is that not the same thing?'

'I can't say. I just know my brother. He is a lot of things but not careless. I need to find out what happened.'

'Can you not leave that to the police?'

'The police? What makes you think of the police?'

'I don't know. Would that not be a natural assumption?'

'Professeur… Raoul and I… there are things the police would never understand.'

Even after all the time he has spent with her, Henri Lefevre finds himself unable to penetrate the ages that seem to layer and shift within her face behind the twenty-six years of her perfect skin, the subtle geometry of her nose and the arc of her lips.

His question stalls at the pale, grey-blue surface of her eyes, with their single green fleck almost hidden in the left iris.

'Such as?'

'I cannot tell you that, Professeur. It would not be fair.'

'Fair to whom?'

'To you.'

He steers her away from the path, walking them beneath an oak where the leaf-shadow ripples the blonde of her hair, all the while fighting to combat the emotional gravity of her attraction.

'Can you not let me be the judge of that?'

'No.'

'Then you must make your own judgement. I only hope it leads you safely back here in time.'

As he reaches out to take her hand, the movement triggers pain in the freshly-stitched wound across his ribs.

RUE EUGÈNIE IMBERT
LA ROQUE-SUR-PERNES
FRANCE

2006

MAY 25th.
THURSDAY

11:52 A.M.

Even through the closed taxi windows, the brittle chatter of the cascade can be heard rising from the narrow cleft beside the road.

'Stop here.'

'I am booked to take you up into La Roque.'

'I shall walk from here.'

The taxi Fabrienne hired from Carpentras, the nearest town she can reach by rail, pulls off the road onto a dry verge.

'But… *Ma'mselle…*'

'I shall also pay you in full.'

Fabrienne hoists the rucksack and waits until the car has turned in the road, then climbs over the low wall to slide down through rich grass until her feet meet a worn path.

She walks along it for a while, lost in the noise and the fine tang of clean water in the air until she finds the log steps Artus d'Horo had inserted into the bare earth for her many years ago.

She descends them sidewise to the cascade. The riven limestone has intrigued her since she was a child… the holes down which water disappears to come riveting out into the air further downslope.

Lifting her head, she glances up to where the Chateau looms above the village, recalling leaves in the wilderness of her hair… the steady thump of Raoul's feet behind her… unable to catch hers as she flew unshod across this ground with a natural assurance… and the exasperated timbre of his calling voice.

She hefts the pack and climbs the bank.

Halfway up the incline she finds the niche in the high wall on her right where Auguste Godenot had erected a seat.

The seat is still there and Fabrienne can discern the newer laths that Artus and then Raoul have replaced in their turn.

The door to the old *Chapelle de Mairie* has remained locked for seven years now and a rusting steel chain spans the eyebolts that run through the frame. The step is as heavily worn in the centre as she remembers but the stone is now flaking from disuse. She hitches the pack and moves on up the hill.

The cobbles feel strange beneath her feet until she leans against the wall and takes off her boots, stringing the laces together around her neck.

She stands upright, allowing her bare feet to flex against the rounded surfaces.

Now… at last… it feels like home.

MAY 25th.
THURSDAY

12:28 P.M.

Black-on-yellow checker-tape spans the width of the workshop yard, and the dirt path that Artus had always been about to pave has been churned by Gendarmerie boots.

Fabrienne dips an arm into the bottom of the murky old water tank until her fingers find the weighted container in its three layers of sealed polythene.

There will be time to collect this later.

She steps over the black earth, keeping her feet in the grass where they will leave little sign. To the right of the smashed door is a small blocked-off window where the flue from the boiler exits through a pane of metal. She reaches over to tilt the zinc flashing above it.

The spare key is still there.

The inside of the workshop is flat and two-dimensional, the image of a hundred and fifty years of hard work burned into a black amorphous invisibility. She looks up to find the old bullet hole that Artus had told her the story of, but now light pours through where the roof has collapsed.

Stepping over charred wood, Fabrienne follows the trail left by the fire where it travelled from the workbench, up the wall, clinging to ancient racks of seasoned timber, until it met the clutter and debris stashed amongst the roof trusses.

She pulls a tool drawer from under the bench and lifts out two charred canvas rolls. Without unfastening the cords she knows exactly what is carved into their handles.

She puts them on the bench beside the blackened remains of a third.

The contents of the next drawer are similar. There is a soot covering that obliterates the graduated scales on rules and coats her hands with a grease-like residue.

She opens another, filled with blackened paper.

In the corner between the benches, the spare timbers have shrunk away in the heat. Fabrienne finds the barrel of the old rifle amongst them.

She reaches over and lifts it out. The stock has been protected by the stacked timber but the metal is as blackened as the wall behind it. The bolt is covered in congealed grease but works easily as she ejects an unexpected live round from the chamber. She picks up the shell and slips it into the top of her pack. Holding the rifle with scorched paper from the drawer, she wipes her prints from it and puts it back in the corner.

Above the rifle is a nail, hammered into a gap in the brickwork. On the nail are several keys, labels burned off by the fire. Fabrienne carefully selects one. It follows the shell into her rucksack.

By a corner of brickwork and shielded from the worst of the fire is an old clock case that Artus had given her as a store for her pictures many years ago. She takes a knife from the tool drawer and inserts it between the door and its casing until she feels the slight click of the hidden latch.

It is empty.

By her feet is an outline in chalk that the Gendarmerie have drawn. She reaches down to touch the edge of it. Her fingertips press through dark layers of grime into the fabric of the rough concrete itself until a sense of very recent history courses through her body…

MAY 21st.
SATURDAY

10.14 A.M.

'Hey, boy?'

Raoul spins around. He'd been totally absorbed in the shaping of a new gear for the wall clock in the Café.

'I didn't hear you come in. Thought I'd locked the door…'

'Maybe you did, son. But a key on the window ledge is a no-brainer.'

The man walks over to the centre of the workshop and rotates slowly on one heel, taking in the century and a half of collected debris hanging the walls around him.

'Is your father… boss… in?'

Raoul slides from the leather-topped stool, finding himself a good six inches taller than the other man, and at least forty years younger.

Where Raoul has a shock of dark blonde hair, this man's is thick and grey, streaked with a little remaining black and tightly trimmed around the temples.

Despite his apparent age he moves with an easy grace and Raoul can see that it makes sense to maintain a distance.

He moves the stool to the corner away from the boiler and places his back against the bench. 'I'm all there is.'

The man pushes his hands deep into the pockets of his overcoat and pulls out a piece of paper.

'Says outside… Auguste Godenot.' He taps the paper. 'I checked it… right here.'

He holds it out to Raoul who takes a look and laughs quickly. 'How old is that?'

The man shrugs. 'Don't know… it's all I got.'

He takes another step towards Raoul.

Raoul feels along the bench behind him until he finds the tool roll. His fingers twitch open the string and it rolls itself out flat across the sawdust and brass filings. His hand closes around the handle of a slender gouge. The outlines of the inlay tell his fingers it reads *Artus d'Horo*.

'What do you want with Auguste anyway?'

The man smiles and backs away a half-step, coming to rest with his left foot slightly behind his right. His knees bend reflexively.

'I'm a collector. I was told he had something old… for sale maybe.'

'If he did…' Raoul hooks the heel of his shoe on the rail behind him. '…it was fifty years ago.'

The smile leaves the man's face. 'Then you must be Artus.'

Raoul laughs again. 'Take a good look at me. How old do you think I am?'

A smile flickers briefly across the man's face, but if last time Raoul found it dismissive… only vaguely threatening… the expression that remains behind unsettles him to his stomach.

'Don't play with me, boy. I've come a long way…'

Raoul returns the look with a stony glare. 'To the wrong place and time.'

The man stuffs the paper back into his pocket. 'I don't think so.'

The hard edge of the bench seems intent on pressing Raoul forward into a conflict he neither wants nor understands. 'Would you mind closing the door on your way out? I have work to do.'

The man shifts around until he becomes a solid shape that blocks the path between Raoul and the door.

'So do I.'

'What exactly is it you're looking for?'

'I think you know what it is… Raoul.'

'If you know my name, what was all the other stuff about?'

The man takes a photograph from an inside pocket and pushes it at Raoul.

'Just to let you know I done my homework. Know this girl?'

Raoul glances at a recent photograph of Fabrienne.

She is on the bridge at Université striding purposefully away from the main entrance with the white stone archway behind her. She is wearing boots.

He hesitates, hiding the surprise in his voice. '… No.'

'And I'm the Tooth Fairy.'

Raoul breathes a sigh of relief as the man turns his back and strides over to the workshop door, but he opens it to let another man step across the narrow threshold. Raoul can see that this one is younger… much younger.

The older man locks the door again and drops the key into his overcoat pocket. 'This is my friend. He's come to help me with the negotiation. What say we all sit down and talk about this?'

Raoul reaches for his jacket, the gouge still tight in his hand behind his back. 'Then let's go to the Café. As you can see, the seating arrangements are a little primitive in here.'

'We don't mind primitive, Raoul. Fact is… I've often been accused of that myself. Don't you believe it though. I always try to be gentlemanly 'bout things. Folk don't often see that side of me.'

Raoul moves sideways along the bench so that the door comes into plain sight.

'We don't often get a chance to meet the Tooth Fairy.'

The older man moves across to block Raoul's view.

'Now… Henri…' The younger man jumps in a way that tells Raoul this is his real name. '…is here as my interpreter, but we're not going to need that, are we Raoul? He also knows a thing or two about what we're here to collect. Isn't that right, Henri?'

Henri nods, a nervous twitch closing the lid of his left eye. Raoul slides back along the edge of the bench until he reaches the corner. The gap there is packed with short lengths of ancient, dry timber.

Without turning, Raoul fights to remember where in the stack the muzzle of the old rifle stands.

'Now, Raoul…'

The direct route to the door is open, but Raoul knows if tries to run they will catch him in a pincer movement… and then there is the lock to get through…

'Raoul, I want you to be comfortable here. First rule of any negotiation… put your adversary at their ease. Puts you in the 'cat-bird' seat. Know what I mean? No? Perhaps Henri here can translate… later.'

The man removes his overcoat. The suit under it is a plain, functional dark grey.

'You and I need to talk first about clocks…'

Raoul slips the gouge, blade first, into the back pocket of his jeans. 'Then why all the drama? I can talk about clocks all day.'

'Don't be smart, Raoul. It's just a device… but then you know something about devices too, don't you.'

Raoul brings both hands out in front of him. 'Get to the point.'

'The point is that… a long time ago… even before you were a twinkle in some mad, drunken bastard's eye… in this very workshop…' He lifts his gaze to the accumulated layer of dust coating everything stacked above him in the rafters.

'…our old friend, Auguste Godenot, was visited by a

priest, and this priest was something else again, Raoul… a *real* piece of work. You familiar with the term?'

'I watch TV.' Raoul folds his arms and shifts his position. He relaxes the muscles in his legs enough to turn his hip slightly. If his suspicions are correct, even a half-step might be an advantage.

'And this priest brought a device for Auguste to repair.'

Raoul laughs nervously. 'Well it isn't here now or I would have found it… and if I do… you can have it back by Thursday.'

'No, no, no, Raoul. I know you don't have that device. What I want is the other one… the one that Artus made.'

Raoul straightens up, at last on solid ground. 'Artus made no device. Not while I was here… and I was his apprentice.'

'Now… I hear that, boy. Honesty always has a certain ring. You looked me in the eye too. I like that in a man.'

Raoul unfolds his arms and hooks his thumbs into his pockets. 'Then we have no further business. So why don't you just leave.'

He spins around, reaching out for the barrel of the rifle. It leaps upwards from the pile in the grip of his left hand. With his right he works the bolt, ejecting the empty cartridge kept in there. A live round enters the chamber as he swings it towards the older man.

The man stands his ground. From the corner of his eye Raoul notices the man he'd called Henri stepping sideways to the door. The older man stops him with a look.

He turns back to face Raoul.

'Have you seen yourself with that thing? It's as old as I am. I can see the rust in the barrel from here.'

Raoul keeps him firmly in place at the end of the gun. 'Is that a chance you want to take?'

'Hell yes. If you want to blow your head off go ahead. Save someone else the trouble.'

The man reaches into his suit jacket below the shoulder. Raoul is so intent on what his hand withdraws that he doesn't see the kick that springs from nowhere, knocking the gun barrel sideways.

At a shout from the older man, Henri leaps on him.

Raoul tries to get the gun up but only catches Henri with the sight, ripping flesh open with the force of his swing. He drops to the floor, pinned by the weight of Henri with blood from the deep chest wound spilling across them both. He tries to kick himself free but his legs are held fast by the older man who lashes them with plastic ties from his pocket.

'Right, Henri. Let's turn him over.'

Between them, Henri and the older man manage to grasp Raoul by the wrists. Henri seems weak and if Raoul had both hands free… but the older man holds him one-handed in an iron grip. The plastic ties bite into his flesh as they drag him into an upright position.

They prop him against the bench, the older man breathing deeply to regain his inner equilibrium.

Henri shakes the dust from his clothes. His hands come away covered in blood.

'I didn't sign up for this. Do you have a first aid kit in here?'

Raoul's eyes give an involuntary flick towards a cupboard on the wall. 'No.'

'Of course he has. But there's no point looking…' The older man rips away Henri's shirt. 'What kind of injury does a clockmaker get? Cut finger?'

He takes a quick look at Henri's wound. 'You won't find anything to cover that. Clean it up with your shirt and try to hold the edges together.'

He turns away to rummage through the drawers until he finds what he wants.

'Here…' He tears off a length of duct tape. 'Now move

your fingers. That's it. It'll hurt like hell when you pull it off but at least you won't bleed all over the rental.'

He stands up to face Raoul. 'Raoul, are you happy now? It didn't need to get this intense. There are easier ways than this, you know.'

'Such as? Perhaps I should just lie down and let you kill me?'

'Now, Raoul... you're the one who's talking about killing here... though I do hear that you're some kind of an amateur in that field. No... killing is the strategy of last resort. You could be so much more useful to me alive. How you come out of this depends on you.'

Henri arranges his jacket to cover the blood stain that has soaked his shirt. It is drying now, blackening in the warmth from his body and the heat from the stove in the corner.

'You didn't tell me he was a killer. I think I would not have come.'

The older man throws him his overcoat to wear.

'Our friend Raoul here is a particular kind of killer. What do they call it, Raoul? Like something Greek or Roman...'

'He's a maniac?'

'Get a grip, Henri. One man hardly makes it a rampage.'

Henri shrugs his arms into sleeves too short for him and stares blankly at the pale beige cuffs protruding. 'I still think you should have told me.'

The older man sits down on the leather stool, his eye firmly on Raoul.

'Where would we be if everybody knew everything... eh Raoul?'

'You seem to know enough about me.'

'Well... that's just the point, Raoul. Enough. I learned to be happy with that many years ago, but you... you couldn't leave well enough alone. And as for your sister...'

'My sister? I don't have one.'

'Raoul… *enough*. She is being well looked after… is that not true, Henri?'

Henri nods vigorously. 'Like a daughter.'

The older man wedges a poker into the burning ash in the stove. 'See, Raoul? And I'm going to be just like a father to you.'

10:55 A.M.

'Henri! Search the drawers.'

'You knew he wouldn't talk. Did you have to kill him?'

The man rolls Raoul over onto his back. With practised ease he reaches over to close his eyelids. 'If he won't tell me what he knows, he sure as hell won't tell anyone else now, will he?'

'I didn't agree to this… wait… you knew all along you were going to kill him… or you wouldn't have used my name.'

'Slip of the tongue.'

'Not even I believe that.'

'Henri. The drawers. Find me that device if you don't want to join him…'

Henri pulls open all the drawers that are visible along the front of the bench but none of them seem large enough to hold the thing they are searching for.

The older man, introduced to Henri only as 'Frank' a few days earlier, kneels beside Raoul's body cutting away the ties.

'Under the bench, Henri. Have you checked under the bench? There's always a hidden drawer in these places.'

Henri peers into the dark, debris-ridden spaces beneath the bench. 'No… nothing.'

Frank spins on one heel, taking in the whole of the workshop at a glance. 'Check out these clocks.'

A collection of partially dismantled cases sits along the

back of the bench. 'Looks like he never finished anything…'

Henri examines them in turn. 'Nothing… just clocks.'

'Try the one in the corner near the boiler.'

'I did. It's too light. The device can't be in there.'

'Humour me.'

'It's locked.'

'Then open it.'

'I don't have the key.'

Frank pushes the gouge from Raoul's pocket into his hand. 'I said, humour me.'

Henri slides the gouge into the gap between the door and the edge of the cabinet and lifts. The door swings open.

'It's just full of paper.'

'Then let's see what it is…'

Frank riffles through the loose sheets. 'These are just circles…'

Henri takes them from him as he discards them onto the bench. 'Not just circles. Remarkably perfect circles, drawn by the same hand. Look… no compass pin holes.'

'By Raoul?'

Henri refuses to look down at the body of Raoul beside his feet. His hands shake as he lowers the papers back to the bench.

'I would say no… but look… if I was to cut these out and put them together like this…' He overlays one piece carefully with two others, the dark pencil lines showing vaguely through the cheap paper. 'This is the ring. The others are a sun wheel and two planet wheels… see?'

Frank peers over his shoulder.

'And what does that make?'

Henri begins to sift the papers into what he feels may be the right order.

'It makes an epicyclic gear.'

'And?'

'And clocks don't use an epicyclic gear… so this wouldn't make a clock.'

Frank deals the papers one by one onto the bench top and stops suddenly. 'What's that one mean?'

Henri picks it up. The encircling arcs are perfectly drawn but the scale is different from the other drawings he'd found.

At the bottom, between the left and right arc is the name '*Artus*', printed so that it completes that part of the circle. At the top is another. '*Oriel*'. In the centre is the name, '*Mignon*'.

He screws the paper into a ball and puts it in his pocket while Frank's back is turned.

'Henri. Open that can. See what's in it.'

Henri unscrews the lid and takes a sniff. His head jerks back, eyes filling with tears. 'I think it's turpentine. He must use it for the varnish.'

'Well… he don't look so shiny now.'

Between them they turn Raoul's body over and lay him face down. Frank arranges Raoul's arms so that his head is supported on them. 'There. That's pretty.'

'Pretty?'

'Look… this guy works alone in his workshop… he does a little varnishing. He's overcome by the fumes from the tin. They meet the fire in the boiler… history. That's something you should know about.'

He nudges Henri towards the door. 'Here's the key. Get that thing unlocked.' He scoops up all the loose papers and folds them into his jacket pocket. 'Ok. Get ready to light up.'

Frank shakes the tin onto the concrete, making his way back to the door. Henri waits in the open doorway.

'What shall I light it with?'

'You could try using the paper you stuffed into your pocket but if you do…' Frank nods to where Raoul is laid out on the floor. '…you will join him.'

Henri hands over the paper. Frank stretches it out flat with a palm. 'Get that fire lit… use a stick in the boiler or something. Get imaginative.'

He steps outside into the daylight, examining the names on the paper. From behind him comes a soft 'whoomf' as the tin of thinners explodes.

Henri follows him into the yard, screaming, hands and shirt cuffs ablaze with soft blue flame.

'Jeezus, Henri.' Frank plunges Henri's arms into the water tank by the door until the flames disappear. 'Shut the fuck up.'

He locks the door and returns the key back over the window.

Fabrienne reels away from the vision she has been given, but holds on to the faint hope that she is not too late to save the rest of her family. Not knowing who to go to first, she takes the easy road downhill towards the river.

MAY 25TH.
THURSDAY

12:57 P.M.

'Don't say anything. Just let me look at you…'

Holding Oriel at arm's length, Fabrienne examines the fresh bruise below her left eye. There are other marks where cruel fingers have pushed deep into the skin of her slender arms. She rubs the skin with the pad of her thumb and watches it crinkle and fold with age.

Oriels' eyes fill with tears that spill down her face.

Fabrienne leans in and kisses them.

'Stop that. You are still beautiful.'

Oriel's face creases into a slow smile. 'It is only when I look at you that I feel old. Sit down here beside the fire. I will fetch some timber from outside.'

'I will fetch it.' Fabrienne lowers Oriel gently into the chair, supporting her weight with her hands. As she turns away, she notices thin red lines around Oriel's ankles and wrists.

The wood is where it has always been, in the corner by the wall protected from the rain by an old piece of tarpaulin, but now the tarpaulin has gone. She looks around the garden and finds it caught amongst the spines of the gooseberry bush at the top of the flower bed. As she drags it away she notices that it has ripped in many places. Beneath it, the hole she dug there as a child has been reopened and Artus' old spade is thrown to one side.

White limestone gleams back at her from the bottom.

The kindling has been scattered from the neat stacks that Oriel always keeps it in. Woodlice mill blindly around in the space where the earth has been scratched to see if it has been recently disturbed, but nothing else has been touched this close to the house.

She gathers a few of the driest sticks and carries them inside. 'Do you have any paper?'

'No. My eyes… I can no longer read… even with this.'

Oriel takes Artus' loupe from her skirt pocket and holds it to the light. 'I sometimes even put it in the wrong way round. The neighbours…'

'It's alright… I know where there is some I can use.'

Fabrienne opens the middle drawer of the sideboard to find it empty. 'Where are my drawings?'

'They took them. They took everything. They wanted to know if you had been digging. I told them it was such a long time ago but they wouldn't listen.'

Fabrienne holds Oriel's shoulder lightly until she stops shaking.

'Not now. Let me make tea for us first.'

Fabrienne opens the kitchen cupboard to find that all the containers, biscuit tins and caddies have been opened and their contents dumped in a single heap on the bottom shelf.

'Oriel… who did this?'

Oriel shuffles herself deeper into the chair until the pain in her back lessens a little.

'He said he was the Tooth Fairy.'

'Do not move from that chair.'

Fabrienne takes Oriel's coat from behind the door and spreads it over her.

'I am going up the hill to Maman's. She will have some things we can use to sort you out. I will bring her back with me.'

MAY 25TH.
THURSDAY

1:08 P.M.

'*Maman?*'

The door swings open at Fabrienne's touch. She pushes it wide and steps quietly into the small hallway that leads to the kitchen.

She peers through the crack of the door into the parlour as she passes. '*Maman!*'

Mignon Merle is slumped across two chaise cushions, her damaged leg propped against a third.

Fabrienne kneels beside her and lifts her hand. It is warm. She rubs it harshly between her own.

'Maman… *Maman*… It's Fabrienne…'

Mignon partially opens her eyes. 'Fabrienne? How long have I been here?'

Fabrienne sits her up straight, carefully lowering her leg to the floor. 'I don't know, Maman. I have only just arrived.'

Mignon smiles through half-closed eyes. 'It cannot have been long. I was waiting for Raoul to…' Her face crumples. 'Why did you wake me? I do not want to be awake… not ever.' Her eyes close again.

Fabrienne reaches across her to tenderly lift an eyelid. Only the white of the eye is showing. 'Maman. What have you taken?' She scans the floor and the small side table.

Mignon tries to push her away. 'Nothing. Just a little… for the pain. The doctor…'

'Maman! Where are they? Show me!'

Mignon's handbag is on the floor beside her feet.

Fabrienne wrenches it open. Inside is an empty brown

bottle from the local pharmacy. Fabrienne reads the scrawl on the label… fifty tablets, to be taken as two, four times a day. It was dispensed only yesterday.

'Maman? Where are the tablets?'

Mignon slides back across the sofa as Fabrienne gets to her feet.

'Hold on, Maman. I will be back very soon.'

Fabrienne dashes into the bathroom and ransacks the wall cabinet, scattering old medicines, toothbrushes and the bottle of black hair dye that her mother still uses, despite her and Raoul's insistence that she no longer needs to hide, but there are no more bottles of tablets.

She dials the emergency services from the hall.

'Hello? Yes. Ambulance. Yes? My name is Fabrienne Merle. No, it is not for me. It is for Maman. She has taken tablets. No, I don't know what they are but I am on my way to find out. I shall be back by the time the ambulance arrives. Yes, we are in La Roque…'

1:15 P.M.

In the Place, Fabrienne arrives to find the pharmacy closed for sieste. She rattles loudly on the shutter.

Bruno Dernot from the café over the road comes to his door. 'What do you want? Can't you see they are closed? You are putting my customers off their lunch.'

'It's Fabrienne…' She calls back across the square, her voice clear and loud in the silence since the fountain fell into disrepair. '…and I need the pharmacist.'

'Then come back later. You always were impatient.'

He slams the door behind him.

Fabrienne rushes across and bangs through into the café.

'It is for my maman. She is in trouble.'

'Mignon? *La petit sou…*? How does she get into trouble? You, Fabrienne, are a different kettle of fish.'

Fabrienne holds up the empty tablet bottle. 'I am trying to find out what was in here. I think Maman has taken them all.'

Dernot returns from behind the bar with an identical one and holds them up together. 'For my Migraine.'

'Yes… but what are they?'

He hands her back the empty bottle. 'Paracetamol.'

'Oh, dear God.'

Dernot removes his apron. 'Is there anything I can do?'

'What about your customers?'

'Stuff my customers. Your maman is the only one in the village who has never complained about me.'

Fabrienne catches the edge of the door on her way through. 'Then in that case, can you take some tea, coffee and a few cakes down to Oriel's please? And something to light the fire with?'

'Oriel? With great pleasure, but I thought it was your maman?'

'It is. But in doing this you will prevent a second problem that I do not have time to deal with.'

'Then go… quickly.'

The few customers Bruno has are watching intently. He throws the apron behind the bar. 'Everybody out. Come again tomorrow if you like and I will feed you for free, but for now we are closing. No, no, put down your coffee.'

He stops an elderly, black-clad woman as she gets to the door. 'Danielle? If you have the time, can you come with me?'

'Where are we going, Bruno?'

'To Oriel's house.'

Her seamed face looks up at him, framed by a host of silver hair. 'She curses the ground I walk upon.'

'Then she will not have far to travel these days… and I cannot imagine Oriel holding a grudge no matter what you might have done.'

Danielle huffs quietly. 'We shall see about that.'

1:32 P.M.

Mignon is still slumped where Fabrienne left her. Her hands are growing cold and Fabrienne chafes them with her own, trying to wake her gently. Mignon stirs, moves her head to one side and smiles. Spittle drools from her mouth onto the shoulder of her cardigan. Fabrienne mops at it with a tissue she finds tucked in Mignons' sleeve.

Outside, a siren cuts into silence.

'In here…'

The paramédical shoulders his way through the door carrying a large equipment bag. Fabrienne pushes the brown bottle into his hand. 'Here… I think they were Paracetamol.'

He studies the label. 'Are there any left?'

'No. I think she has taken them all.'

'Do you know how long ago?'

Fabrienne shakes her head. 'No. But she was still awake when I arrived here. Will she be alright?'

'Let's get her in the ambulance and stabilised then see what we can do. Move aside a moment, please.'

'Can I come with her?'

'Of course you can. Do you have a car?'

'No.'

'Then you get to ride with us.'

2:11 P.M.

'*Maman. Maman.* Hold my hand…'

The darkened glass of the ambulance window beside Fabrienne displays the unfamiliar streets of Avignon.

'We are almost at the Hospital, Maman. Soon you will be well again.'

Fabrienne throws a defiant look at the paramedic sitting across from her. 'She will… won't she.'

He disengages her hand so he can read Mignon's pulse.

'I gave her an injection that should stabilise the effects of the tablets and prevent further damage. We carry it with us now, so few people are aware of the damage Paracetamol can cause.'

He checks the straps holding Mignon to the stretcher as the ambulance lurches into the arrivals area. 'It will all depend on how long it was in her liver before we got to her.'

'There is a transplant?'

A professional smile flits across the paramédical's face.

'There remains that possibility… but for now only a possibility. We have to be sure that she would never try this again. There are so many deserving people… so few organs available.'

The back doors fly open.

Fabrienne is ushered aside as the stretcher slides out. She follows its flight through doors along brightly lit corridors, seeing nothing except *Maman.*

2:15 P.M.

There is no reply to Bruno's knock at Oriel's door. Danielle turns away, looking at something at the top of the garden.

Bruno Dernot knocks again.

'Oriel? It is Bruno from the café. Fabrienne has asked me to call.'

The door opens and Oriel wavers before him. At the sight of her he drops the parcel. She stumbles back into the kitchen and he moves forward to catch her.

Danielle turns at his raised voice to see him standing in the kitchen with Oriel clasped in his arms. Her hands are draped around his shoulders, her head rests against his neck.

'I see she hasn't changed much…'

'For God's sake, Danielle. The woman has collapsed.'

'A familiar ploy…'

'Danielle, grab her feet. Help me get her through into the parlour.'

Danielle bends to grasp her by the ankles, noticing the marks left by the plastic tie. 'What has been happening here, Bruno?'

'I don't know… but pick her up quickly. She is shaking fit to die.'

Between them they manoeuvre Oriel into the chair by the hearth.

Danielle begins to build a fire from the old magazines they have brought. 'Look how thin she is. When did she last have a good meal?'

Bruno retrieves the bag, unwrapping biscuits, cake and tea. 'I don't know… she went completely to pieces for a while after Artus… but let us see what we can do now.'

Danielle piles kindling on the growing flames. 'Where is Fabrienne? She was never where you wanted her to be… and always where you didn't.'

'She is seeing to her maman. Mignon is very ill.'

'Is that what all the fuss was about? That little *souris* of a thing?'

'Mouse or not, she is still Fabrienne's maman.'

'I suppose so.' Danielle gets up and walks through into the kitchen to stand by the window, staring out with a curious expression at the hole that has been freshly dug at the top of the garden.

2:35 P.M.

'Oriel! Oriel! Wake up woman. I know you are stronger than this.' Danielle slaps Oriel's face with both hands to attract her attention. 'Snap out of it. Now that fool Bruno has gone I want to know what really happened here.'

Danielle slowly swims into focus before Oriel's eyes.

'Danielle! What are you doing here?'

'Dernot brought me. He thought I might be of use.'

'And how long has he known you?'

'Oriel… leave the past where it lies. Dernot will be back soon. What did they want? Everyone knows you have no money to speak of.'

'I don't know… some kind of clock. Fabrienne might know. I saw her with something that she and Raoul… Can you move my leg please? Ah…'

Danielle straightens up again. 'Why would someone think that you had it?'

'Had what?'

'No matter. It is better this way. Trust me.'

'Danielle, I have known you since I was a child… that is the one thing that I would never do.'

34

Danielle refills the kettle at the kitchen sink.

As the water pours dispiritedly from the tap she peers across the garden to the hole beyond the gooseberry bush.

'Oriel? Did they dig the hole? The burglars, I mean?'

'Yes. They made me tell them where the garden was last dug up. I told them it was many years ago, when Fabrienne was a child… but they were not burglars… they were thieves. They took Fabrienne's drawings, even the ones she did of Artus. They stole my memories.'

'Don't worry.' Danielle stares into the pattern made by the drowned leaves from the teapot, trying to discern a future hidden there, then looks up again to the garden.

'I think you're about to get some new ones.'

3:47 P.M.

The doctors have left and Fabrienne appreciates the silence in which she and maman find themselves.

There is a cannula inserted into the back of Mignon's hand and Fabrienne watches the drip of fluid, counting the periodicity it as if it were a liquid pulse.

Mignon's eyes are wide open and fixed on a point beyond the ceiling tiles. Fabrienne sits back into the chair to await the results of the tests they have just taken. So far they have seemed positive.

'Fabrienne…'

Fabrienne sits up sharply. *'Maman?'*

Mignon's eyes remain unfocused but her voice is much clearer than before. '…you must find your father. He must be told about Raoul.'

'Is that a good idea, maman?' Fabrienne swallows down the bitterness of an old lie. 'He never came to find *us*. Try to sleep for a while.'

'Your father was a good man until the government sent him to Lebanon. When he came back he was changed but he would never speak of the things he had seen there. It is only fair that he knows.'

'War does that to everyone, Maman.'

'Not like this, Fabrienne. I listened to his dreams. I know some of the things he saw and did… the children… the women… and when he touched me… I do not wish to even think about it… but he must be told about Raoul.'

'Maman… if there is a God… Raoul will find papa. Now go to sleep while I check on Oriel.'

6:18 P.M.

Smooth white stones are arrayed across the bottom of the hole in Oriel's garden. They are as Fabrienne remembers them, curved like the vertebrae of a large, sleeping creature. She jumps down into the hole and picks up the spade.

'Wait.'

Fabrienne turns to find Danielle standing over her.

The old woman holds up her hand. 'You do not need to do this.'

Fabrienne turns the tip of the spade under a large, central stone to prise it loose. She lifts it out of the hole and places it beside Danielle's feet.

'Perhaps. We shall see.'

Danielle steps back a pace. 'You may see more than you wish to.'

In the space where the stone has been, Fabrienne places her foot on the spade to push. The blade sinks easily into hollow earth.

She discards a spadeful of soil and a small thing, hard, round and smooth, rolls back into the hole. She bends to pick it up. It is a dark bead, made from a heavy, polished brown stone with a hole drilled through the middle.

She breaks open the clod of earth to discover several more strung along the remnants of a cord.

The next spadeful brings up a blackened cross.

Danielle reaches down to take it from the blade. She offers her other hand to Fabrienne.

'Let's take this into the kitchen. I will tell you all there is to know.'

The kitchen is empty. In the parlour, Oriel sits nervously

beside a hastily made fire where she rocks slowly, hugging her knees to her chest.

Danielle lifts the kettle onto the gas and the ring erupts beneath it in long yellow flame.

'Artus never could do gas.'

She hands the crucifix to Fabrienne who rinses the earth from it in the sink. Under her fingers it comes up clean but the tarnish remains.

'Here… give me that.' Danielle holds out her hand. 'She must have something in here.' She opens the door to the cupboard and steps back in surprise. 'And Oriel always pretends to be such a tidy person.'

She dips her finger into a smear of ketchup oozing across the bottom shelf and rubs some onto the cross. From beneath the oxide, smooth metal gleams in the yellow of the lit gas. She tosses it back to Fabrienne and opens a packet that Bruno has brought from the café. 'Tea?'

Fabrienne holds up the crucifix. 'A name.'

'Tea first… this will involve Oriel and I want her awake enough to listen.'

Oriel is staring deep into the flames, perhaps seeing the same dragon's tongues that Fabrienne has always known it is made from.

Danielle brings the tea things through from the kitchen.

'Dernot has gone back to the café for more things. Everything in the cupboard here has been spoiled so he's replacing it from his own. I think I may come down here to eat instead. Oriel cannot be any worse a cook.'

Fabrienne senses her level of unease. Danielle's fingers are in constant motion and for the first time in Fabrienne's memory she hears uncertainty rather than bitterness in her voice.

'What are you doing here, Danielle? I thought that you and *Grande-maman*…'

'And you thought right, child. Oriel and I once shared a passion for something…'

'You mean Artus?'

'Amongst other things… and looking at your *Grande-maman* I can see that this is not yet the moment. She is not strong enough.'

'Are you surprised?'

'No, but I should be. She always pretended to be strong. Right from the moment she first defied me.'

Fabrienne kneels beside Oriel's chair and tries to engage her eyes. They turn towards her but are so filled with tears she accepts it isn't the present she is seeing.

'*Grande-maman*… I am more sorry than you can know, but this is my fault and I have to leave you. Maman is safe in the Hospital in Avignon and I know that, despite all other considerations, Danielle will allow no more harm to come to you. Bruno will see to that. We have always known he is in love with you. I have been shown a challenge and whatever it turns out to be I know it will define me and I can't lose sight of that. It will not allow me to. Hold on tight until I return, perhaps with the reason for all our lives. But for now I must leave you alone with Danielle… and your memories.'

CHRONICLE

IX

ANTIKYTHERA

2006

JUNE 5th.
MONDAY

8:45 P.M.

The dusk-dark hills of Antikythera shelter the natural bowl of Potamos Bay and, as the ship draws into their shade, scattered buildings appear... white, squat, almost biblical... nested in night-gardens and profiled by sparks of electric light that sway suspended.

The breath of movement through the evening air cools Fabrienne's skin, making her tug at the linen jacket around her shoulders as she makes her way down to the loading deck. As she waits, a small open truck drops towards the harbour. Summoned by the ferry's approach, its bright beams skip amongst the waves. The tarmac beneath its wheels seems an unnatural absence where the land either side is scrubbed ochre dust.

Under the harbour floodlight, Fabrienne sheds her rucksack beside the ramp and settles down on it to wait.

The truck lights sweep by again, ignoring where she sits.

Behind her, she hears the ramp begin to withdraw... the bright hydraulic hiss of the rams... hammer-blows from clamps thumping it securely into place... screws bending water into a dark turbulence behind the ship.

She hears the howl and pulse of bow thrusters as the ship rotates completely before it settles to power out beyond the arms of the bay.

Eyes closed in thought, Fabrienne realises how hollow her plan sounds, even to herself… and, for the first time in her life, how truly alone she feels.

The harbour light above her is extinguished.

In the sudden dark there are footsteps, and fingers that tap lightly against her shoulder. She stands quickly, knees bent at this intrusion, peering into the shadow of his face.

Above him, brighter stars are filtering a graduated sky.

'I'm sorry. I didn't mean to startle you.'

His English had been perfect, yet, without thought, she lapses into her native French.

'You didn't.' She eases herself upright. 'I am…'

He replies in kind. 'You are alone.' He reaches down to help lift her rucksack.

She catches his arm. 'Sometimes I like the chance to be alone.'

He straightens as she swings the bag over her shoulder.

'As you wish. I only wanted to help.'

Behind Fabrienne the jetty is empty. The safety of the ship is now little more than a few diminishing points of light against the sea, taking with them the last of her choices and regrets.

In the darkness, all that remains is this man… and a battered Renault 4 parked against a nearby house wall.

'I am to meet someone. I have a letter. His name is…'

She fumbles in a pocket on the side of the bag, retrieving a small, crumpled sheet of paper.

He takes it from her and smoothes it between his hands.

'Barnard… *Professeur* André Barnard.'

'You can read it in the dark?'

'No, I am it in the dark. And in the dark as real as you are… Fabrienne Merle.'

He turns away and, with the lights from the houses now revealing his face, she recognises him.

'I saw you on the boat.'

He kicks the leather bag on the ground by his feet. 'I have been to Kissamos for medical supplies.… but mostly cigarettes for Alec. And I saw you, too.'

'Why did you not speak to me?'

'Sometimes I like the chance to be alone.'

He picks up his bag. 'My car is over here.'

9:03 P.M.

Fabrienne tracks the erratic weave of tarmac as it winds the slope between subtly-lit houses.

'Wouldn't you be better using headlights?'

'They don't work… but when we get to the top there will be light enough to take us where we are going.'

Fabrienne reaches for a seat belt and notices his smile.

'You won't find one. Like me… the car is very old.'

She braces herself against the side door and studies him.

The faint glow from the Renault dashboard delivers a yellow-orange cast across his face, profiling the narrow Roman nose. In this light he looks no more than thirty.

Perhaps in the sun he will look the age she knows he is.

A crack has opened between the door and frame and the evening air is whipping through, chilling her arm.

'What happens if something comes the other way?'

'The door…'

'You mean I should jump out?'

His laugh is startling, even above the engine grinding away in second gear. 'I mean don't lean on it.'

His tanned fingers twist the gearshift, slamming it to the dashboard. 'The catch was fixed by the man who fixed the headlights.'

Fabrienne pulls the pale linen jacket around her. She shuffles away but holds tight to the handle.

He glances across but his attention is evidently elsewhere. 'When we reach the top I will stop and close your door again.'

Within moments they crest the slope onto the north-south ridge that runs the length of the upland and, through smears on the window where a spread hand has brushed away the dust, the sky flares against the horizon.

Fabrienne raises her hand as a last arc of setting sun pours light into her eyes. Turning round in her seat she sees Potamos Bay below them suffused with blackness, relieved only by shards of house light. Out to sea, the superstructure of the ferry glows bright as it escapes the shadow of the island.

The car begins to slow, swinging across the narrow strip of road towards an outcrop of rock. The engine stalls as it comes to rest against it and the door swings wide the instant Fabrienne lets go of the handle.

André Barnard climbs from the driving seat and taps on the windscreen for her to join him.

He points along the narrow strip of beaten roadway, little more than a pale, twisting ribbon along the spine of the central ridge. 'Welcome to Antikythera, the coincidence of two worlds.'

To Fabrienne's East the island is full dark. To the West, earth, sea and sky are veiled in the reflections of a fallen sun while the land below seems scooped by a giant hand into sinks and hollows in which night is already pooling.

In the southern distance is a ruined tower, sliced vivid by sunset and shadow. Fabrienne turns to face him.

'And which world do you prefer?'

He looks away from her abruptly and slams shut the passenger door.

'Get in the other side. Climb over the seats.'

Fabrienne slides across the seats and nudges the door.

She glances back at him across the deep shadows within

the car, intrigued by the way he combs his fingers through his dark blonde hair as if to brush the sunset from it.

'I'm sorry. I didn't mean to intrude.'

'Why should you feel that? I asked for you to be here.'

'I thought it was I that asked?'

'You did.'

'Then how…?'

The engine breaks into life with a judder that shakes the car.

André lurches it back from the rock where it was resting.

'Let us say for now that both worlds may need each other… in order to exist.'

9:16 P.M.

On their approach to the camp, the arc of darkness has eroded the stone face of the ruined tower until only the top course attracts any light.

On a small flattened area close by, three green tents are pitched in ray formation, their entrance flaps thrown back to encourage the heat of the day to leave. In front of them, a ring of loose stones embrace the cold remains of a scattered fire.

The car halts beside the ruin, front wheels nestling on rocks placed there for the purpose. Fabrienne waits until André comes around to let her out. He offers his hand but she hefts the rucksack and climbs from the car unaided.

Climbing the western slope in the fading light, a slender figure in worn jeans and a white top is struggling under a huge bundle of gathered timber. Behind her, another girl is carrying a large yellow bucket.

André ushers Fabrienne into the space between the tents, dropping his leather bag into the dust.

'Alec?'

A face appears at the flap of the central tent, eyes drowsy, black hair spiked and careless. Alec shuffles from the tent, tee shirt creased and awry, sleeping bag held tight around him. André kicks the leather bag towards him.

'This is Alec Ryan, our token Idle Englishman. I will never understand why his University had good enough sense to help pay for the dig then insisted that he came along too.'

Alec opens the bag at his feet and sifts through it for his cigarettes. 'That's because we Idle English never trust the *louche Français* to get anything right by themselves.'

Fabrienne watches Alec's face for a smile. It is slow in coming, but she is relieved to see that she has walked into a humorous situation.

'And why might that be?'

'And you just rode here in his car?'

'So?'

'That's French.'

'So am I.'

'Ah… but…' His eyes contrast the unblemished planes of her skin against the creased linen jacket.

'Alec…' Barnard gestures toward the bag. '…get your cigarettes out of there and leave Fabrienne alone.'

Alec splits off a pack from the carton. 'Want one?'

'No, thanks.' Fabrienne is watching André walk away. 'Where's he going?'

'To his tent. He doesn't sleep with the riff-raff at this side of the tower. He likes to wake with the sunrise.'

'So where do I sleep?'

Alec indicates the flap of his own tent. Fabrienne hitches the rucksack further onto her shoulder.

A girl steps between the tents carrying a bundle of brushwood above her head. She dumps it beside the circle of stones and takes a deep breath, hands on slender hips.

'Whatever he was saying… don't listen.' She embraces Fabrienne, rising up on her toes to offer a kiss to both cheeks. Her brown, page-boy cut brushes lightly against Fabrienne as she does. 'I'm Manon. I'm new here, too. You must be Fabrienne. Oh… and it's your turn tomorrow for the firewood.'

The other girl, olive-skinned, almond eyes and black hair scraped into a ponytail through a small headscarf, arrives behind her with the water. She lowers it gratefully by the fireplace and reaches for Fabrienne's hand.

'Hi, I'm Veronique. Where is André?'

'Gone to his tent… I think.'

'Ah. Good. I wanted to walk up to the sunset with him and I thought for a moment that perhaps…'

Alec rolls back out of his tent, this time fastening a pair of ragged denims.

'He's still here. Picking up Fabrienne made him late. He won't go tonight.'

Veronique turns to the hearth, visibly crestfallen.

'Is the fire not lit yet?'

Manon is breaking firewood in the hearth, her face set hard as she snaps wood with her bare fingers. She kicks the sticks into a tangled heap within the circle.

'You can see it isn't.'

'Then when will dinner be ready?'

'As soon as you…'

Fabrienne interrupts by shaking dust from her rucksack.

'Ok. Where do I put my things?'

Manon strikes a match into the dry kindling. The flame licks amongst it to catch the air with a thin strand of smoke.

'Take your pick. You can share with Alec… or you can be sensible and share with either me or Veronique. Or we can share and you can have a tent to yourself. Maybe you should do that tonight. See how tomorrow goes, eh?'

She kicks timber into the glowing flames. 'And if we all like the smell of each other who knows what might happen. Take my tent over on the left there.'

Fabrienne nudges her rucksack to the far end of the tent. The simple comforts of maman's kitchen feel distant now in the aftershock of an Aegean sunset.

Manon pokes her head under the canvas.

'Here… pass me that sleeping bag. Oh… and the little plastic bag under it. That's right.'

Fabrienne hands over a small toilet bag, then a towel she found she was sat on. In one corner a pair of jeans dishevel into a heap with a green tee shirt.

'These as well?'

Manon takes them without a word.

Fabrienne unrolls her sleeping bag. Below it there is room for little more than another pair of jeans, two or three shirts, a simple wooden flute, a small canvas bag of hand tools and a dark, oblong box. She wraps the spare clothes around the box and slides it behind the pillow of the sleeping bag.

A scent of burning timber infiltrates the walls of the tent, along with an uncertain aura of warm food. Fabrienne unfastens the boots she has been forced into for forty-eight hours straight and stands barefoot outside the tent.

The fire has been tamed into a concentrated area where Alec is fussing with an iron stand that straddles the hearth. The shaved earth around it is speared with tiny flints.

Fabrienne steps forward. 'Smells weird.'

He turns, startled, noticing her bare feet. 'No wonder I didn't hear you. How on earth do you walk on this stuff?'

'Mis-spent childhood.'

'I know… you *Français* are all poor as *Église souris.*'

She ignores the jibe. 'So… what does it take to learn to cook something that smells as evil as this?'

He holds up a small silver implement, rattling it on an empty can.

'*Un Homme Anglais. Un ouvre-boîtes!* See… you French can't even call a bloody can-opener a bloody can-opener.'

She sits down on the earth beside him.

'That's because *nous Français* never learn to use one…'

9:56 P.M.

Wrapped in her sleeping bag with the mosquito net across the open end of the tent, Fabrienne hears André's footsteps as he leaves the camp. She hears them turn and take the path away from the tower. She opens the end of the tent to peer out and watch his footsteps taking him slowly northward until they find the road that runs the ridge to Potamos.

He pauses a moment, head down in thought, the western side of his face flickering in the glow from a remnant cloud.

Fabrienne holds her breath, fighting an urge to climb out of the tent and join him, but tonight would be far too soon. She hopes she has bought herself enough time on the way here to be able to spend it wisely.

André shakes his head sharply then returns to his tent.

Before his footsteps fade into a workshop memory, Fabrienne comes to realise just how many years she has been waiting to hear them.

GALANIÁNA CAMP

JUNE 6th.
TUESDAY

6.15A.M.

André Barnard sits up suddenly. The inside of the tent is still quite dark, back-lit by the reflected glow from the early morning sun striking the tower above him. From outside, further down the slope, comes the sound of a flute.

Peeling back the tent flap, he stares down the hill.

A figure sits by a rock some twenty yards downslope. In the blue of the dawn light, the linen jacket they are wearing is a fashion he has tried not to think of for some years.

For one moment, in which sleep and dreams chase each other in a mélange of time and consequence, he thinks… but no… it never can be.

As his heart slows, he remembers who it must be.

He ties back the flaps and sits silently in the entrance to listen to Fabrienne play.

Around her, a small gather of nervous goats are standing sideways across the slope, one eye on her and one on the sea. He hears the clatter of their hooves pushing at small stones for a better grip. They seem poised for flight as if she is keeping them where they do not want to be simply by the power of her music.

His attention is caught by notes that rise and fall in a scale at once alien and familiar. His eyes close for a second to allow his thoughts to clear.

The music stops abruptly and the air around him echoes to a dull thudding of goat bells as they escape downhill to the greener shrub.

When he opens his eyes again, Fabrienne is watching him from below.

JUNE 6th.
TUESDAY

8:37 A.M.

The excavations are marked out in overlapping circles that mirror the terracing Fabrienne had noticed the evening she arrived.

'This is an unusual dig.'

André hands over the canvas bag filled with small hand tools for her to carry.

'It's my own design. Intuition informs me where to dig the first circle. If we find anything, we extend that area by overlapping the first with four other circles, each three metres wide, until we find something else. This gives us a sense of the lateral direction that the dig will follow. If we find nothing, we move on. If we find a wall we dig along it until we find a junction.'

The excavations range in an arc towards the southern end of Antikythera, exposing a curved wall as they go.

Fabrienne can see that they leave more room for working than a plain trench, and that artefacts dropped by the men who built the walls will also be unearthed.

Alec has been left behind at the camp, washing those fragments through a filter. Manon and Veronique are visible below her, working in adjacent circles.

'Where shall I start?'

André leads her to the edge of a box where the earth has been squared off by sharp blade-strokes of a spade.

'Start here. Alec has removed some of the soil from this structure but we still don't know what it is.'

Fabrienne lowers the canvas bag to the ground.

'What have you found here already?'

André shrugs. 'Other than the box itself, nothing much of interest. As you can see, it is one meter by just over two and we have taken out perhaps half the soil.'

'Do you still have the things you found?'

'Yes, back at the camp. They will form part of a batch of items for the next boat on Thursday.'

'What were they?'

'A bronze shard that could have been from anything… a shallow bowl…small, broken amphorae… scent containers perhaps. Who knows after all this time.'

'So, nothing you considered of significance?'

'Only an arrowhead struck from bronze. The Romans left hundreds of those around.'

'Which direction was it pointing?'

André's hand reaches up to cup his chin. 'Why would you think that significant?'

'Who knows after all this time?'

'Here…' He takes a pair of metal pins from his shirt pocket. They are wound together by a fine string. 'In case you discover anything else you might think significant, you can mark out the line.'

She leaves them on the wall. 'You didn't tell me the direction.'

'Alec found it. You'll have to ask later.'

Fabrienne opens the bag. 'Where do you want me to start?'

He takes the trowel from her and turns her hand palm up. 'I put gloves in your bag. Use them until your hands harden. We have little medical treatment here and if you can't dig you are just using up food.'

Fabrienne searches amongst the tools for the gloves. When she finds them they bring a smile to her face. They are like the ones Oriel had given her as a child.

'Can I ask why we are not excavating by the Temple of Apollo?'

André hands back the trowel. 'How many times do we have to disturb the poor old boy? He's been dug up enough. No. We dig here.'

'Why here?'

André studies the sun, guessing around three hours until midday. The edge of the exposed wall is dusty from the winds that graze the island. He hitches himself up on it.

'Have you ever played a hunch? There is something here. But I'm not quite sure…'

'Not much of a hunch, then?'

'Don't be flippant. I have enough with Alec…'

Fabrienne pulls herself up onto the wall beside him.

'You realise we shouldn't be treating archaeological finds in such a cavalier manner?'

'We will not be the first to sit on this stone and, if I am right, we will be only two amongst thousands.'

'What leads you to think that?'

André's hands find their way into his pockets, he draws his shoulders inwards and his head tilts, like a bird listening to movement below the surface of the soil.

'I hear their voices.'

Fabrienne studies him with care as she becomes aware that he has not spoken in jest. His glance is so direct that she is forced to turn away, catching sight of Veronique kneeling in the distance.

'Do the others… are they aware…?'

'No, no. And it isn't what you're thinking.'

She slips off her boots into the small trench beside the wall where they hit the dust with a satisfying thud.

'And what am I thinking?'

'That I'm mad, of course. What else?'

'How about my own thoughts?' She swings her feet in

the space before her, spreading her toes wide and even.

'To hear voices doesn't mean that you are mad. But to follow what they say can lead you there. Is that not so?'

'That wouldn't make me the first. But these voices are different. They don't tell me anything. They just are.'

'They do not talk to you?'

He laughs out loud. 'No, not directly. I only feel them as I'm falling asleep. Perhaps they're too discerning to discourse with the likes of me.'

From the corner of her eye, Fabrienne sees Veronique stand up and stare towards them.

She lifts a hand but Veronique turns abruptly away.

André pushes his fingers through his hair. She has seen him do this in the car but, outside in the light, she now reads into this far more than mere gesture.

'Do you recognise them?'

'I don't always know the language… odd words only… a mixture of Greek, Roman… sometimes Arabic.'

He clasps his hands again, fingers intertwining. 'It's like standing at the edge of a party where you don't know the host and don't understand why you were invited.'

'Is there nothing else that you recognise?'

'Yes, there is, but I can't refine it. Tell me… how would you define civilisation? I hear it in the way they speak… the confidence in their voices… I think…'

He stands up, his spread arms encompassing the visible land. 'No, I don't think… I don't know how, but I *know*… that beneath our feet lies a city… and that here were civilised men.'

11:15 A.M.

Fabrienne rests her trowel on the wall to lean against the structure she has been steadily emptying. Perspiration soaks the back of her cotton work gloves.

Two hours of excavation have produced nothing of any significance except a pile of sifted earth.

She shades her eyes from the sunlight.

Veronique has disappeared from the adjacent circle. Her tools lay abandoned at various points of the dig. Fabrienne catches sight of her, almost back at the tower, climbing the slope empty-handed. As Fabrienne turns, she notices the empty yellow bucket that has been placed silently behind her.

Manon waves to her from three circles away. Fabrienne waves back with the bucket as Manon makes her way over, picking a route carefully through strings and tapes.

Fabrienne helps her onto the wall. 'What do I do with this?'

Manon shrugs off her tee shirt and throws it carelessly over one shoulder. She is naked underneath. Her breasts are small and pointed and her skin glows like warm honey.

'There are several things. You could wear it, pee in it… or fill it with water from the spring.'

'It's not my colour. What if I pee in it?"

Manon grabs the bucket from her. 'Alec would drink it. I saw the way he looked at you. Come on, I'll show you where the spring is.'

She takes Fabrienne by the hand. For half a second, Fabrienne remains rooted, then follows willingly, leaving her boots behind.

As they help each other over the wall, Fabrienne takes a long look at the scree slope they are about to descend.

'How far down is it?'

Manon waits for her, feet braced against the slope. 'Not far. It emerges on a stone shelf fifty metres above the sea.'

'Where does it come from?'

'It gets filtered through the basins… you know… you must have seen them yesterday when you drove over?'

Fabrienne slides down to join her.

You mean the terracing?'

'Yeah. André says it filters down into an aquifer. When that fills, it runs off to form the spring.'

'Is it clean?'

Manon grins at her. 'Are you?'

Fabrienne brushes dust and perspiration from her arms. It had been a while since she'd dug with such a degree of concentration. She smacks the dirt from her shorts.

'I guess not.'

'If you don't mind cold water you can shower in the spring.'

'In this heat? Cold is the only kind there is.'

Manon seems to glide over the loose surface as it slides them ever more steeply towards the sea.

She scrambles across a large rock and holds down her hand for Fabrienne to catch. 'It's over here…'

The spring bounds from a cleft in the hillside. It arches from a natural spigot to land on a large flat stone. Rainbows chase the air around them in the slight breeze.

Manon holds her fingers tightly. 'Come on…'

She pulls Fabrienne with her around the top of the cleft and slides on her backside down the scree until they reach the flat stone.

Spray saturates the air and Manon's upper body glistens like frost as she spins around in the mist from the fall.

'Take off your clothes… come on.'

She sheds her boots and jeans, throwing them and the tee shirt up amongst the rocks above the cleft, then turns to stand naked in front of Fabrienne.

'Your turn…'

Fabrienne hesitates. 'I think I'm alright as I am.'

Without a word, Manon dances through the waterfall, grabbing and embracing Fabrienne so quickly that she has no choice but to follow her under the water.

The force of the flow quickly unpicks Fabrienne's hair from the style she has pinned it into, plastering it around her head and shoulders.

Manon reaches up to push it from her face, drawing her closer. 'You really are quite something… but then you know that.'

Fabrienne shields her eyes from the rushing stream and opens her mouth under it, allowing it to overspill and gush between them. She closes her lips to drink the sweet water down, shivering violently as it chases the heat from inside her body.

'You mean… as an archeologist?'

Manon steps from the waterfall into the mist beside it, spreading her arms and tipping her face into the warmth of the sun with a smile. 'You know what I mean…'

Fabrienne steps out to join her. 'Yes… I do.' She pulls her hair together at one side, winding her fingers in it to twist out the water. 'I'm flattered… but I don't know what else.'

Manon relaxes her arms. She follows a rivulet of water along Fabrienne's skin with a fingertip until it filters into an open hand.

Fabrienne gives no sign of pulling away. Instead, she stares deep into her eyes while her own fingers tighten around Manon's.

Manon turns away, unable to sustain the pressure of that stare. 'What did you see?'

Fabrienne shakes her head and smiles. 'Sorry?'

Manon lets go of her hand. 'What did you see?'

'Where?'

Reaching the tee shirt from the rocks above, Manon rinses it under the falling water. 'You know where… how do you do that? I have never been looked at… no… into… that way. I felt you…' She clutches her hand in front of her stomach. '…right here.'

Still naked, she throws the tee shirt onto a rock beside them. Reaching out for Fabrienne, she is shocked to find this time her embrace is allowed.

Fabrienne folds her arms around the smaller girl. Closing her eyes, she moves them both gently under the falling water, hoping that it will wash away some of the sadness of doubt she had found inside.

Manon is held tight, feeling her world turn, allowing the loneliness of her simple life to rise to the surface where the water fails to wash away any of her growing indecision.

She moves her arms to Fabrienne's waist and slides them under the drenched cotton of the tee shirt to make closer contact with her skin. She stops. Her arms fall limply to her sides as she turns away.

Fabrienne catches her arm. 'You were not to know.'

Manon studies the washed stone beneath her feet. 'I… I'm…'

Fabrienne's finger touches her lips. 'You are not anything. There is no need for regret between friends.'

'Is that what we are?'

'I hope so.'

Manon continues to dress in silence.

Fabrienne fills the bucket. 'Is Veronique your friend?'

'No. At least… not in the way you mean.'

'And how do I mean?'

'Not like I… you know.'

'Like what? Nothing happened here.'

Manon picks up the bucket but Fabrienne takes it from her. 'It's my turn.'

Manon snatches it back.

'I'll take it. It's what friends are for.'

Fabrienne throws off the confines of her sleeping bag and crawls out into the night. To the west, the moon sails the close horizon, beating a metalled path to the rocky outcrops below the headland. She turns her face to the stars that rail across the arc of blue-black night like a silver stain, splashed and irremovable.

She listens to the night-wind and the voice echoes it carries. They are many, as André has said… and for the most part indistinguishable… riding the fine edge of audibility.

Stillness falls, but arching above it are fragments of a language she does understand.

She strides deliberately across the hearth, keeping the bulk of the tower between herself and André's tent.

Making her way around it, she pauses, one foot on a loose rock. The voice is louder here. Fabrienne sits down to listen.

JUNE 7th.
WEDNESDAY

7:36 P.M.

Fabrienne's knees are drawn tightly to her chest, her chin resting on them. Her breathing is slow and shallow, pausing occasionally.

Her eyes see nothing but the tracks of the setting sun on moving water, distracted occasionally by a cormorant that fishes the rocks a few metres from the shore. From this elevation it is little more than a fleeting shadow whispering amongst the waves.

The car engine has been audible for a while now, and she is not surprised to hear it halt against the rock behind her.

She allows her head to tip forwards, closing her eyes against the light. André settles beside her, his back propped by the rock.

'I didn't think to find you here.'

She lifts her face, eyes still closed. 'I shouldn't have come. This is your private place.'

André stretches his feet out in the dust. His heels track through the sharp, flinty earth while his fingers search amongst the cotton cloth of his shirt, his trousers.

'What are you looking for?'

'This… I have been meaning to give it to you.'

He holds out a small arrowhead beaten from bronze, the edges as sharp as the day it was made. 'Open your eyes and you will see…'

Fabrienne focuses on it slowly, turning it so the sun flecks the edges. It fits so neatly within her fingers. There are marks across it where the bindings have faded with time.

She squeezes her hand around it. Tiny cuts appear in her

63

palm. Time itself is seeping both ways between them.

'How old would you say this is?'

André reaches out a finger to touch it. 'I'd thought it was early Roman, but it could be much older. I was hoping you'd tell me.'

'It feels somehow inconsistent in Time.'

'Like you and I?'

Fabrienne recalls his expression the first time they had brought the car to rest against this same rock. He had peered across the waves as though searching for something missing from his life.

'I was wrong to come. I should not be here.'

André pushes his hands deep into his trouser pockets where they ball into fists, straining the fabric.

'Why not? It is not my private place.'

'But it is a private time. You do not like Veronique to accom…'

He stops her with a laugh and drops his gaze to the soil, tracing a pattern in it with his heel that somehow resembles the arrowhead.

'Veronique… I do not need that much *need*…'

'She is in love with you.'

He spins around to face her, trying to penetrate the depth of her eyes for meaning but can find only the light reflecting there. 'How can you say that? How long have you been here?'

'Long enough to recognise a woman in love.'

'And a man… how does a man in love look? What is it you see that…'

'He looks like you.'

André takes a deep breath and lets it out again slowly.

'I asked for you to come here because Henri Lefevre said you are the most intuitive archaeological artist to come out of university in years… and that he could think of no-one better to help me find my city. I also heard that your work rate was second to none. Now I have seen that energy for myself, I have to ask what it is that *you* are looking for.'

'The Moon in a puddle.'

He tips his face to the darkening blue. 'Isn't that… you know… up there?'

Fabrienne scratches a matching sign in the dust with her heel. 'Depends what time of day it is….'

'And what time of day is it where *you* live?'

'It's felt like evening for some time now. Most of my life in fact… but now that I'm here, maybe the night will roll over me while we sleep.'

'And in that bright new morning?'

'It will not be bright… and it may not be new… just one that was postponed earlier.'

'So how will you tell?'

'It will be in people's faces.'

'Is that why you were studying me?'

She turns sharply. 'When?'

'The morning after you arrived. You were playing your flute to the goats. Where is that by the way? I haven't heard you play it since.'

She reaches inside the open neck of her shirt to lift out the flute. It is narrow, tapered and worn. The wood is a mixture of darkness and light, whorled like the fingerprint of an old olive tree, the reed a rough cut an inch or so along the stem.

She holds it out to him. 'That's because I haven't played it since.'

'Play it for me now.'

'No.'

'I see. I'm not enough of an old goat to pique…'

'*Au contraire.*' Fabrienne tucks away the flute. 'I'm quite sure you are.'

'And that is the problem?'

'Not at all.'

'Then why were you looking?'

'Is it against the law on Antikythera to look at someone?'

'No, but that wasn't a look. That was an invasion.'

'Is that why you have avoided being alone with me?'

'Is that even possible here?'

His hands appear slowly from his pockets. He drops them into his lap where the fists uncurl. 'Your look made me turn away my attention… and in that moment, the doors of my conscience flew open like the wings of escaping birds.'

'And you have been trying to gather them back in ever since. But why? Birds are meant to fly… and so are ghosts.'

'Since your look left me with little but empty rooms, ghosts and birds might seem better company than none.'

Fabrienne raises the flute to her lips, fingers dropping into place along the stem.

With a gentle hand, André pushes it away. 'I don't want you to play to my ghosts,.'

'Are you afraid that I might bring them back?'

'I am not afraid of ghosts.'

'Are they the ones who talk to you in the night?'

'No, those voices are memories, impregnated deep into the soil. We are disturbing them… that is all. Only now…' His face clouds over as his thoughts sift amongst self-doubt and repression. '…since that look… do I feel that I can talk more openly about them.'

'And which of your ghosts are you still in love with?'

He leans his head against the rock, and sighs deeply as a blue cast shifts the spectrum around them, alighting on their faces, in the air and on the rocks. 'You have no right…'

'I know…' She reaches out to touch his arm. He withdraws quickly and she stands to walk away, picking up the short jacket she has brought with her. '…and I am sorry.'

She has taken no more than three or four steps when she hears him speak softly to himself.

'And so am I.'

She hesitates a second, then sets off alone.

'Wait… come back. You owe me something.'

She stops mid-stride at the sound of his voice but stays facing away from him along the rutted track towards the camp. 'You already have my apology.'

'I would like an explanation.'

'For what?'

'For why you are here.'

'That is simple. I am here to lay a ghost.'

'I thought you said they didn't exist?'

'No. You said that. I am all too familiar with them.'

André stands and shakes the dust from his clothes.

'Then perhaps you would like to come with me to meet the boat?'

She turns around… the car is a forgotten presence… leaning heavily against the rock by a section of corroded bumper.

André opens the door for her. 'From Piraeus. It will be here soon.' He sees the look on her face. 'Don't worry. I don't mean for you to be on it.'

'Are we meeting someone?'

He shakes his head, fingers travelling his hair in an ever more familiar gesture. 'No, just more food for Alec to ruin with his interminable ketchup.'

Behind her, black bin liners on the rear seats rustle and clank with the debris of living out of a can.

'Can we buy something fresh from the boat?'

André slides behind the wheel and slams the door shut.

'Of course, although it won't keep once we get to camp. Perhaps you could eat it raw on the way back. At least it will be free from Alec's chemicals.'

TO LIMÁNI TOU POTAMOS

The car groans down the steep hill in first gear. André dabs ineffectively at the brake as they approach each turn.

Lights are coming on in the houses they pass, filtering an electric glow through shutters and curtains into the well-tended, rich-soil gardens within their walls.

Below them, the concrete ramp of the jetty is etched bright under the stark glare of the harbour light. Across the bay, green- and red- lit buoys heave on the swell, weaving patterns into the shadowy water.

André pulls the car into an empty space and checks his watch in the glow from the dashboard.

'We are early.'

'That's my fault.'

'Don't apologise too easily. Save it for when you really need it.' He steps out of the car. 'Will you help me with the bags?'

'Of course. Where do they go?'

'Grab a sack and follow me.'

The small open truck is beside the jetty. They swing the bags over the side onto a pile already there.

André walks along the ramp to rinse his hands in the sea then jumps from there onto a low wall to take a closer look at a bright orange rib moored bow-on to the harbour.

Fabrienne is waiting by the car.

André's gaze flicks from her to the sky, out across the empty bay and finally, for a moment again, to the rib.

'Would you like a drink while we wait?'

She hesitates, visibly. 'Would you?'

A few yards beyond the road there is a door in the gable of a large house. A single light swings over it on a wire, tormenting the shadows in the evening breeze off the water.

Inside, a small room holds a crowded, makeshift bar. The four tables are full and the air pulses with cigarette smoke and conversation.

Through a window comes the sound of chickens in loud dispute, claws scratching at unforgiving soil.

André finds a wooden stool for her beside him at the counter. 'What would you like?'

'Nothing. Thank you.'

'You must have something.'

'A little soda water?'

André orders in Greek. The old woman behind the counter shakes her head.

'She says no soda… what else would you like? Ouzo with a little water?'

'Thank you, but no. I can't drink alcohol.'

'Is that a medical condition?'

'No.'

Four men at a table in the corner begin to laugh out loud. They raise their glasses in salute.

One of them speaks to her in perforated English. 'We make up for you. You job sit look pretty for us. *Vale?*'

André tops up his ouzo with a few drops of water from a jug on the bar. The old woman touches Fabrienne's hand with a finger and for a moment they study each other. The woman goes through into another room, returning with a segmented orange on a plate. She puts this in front of Fabrienne then returns to her stool in the corner where she begins to rock gently, toying with a string of wooden beads from the pocket of her black dress.

André's face holds a new expression, one that Fabrienne hasn't seen in the short time she's been here on Antikythera.

'What was that about?'

Fabrienne shrugs. 'Kindred spirit?'

'Are you always this enigmatic?'

Fabrienne strips the peel from a segment of orange.

'Only in company. Alone, I am the soul of indiscretion.'

'Lady!' A man at the corner table motions for her to attract André.

As she brings this to his attention, the man lifts his glass in salute. André ignores him, leaning back against the bar.

He taps his glass on the counter and the old woman splashes a fresh shot in it.

Fabrienne passes him the water jug. 'Who is that?'

'Who is who?'

'Does it take one enigma to recognise another? Or is this just a coincidence?'

'I am sorry. His name is Fernando.'

'Sounds demonic.'

'Fernando Fuentes… and he is.'

Fabrienne twists around on the stool.

The man is younger than André, yet his angular face is more weathered. His small neat goatee barely covers the cleft of his chin. His eyes are unusually dark, even in the tanned brown of his face. There is a suggestion of receding hairline but, where it has been pushed behind his ears, the hair is coarse and long, streaked with blonde.

'Tell me about him.'

André reaches for his glass. 'He is a diver.'

Fabrienne holds it to the bar. 'So are you.'

He disengages her fingers from the glass. 'I was.'

'Once a diver… always a diver.'

He pushes the glass in her direction.

'Is that not the same for alcoholics?'

'I am sure so. Will you dive with me?'

'No. Will you drink with me?'

'No.'

'Then don't dive with anyone else here.'

She glances quickly to Fernando and back again, making

the comparison obvious to both men.

'Perhaps there is a similar genetic component to both.'

André pushes a note across the counter. The old woman rattles noisily with a tin box. He holds up a hand until she stops.

He checks his watch. 'The boat is due.'

8:53 P.M.

Fabrienne can sense the throb of the ship's engine on the air before it swings into the tight curl of the bay. The waste truck pulls toward the water's edge, peppering the wave tips with light.

André leads her over the apron and onto the harbour side, avoiding the iron mooring rings caulked into the stone.

The bright orange rib rears to the kick of a wave from the oncoming ferry. Diving gear lays disassembled on the dock beside it.

Fabrienne shivers suddenly. 'Is that Fernando's boat?'

'Are you warm enough?'

'I left my jacket in the car.'

André hops over the low wall onto the jetty. 'I'll get it.'

The bar door opens as he strides away.

Fernando and his friends take the short walk down the slope to join Fabrienne. She turns her back to them, studying the sheer blackness of the sea under the approaching ship lights.

Through her thin shirt she senses the heat radiating from Fernando's body. There is a sweet scent of anise and alcohol on the air.

'Hello, Fernando.'

'*Hola, cosita bonita.* So… he tell you all of me. What do I say?'

André steps in to slip the jacket over her shoulders.

'I told her nothing about you. There is nothing worth

saying.'

Fernando's laugh resonates with confidence. 'This not always same, Pretty Thing. You know he have *mote…* you say… nickname?… *para mi* ?'

'I can imagine.'

'He call me *'Monstro'.'*

André takes her arm to lead her away. His fingers feel safe and strong through the thin layer of silk-lined linen but Fabrienne resists. 'Why?'

Fernando lets out a whoop. *'El Cazón Terrible.* The Terrible Dogfish. I say he Pinnochio. *Es razón por la* big nose.' He brushes past them to reach the moorings and check the bights that hold them to the rings.

She tugs the jacket more closely around her shoulders.

'You are from Spain? *Español?'*

'No Español… Soy filipino.'

André releases her arm. His fingers curl into fists.

Fabrienne takes hold of his wrist and relaxation ripples through his body.

He stares hard at her touch. 'What are you…?'

Fabrienne slides her hand until their fingers interlock. The sensation spreads through him again, chilling the anger rising from his stomach.

Fernando notices the movement of her hand. 'Pretty Thing… be careful. *Ver con los ojos, no con el corazón.'*

André's fingers stiffen within hers.

Fabrienne increases her grip and presses forward until she can scent again the anise on Fernando's breath.

'What do you mean by that?'

Fernando returns her stare. 'I mean see with eyes… not with heart.'

Fabrienne stands her ground. 'I know exactly what you said. I asked what you meant. I see things my own way and I can see that… if I was interested enough… I would find my own *mote* for you.'

Fernando bares his teeth in a grin. 'Then make it pretty one, Pretty Thing. Not like him, eh?'

Fabrienne grins back at him. 'I bet you have other names, too. And I bet you both deserve each one of them…'

'There is one he do not deserve…'

Fabrienne senses André's grip relaxing, his hand ready to slip quickly from hers.

She increases her pressure. 'And what name is that?'

Fernando slips his hands safely into his pockets.

'The one when I call him brother-in-law.'

9:47 P.M.

The worn gearchange clashes against the dashboard. André shakes his hand to free the trapped knuckles.

'I didn't know you spoke Spanish.'

Fabrienne is staring at the windscreen as if the force of her anger could send it shattering amongst the stars that glare back at her from above the ridge.

'I do many things that you do not know.'

André throws the car around the bends as fast as it will climb, the engine protesting, forcing him to change gear.

'And now I see there are things you do not do.'

Fabrienne is holding tight to the door handle. 'Then you saw wrong.'

When they reach the top of the hill, the car coasts slowly out onto the road that traverses the ridge. Without warning, André slews it hard to the right. The car is brought to a halt by the large rock from where he had collected Fabrienne on the way down.

She tries the door. It has jammed. She turns sideways on the seat to kick it open, tumbling broken window glass out into the dust.

André remains in the car, hands gripping the wheel, his

expression in the dash-light dark and impenetrable.

The car sidelights are still on, reflecting in the fractured glass from the door. She sweeps it aside with her foot and sits down, slipping her arms into the jacket sleeves.

The heat of the engine fills the air around her with the taint of leaking oil and gasoline. There is another smell that takes her a while to identify… overheated plastic. The lights flicker and die.

She hears André get out of the car, leaving the door open. Footsteps track around from the other side. She hears the scrape of a cigarette lighter wheel.

'I thought you didn't smoke?'

'Then you thought wrong. Not really our night, is it.'

Fabrienne shrugs herself away from the warm surface of the rock. 'I'll walk from here.'

Halfway back to camp, she hears the approach of tyres on gravel. The car appears, rolling slowly beside her.

André pushes the door wide. 'Get in.'

'I am walking.'

The car slides slowly alongside her with the door open.

André shouts. 'Please?'

Fabrienne slips into the car while it is moving. She slams the door behind her. 'What is this all about?'

'I apologise.' His voice sounds tired. 'This is not about you. I didn't know Fernando was on the island.'

The road in front of them is a dark ribbon. André keeps them vaguely within the margins of dust at either side, the sound of rolling tyres filling the silence between them.

'Why do you not put on the lights?'

'I told you. I have broken them.'

'Oh… and the brakes too? This is why you didn't stop?'

'They need vacuum. No battery. No engine. No brakes. I will fix it tomorrow.' His right foot stabs at the rock-hard brake pedal.

'If there is a tomorrow.'

Fabrienne braces herself against the dashboard. 'What happens when we reach the camp?'

'I am still working on that. As a last resort there is always the tower.'

'And if we miss the tower?'

'There is a long but very quick downhill run into the sea. The place where you seem to want to be and I do not.'

The car rumbles on, the slope beneath the wheels being enough to keep it moving but little else.

The top of the tower begins to rear against the stars, its bulk an impenetrable shape of black.

'How do you know where I want to be?'

André jerks hopefully at the handbrake lever and feels the remaining few strands of cable snap. 'Because I do my homework. And because you have been doing yours.'

'And what did I find?'

'You found my friends. People I have worked with for years. Did you think they wouldn't tell me that you had been asking questions?'

'I was not afraid of that.'

'Then what are you afraid of?'

Fabrienne points through the smeared glass of the windscreen into the night sky where stars stream above them. 'Those…'

The stars absorb her… Orion courting the horizon while Argo Navis sails the southern reaches of the Milky Way… until she is suddenly aware of André's voice in the darkness.

'They are too far away to be afraid of.'

She lowers her hand from the prints she has made on the glass. 'And so are you.'

'That didn't stop you looking.'

'But I didn't know what I would find. I hadn't thought that you might be broken.'

'Broken?' He laughs. 'You could say that I suppose. But 'broken' supposes a thing can be mended… like this car… and I have tried, despite what you might have heard.'

'I have noted your ability as a mechanic.'

They are slowing gently as the slope recedes. Fabrienne places both feet firmly on the floor and turns to watch his profile slide against the night sky.

'And in the dark… you smell like Fernando.'

8:30 P.M.

André shuffles down beside Fabrienne on the coir mat by the hearth. 'The arrowhead. Alec said that it pointed North East. He thinks.'

Fabrienne moves over to make a little more room for him. 'He *thinks*?'

'He *is* English.'

Fabrienne's cup is empty. She picks up a little of the dust to wipe clean the inside of the enamel. 'That sounds like an excuse.'

'Not to notice these things is inexcusable. Here… let me rinse that and get you some more coffee.'

'I think I've had enough. I may not sleep tonight as it is.'

André settles back. 'You've been at the dig all day.'

In the relaxation of his movement, Fabrienne can sense a poise he maintains between the two worlds that influence his life, but it is too late now for him to stride off and revisit the halls of his past.

'I admit to having taken time out for a shower.'

'So you found the spring…'

'Not exactly… I was shown it.'

André stretches out towards the ring of stones encircling the fire. 'I noticed Veronique was missing for a…'

Fabrienne heads him off. 'No. It was Manon.'

'Ah…'

'And what does… 'Ah'… mean?'

'I'm not sure…'

'You are beginning to sound very like Alec.'

André stands and knocks the dust from his trousers.

'On that note, I shall bid you goodnight.'

Fabrienne watches him stride the hearth in a single step.

Warmth from the fanned embers searches the heat of the sun impregnated in her skin. Soon, the light will drop entirely and the air around her will turn to the shade of blue she has come to love.

11:21 P.M.

Fabrienne awakes to the sound of a gentle wind teasing a layer of dust against the shallow walls of her groundsheet.

She turns over, rearranging the bag beneath her head, pushing clothing on to the top of the wooden box so that her neck can relax. She drifts back into a dreamless sleep until the sound of a zipper brings her back to consciousness.

The end of her tent is sliced apart, starlight visible through the opening and, silhouetted against it, a figure is pushing a sleeping bag through the mosquito net. The zipper slides down again, closing out the night.

Fabrienne remains motionless as the figure struggles into position beside her.

She tries to detect a scent but they had all been around the fire until late, sharing a pungent dish concocted from mountain greens and a few cans. Where no-one has time for toiletries, it is inevitable that they share an aura of musk.

The warmth of another body stretches out against hers.

An arm is thrown lightly across her shoulder.

A hand touches her hair.

The fingers lift and separate it into strands.

Fabrienne hesitates a moment. The sensation of touch in the familiarity of darkness is almost beguiling.

'If that hand belongs to Alec I will tear it off.'

'If I was Alec, I would do it myself.'

'Manon?'

'Hmm…'

'What do you want from me?'

Manon snuggles closer. 'Nothing.'

Fabrienne can feel the heat between them energising her skin. The material of the sleeping bag seems to melt away, leaving her unprotected.

'I don't believe you.'

'Sometimes I need a friend.'

Fabrienne relaxes a little. 'You know that's all I can give you.'

Manon shuffles in to fill the small gaps that are being created. 'I don't want you to give me anything… I want to *steal* it.'

'Why?'

'Because, when you take it back I will know it was never mine in the first place and so it will not hurt.'

Fabrienne reaches across but finds her response held back by Manon's arm and her low whisper.

'Don't touch me again like last time. I only want you to warm my back.'

TO SKÁPSIMO
GALANIÁNA

JUNE 10th.
SATURDAY

9.35A.M.

The box Fabrienne is excavating is aligned directly North to South. She has checked it with her compass… finding it out by five degrees… until André had shown her the calculation that took her to true North.

'…but how would they have known? They had only an iron lodestone… and that would have been rudimentary at best.'

André had glanced up into the sky. 'They had the stars, too, don't forget. Anyway… in all probability it's just coincidence.'

She had teased him then. 'Like your voices?'

'I don't understand.'

'Is it just coincidence that you are here to listen to them?'

'No-one else hears them.'

'Perhaps 'no-one else' is the person they have been waiting for.'

10:03 A.M.

'Show me where you found it.'

Alec shuffles around the box, trying to remember.

'Exactly…'

He shrugs off her insistence but Fabrienne keeps him firmly on her hook. 'Close your eyes for a moment…'

'Whatever good that does…' He reaches into his pockets for his lighter and a cigarette. 'I need to think.'

Fabrienne snatches away his cigarettes. 'Look. I think this

is important even if you don't. I have been excavating this box for hours and there is nothing of any significance except the arrowhead you found. So tell me. Exactly where was it and where did it point?'

'Oh… I don't…'

'Close your eyes. *Now.*'

'Alright…' Alec closes his eyes and feels his way around to the end of the box. 'I think it was about… there…'

He points, eyes still closed, at a place around two-thirds of the way along the box. '…and it pointed North… or is that North West? To the right, anyway… from where I'm standing.'

'That's North East.'

'I always did get them mixed up.'

'Thank you, Alec. That's good.'

'Can I open my eyes now?'

'Do you have to?'

Fabrienne studies him without return. He sways slightly on the balls of his feet as if the breeze is blowing him. He is so slender as to be almost without substance. His hair, which at first she had thought was an affectation, is the result of it never having seen a comb the whole time she has been there.

He blinks in the sunlight. 'Hey… that works. I saw it clear as day.' With the point of a steel peg he draws a line across the earth in the direction he has remembered. 'How do you do that?'

'It's easy. I just remove all of the distractions.'

'Such as?'

'Such as you trying to see my nipples through my tee shirt and you won't because I'm wearing a bra.'

'Who *are* you?'

'I'm the Thief of Hope.'

Fabrienne places her compass in the centre of the line, wriggles it down into perfect alignment, compensates in her head for Magnetic to True and reads off the dial. 'Nine degrees, fifteen minutes… what lies in that direction?'

Alec shakes his head. 'Europe?'

'Yes, obviously. But where exactly.'

'Is this relevant?'

Fabrienne stares at his lack of interest. 'I'm surprised at you. Everything is relevant. Of all the people here you must be aware of that.'

Alec glares at the compass until the needle sews its image into his retinas. 'Yes, but… this place… it's so… tight. Do you know what I mean? It laces itself around you like an ill-fitting shoe. It seizes your attention and doesn't allow your mind time to breathe.'

'Isn't that why you came here?'

'Yes, it was. But perhaps that was a mistake.'

'You cannot run away from duty. You have to stand and fight its corner.'

Alec leans uncertainly on the edge of the box, his long slender fingers wrapping against the stone. 'How much do you know about me?'

Fabrienne's face lights with more humour than Alec has seen since her arrival. 'Almost everything.'

'Almost?'

She recognises the need for discovery behind his eyes.

'Sometimes, almost is enough. Now… do you wish to be a part of this or not?'

'A part of what?'

'Time will tell. Do we have a map?'

Alec scratches his head, his hair rearranging itself into chaotic familiarity. 'I think there's one in André's tent but he has gone down to Potamos Bay to order supplies.'

'Then go and steal it.'

'Can't we just borrow it?'

'Stealing is safer. Ask Manon.'

Fabrienne waits with her back against the stone wall, watching the play of wind on the sea. Air streams at height above the ridge, leaving an area of low pressure at the shore which it returns to fill. The coiling backdraughts would pull an unwary sailing vessel hard against the land.

Some distance out there is a disturbance where the wind searches the surface. Strong waves ripple back in against a shoal of rocks from which the cormorant dives repeatedly.

She hears Alec's boots coming down the path well before he appears.

They shake out a large paper map then align it with the compass and pin the corners with stones. With a piece of fine string from her toolbag she extrapolates a line at nine point two five degrees.

Alec bends over the map. 'What have we got?'

Holding the compass down with one finger, Fabrienne adjusts the line as finely as she can.

'It passes straight through the Acropolis.'

'At least we know where that is.'

Fabrienne folds the map neatly along the creases.

'If we knew how long this box has been waiting for us to find it, we might also know *when* that is.'

CHRONICLE

X

KALENDIS
MARTIUS

86 B.C.

KALENDIS MARTIUS
DIES MERCURIS

DIEI HORA SECUNDA

General Lucius Cornelius Sulla steps from his tent into the dead of night. His hair is thick, white-blonde and freshly oiled. At fifty-one years his body is no longer the hard temple it once was, though his conquests have led to this patchwork of pale white and rosé skin having been traced by the willing fingers of many women.

All around him, the camp lights have been extinguished but his eyes search the darkness for the signs that he knows are there. The ground between himself and the walls of Athens is quiet and still, but his heart beats with the awareness that the silence is filled with earth-cloaked men, laid on the glint of their weapons, waiting for his word.

He studies the rotation of the stars for inspiration. They say a New Year begins today… for him and for all of the Roman Empire… and he hopes that the collapse of Athens with its continued intransigence against Roman rule will ensure his name outlives him.

Piled against nine hundred *pedes* of wall as a living insult to the Greeks are timbers culled from their sacred forests of the Academy and Lyceum, to which he has laid waste.

Tracing the eastern horizon, the shadowy columns of ballista reel under the hands of last-minute carpenters.

Catapulta skulk in the lower darkness, primed, hunched as whipped dogs, waiting for siege towers to propel their platforms against the sky.

Marcus Germanicus approaches Sulla warily, hardened earth night-crisp beneath his feet.

'We are ready, General.'

Sulla licks a forefinger and holds it up into a breeze that carries the vile stench of five-month-old latrines and the rotting feculence of ten thousand pairs of Roman mules over the walls and into Athens.

'The wind has turned, Marcus. The Gods are with us this night. Send first to light the bonfire and let them eat their own smoke.'

'But the light from the fire, General?'

'Even the fox needs the moon.'

From the darkness, a flame is struck at the foot of the bonfire. Within minutes a dense, acrid smoke from the green timber is powered over the wall by the breeze. The inner city becomes a place of ghosts, coughing harshly out of the mists.

The first stones land between the gates.

Fifty *pedes* of masonry crumble into the city below, shattering the tiles and rafters of a wide shelter, crushing hundreds of cowering women and children.

The air fills with screams as Roman arrows hurl through the gap, taking down the defenders ordered into the breach.

Stones fly above their heads to break the columns of temples behind them. Quoins of polished marble shiver under the blows into pale slivers that scythe the compound, lacerating flesh and eyes.

Accompanied by a clashing blare of trumpets and the sharp, adrenalising beat of a hundred drums, the first ranks of legionaries hurl themselves into the path of arrows the Greeks have held in reserve. They lance from the inner walls onto the heads of soldiers who have lifted their shields, creating a *testudo* against them.

The shafts break and skitter against leather and metal,

few finding their mark in soft, yielding flesh.

Senses blinded by smoke and a chaotic howl and thud of instruments, the Greeks are herded through the Cerameicum and driven on into the Agora, where they find the backs of their comrades pressing against their own.

The Romans draw back out of reach of their swords.

The sound of trumpets echoes away.

The drums decay into silence.

The darkness now overflows with the screams of the dying and the harsh breath of exerted men yet, to Marcus, this perverted silence is one in which a soldier hears nothing beyond that which he expects to hear.

Beyond the Cerameicum, a cockerel is silenced mid-crow.

DIEI HORA QUINTA

Sulla appears openly at the breach. He is flanked by the Senators and Exiles sent to accompany his campaign.

'General, we implore you. Cease the killing. Isn't it enough that you have Athens?'

'How can you petition so, Tullius? Are these not the people who exiled you?'

'There are few in this city support King Mithridates, but their politicians were held in thrall by the buffoon Aristion, who is slavish to his every edict. They fled long ago. Only Aristion remains… barricaded in the Temple. You cannot blame the citizens for his errors.'

'How many times has Athens been taken?'

'That I cannot say. Many times perhaps.'

'But I can make certain this is the last.'

The Senators have grouped behind him. 'General, We feel that no good will come of sacking the Temple. We counsel that you wait him out.'

Sulla rounds on them angrily. 'I wait for neither God nor buffoon.'

Tullius dares a hand on Sulla's arm. 'Time and season in all things, General.'

Sulla shrugs him away. 'This is my time, Tullius, and my season. Do you know how long I have waited to feel Athens under my feet?'

'We are in receipt of fresh orders from Rome, General. Even you must obey a directive from the Senate, especially when it originates from Cinna himself.'

'Was Cinna here today? Has he shed blood on the field as we?'

'As representatives of the Senate we have stood with you and borne witness to your greatness and wisdom. We now beseech you to allow us to conduct this matter on behalf of a power greater than your own.'

'There is no power greater than mine today.'

'The Senate…'

'Is not here. I am.'

'Might we remind you, General, that one day you will wish to return in triumph to Rome?'

'When I am ready.'

'Then may we also remind you, General… that the Senate will be waiting.'

'Do you threaten me? Where is my Scribe! I wish it to be noted that when I sought to drag Aristion out by the heels, I was threatened by a politician. I refuse to sit in attendance to a fool who publicly maligns the name of my wife.'

'Aristion is already besieged in the Acropolis by Gaius Scribonius Curio. He has the gift of words and the patience that we require.'

'Is he to *talk* Aristion to death?'

'Even in war, General… one should always find time for diplomacy and honour.'

'And after a diplomat has clasped your hand, Tullius… be sure to count your fingers.'

DIEI HORA DUODECIMA

The parched earth surrounding Athens is broken and red… hard enough to shatter the blades of wooden spades.

The expected spring rainfall has not materialised and old latrines are being re-opened for ease of digging. Within the walls, thick layers of Greek blood shred and curl as if the city has been visited by the early hand of autumn.

From the roof of the Parthenon, an occasional flurry of arrows falls short of the ring of legionaries waiting in the Temple Square under Curio's command. They force a swift raising of shields but little else.

Beneath a wide canopy, Curio occupies a seat in full view of the Temple entrance.

'How long do you think this will take?' He turns slightly in his chair. 'And is time really of the essence, Tullius? Sulla has been reined in and we can bring this to a glorious conclusion. I believe that to be far more important than a day or two?'

'You believe correctly, Gaius. But there is a degree of urgency in our mission. In our absence Rome is becoming increasingly volatile.'

'And whoever can decipher the direction of that volatility can control it. Is that not the purpose of this visit?'

Tullius glances over his shoulder, aware that slaves have ears and some of them, still, their tongues.

'It appears you are extraordinarily well-informed, Gaius, but also involuntarily vocal. I urge you to mention nothing within earshot, however obliquely.'

'I am confidently safe within my own camp. Is that not why I am entrusted with this task?'

'Gaius, you carry the ability to be an honest man. Stay honest and all good things will befall you. I assure you, we shall speak on your behalf in the Senate when we display our surprise at the things we find here.'

A trumpet resounds from the gateway of the Temple.

Curio sits bolt upright as three figures appear. Dressed entirely in white, they shuffle across the open space.

As they near the canopy, Curio can see that their skin is grimed with sweat and the scabs and sores of weeks without proper food and pure water. They halt a few feet away, their legs trembling beneath them, bodies swaying from total deprivation.

Beneath the grime these are old men, priests most likely, a caste not unused to politics itself.

Curio understands innately why Aristion has sent them. These are the most fragile of the shields behind which he hides. He takes pity on the fact that they have been deemed dispensable and motions them to be seated.

Fully expecting to be killed, they are taken aback by the gesture. 'General…?'

Curio laughs abruptly. 'No. I am not Sulla. Have no fear for your life. Be seated.' He pulls forward his chair. 'I offer my own seat. Does that sound like Sulla?'

Cautiously, the priests lower themselves into the offered seats. Curio stands, his broad back shielding them from the sun streaming under the canopy.

'And what have you to offer?'

The priests share a common glance. 'We are here to request an audience with Atticus.'

'There is no such person here.'

'A moment, Gaius…'

Under guise of a friendly restraining gesture, Tullius'

fingers tighten remarkably around Curio's forearm.

He addresses the spokesman for the priests.

'I am he. Of what do you wish to speak?'

Curio shakes his arm free. 'Wait… I am told you are Tullius. I know that Atticus is not a Senator, yet those are Senatorial robes. Are you an impostor?'

Senator Crassus takes his arm and leads him away.

'Gaius… Gaius… calm down. There is nothing here that will dishonour you. Sulla would not have countenanced Atticus' involvement in this expedition if he had known. You know how he despises intellectuals. I know not by what god-given gift you yourself manage to survive Sulla's company.'

'Do not seek to flatter me, Crassus. Sulla *must* have seen him. I myself have seen them share a table.'

'Seeing is not knowing, Gaius. Sulla knows Atticus only by reputation. I can not know what you have seen, but I know they have never been introduced as such at table. So I beg of you, for the sake of your own future, please allow this small deception to continue.'

'Then where is the real Tullius?'

'He is keeping out of sight for the moment. Visiting friends in the countryside outside of Rome. You may know him also as Cicero.'

'Cicero? As verbose an asp as you would wish to find in an otherwise placid nest of vipers?' He places his hand over that of Crassus. 'I see which way lies safety. I will accede to your request… but don't forget the woman.'

A chair has been brought for Atticus. He leans forward eagerly to listen. The priest's voice is cracked and broken, his emaciated hand constantly massaging his throat.

Atticus waves to the Centurion who has brought the chair. 'Bring wine!'

The priest holds up an unsteady arm that falls to his lap.

'Not wine. We dare not. Water, if you will. I fear wine may kill us in our present condition.'

'Here…' Atticus passes a flask of clean water. The priest drinks lightly from it before passing it to the others. He gulps air greedily as if breath has been denied him for days, then clutches his stomach and doubles over in pain.

Atticus snatches the flask away. 'Centurion?' He holds the flask high in the air away from them.

'Just water, Senator, I promise you. I myself have drunk from the same…'

'Wait…' The priest beckons the flask from Atticus' outstretched hand and sips again. '…it is as he says. But it ceases to be just water after so many days with none. My body was not prepared. It is better now.'

He passes the flask to the others. 'We thank you.'

'Do you require food? No… of course you do.'

'A little wafer… something light or blessed. My mouth has lost the taste for…'

Atticus sets the flask aside where they can reach it.

The priest steeples his fingers. 'I thank you for your kindness, but before I entreat with you, may I ask one question?' He shuffles uncomfortably on the chair, the hard wood pressing urgently on pelvic bones stripped clean of all excess. 'By what sign are you sent?'

'By this…'

Atticus turns his back to them, parting the folds of his toga to display the bright serpentine scar that writhes across his back from left buttock to right shoulder blade.

There is a gasp from one of the priests. 'It is as we were told. Forgive us. We were instructed to ask this of you.'

'It matters not. It gives no pain.'

The priest sits forward in his chair.

'May we ask…?'

Atticus shrugs lightly.

'My mother was an adulteress and when my father beat her she gave up her guilt. He drowned her in a bath of boiling water. I was bound and at her breast when he threw her in. She had thought he would not harm her while she held me. As she screamed he filled her mouth with his sword and plunged her head beneath the surface, holding her there until he was sure she was dead. My nurse plucked me from the water and hid me with relatives from my mothers house in Etruria.'

'And your father…?'

'He died an old man.'

The priest reaches again for the flask. 'Occasionally, this world seems to carry little in the way of natural justice.'

Atticus hands it to him and, as it passes between them, his fingers are touched by the priest in a wasted gesture of sympathy.

'On the contrary. I acquired an education and gathered my wits beneath me. When I had garnered sufficient favour, I had him killed.'

'But even so, the swiftness of a knife is not…'

Atticus dismisses the sentiment with a slow shake of the head. 'This time the water was cold when they began.'

The Centurion has returned with a plate of hard dry bread. Atticus takes it from him impatiently. 'What is this?'

'It is from my own ration, Senator. We too have been here many months.'

The priest snatches at the crumbs, ignoring the thicker pieces. 'We assure you, it is indeed a feast.'

'It is not my vision of hospitality.'

'Hospitality is an embarrassment if the recipient is given more than he can take.' His fingers steeple again in gratitude. 'How may we entreat with you?'

Atticus spreads his legs carelessly into the space between them.

'I expect you to plead for the life of Aristion.'

'We care nothing for Aristion. Do with him as you will.'

'Then why have you not thrown him out at our feet?'

'There are those within the Temple who see Aristion as their only hope of survival. They bear arms against those of us who suggest this may not be the case.'

'Then what will it take to end this stupidity?'

'As you are aware, in the Order of The Temple there are many priests and priestesses. If I can guarantee Aristion and his men immunity, they will not carry out their threat of indiscriminate slaughter. We ask that you offer them safe passage.'

Curio's voice roars in from the far edge of the canopy.

'As far as the nearest galley... where they shall be put to an oar!'

The priest bows his head in that direction. The potential of the day is wavering. Curio's interjection shows it may not be advancing as he had hoped. The few crumbs of bread are already being rejected by his stomach. His throat convulses rapidly. He reaches for the flask of water as Atticus speaks.

'I agree to this condition.'

The priest's hand stops mid-air. 'You do?'

Atticus passes him the flask.

'Is it to be so easy? We thought to negotiate.'

'There will be no negotiation.' Atticus takes all three of the priests in with a single glance. 'We know our real purpose in this. The sooner it is expedited the better.'

'They will not be killed?'

'Their fate may be no better than Curio suggests, but they will live. All that remains is to understand how this shall be brought about.'

'Leave this now to us. There will be no need of entry by your soldiers. All we ask is that you respect our place of dedication to the Gods. Beneath the Temple is a secure chamber. We will show it to yourself alone. By sunset, Senator, your victory shall be complete.'

Curio has turned his face away in anger. Atticus escorts the priests to the edge of the canopy and raises his voice.

'I'm afraid *my* victory may be far in the future. This moment belongs to Gaius Curio.'

Curio spins around to address the priests.

'If that is to be the case, then I wish you well.'

The priests steeple their fingers before him.

Curio returns the gesture with a smirk.

As Atticus stares after them thoughtfully, Curio taps his arm. 'There is a woman… or so I am informed?'

Atticus bears up under a sudden flush of despair.

Ordinarily, this man's thoughts cannot find their way from within a sieve.

'Why should a woman trouble you?'

'I am told she is of incredible beauty. That she is a thing rarely seen this close to the centre of the world.'

'And your particular interest would be?'

'We have not yet discussed payment for my honesty. Perhaps if you have no need of her when this is done?'

'She is an integral part of this. As vital to our success as are yourself, Curio. For now she must remain inviolate. However, once she has been interviewed in Rome, there may be little further use for her.'

'Then tell them not to mark her face. I cannot counsel myself to that. Although there are other afflictions… certain marks… that…'

NOCTE HORA SEPTIMA

Rough hands propel the priests through the darkness of the inner Temple, their eyes as yet unadjusted after the brilliance of the square outside.

They find themselves thrown at the feet of Aristion, a short, stocky man whose skin is burned black by his refusal to shelter from the sun and whose eyes burn dark with the madness of a claustrophobia induced by weeks spent within the cloisters of the Temple of Athena.

'Well? Do we fight our way to the arms of Pluto? Or are we to sit here in anticipation of Sulla's visit?'

The priests help each other from the floor, noting the way Aristion constantly shifts his weight from one foot to the other.

'Neither shall be necessary, Your Greatness.'

'Neither? Are you telling me that the Rom…'

'We have secured your safety… and that of your men.'

'Our safety? From a Roman? You lie! Are you so ready for death that you would lie t…'

'It is the truth. I have the word of both Curio and Atticus that you shall not be harmed. All will be allowed to live.'

Aristion paces the floor of the entrance hall. 'This is a trick. What did Sulla have to say? I cannot believe that he would allow me to live, especially as I have publicly insulted his whore…'

'His wife.'

'Whose side are you on?'

'The side of reason, Your Greatness. For the moment, Sulla knows nothing of this. We must move before he hears of it.'

'And when he finds out?'

'Atticus assures me that you will be long gone. His assertion was that you would be transported from Piraeus on Curio's own ship.'

'And when Sulla finds me gone?'

'One can only imagine his sense of outrage.'

Aristion fills the hall with a bright ring of laughter.

'Much like your own when you asked for bushels of corn and I sent you pepper.'

'Your Greatness does what he can in times of need. We understand that.'

'You have fared reasonably on it.'

'I assure Your Greatness, the taste of your generosity has never been far from our mouths.'

'So, priest. What are we to do to bring this about?'

'You must accompany us into the Temple Square. A seat is being prepared for you there and you may speak safely to Atticus and Curio for reassurance about your conditions. You will then be transported to Piraeus by chariot. At that time your men will exit, leaving the Temple and all other persons remaining within it intact. All their weapons must be left behind by the door. The Romans will enter to see that this has been done in accordance with the entreaty and, if this is found to be so, they will be spared without exception.'

'You have done well, priest. But we shall not leave yet. I will wait until sunset.'

'Why should that be, Your Greatness?'

'They are still the enemy, priest, and the sun will be in their eyes. I do not expect you to understand that.'

Aristion swaggers across to the centre of the Temple Square.

The flat evening sun catches the woven gold thread in the hem of the cloth that covers a table there. A flask of wine has been laid upon it, surrounded by wooden cups, their gilded rims burnished crimson in the light.

Aristion stands behind the single chair and waits to die.

From under the canopy, Atticus and Curio appear. Their robes are singularly well arranged and clean in stark contrast to Aristion's own condition.

As they approach the table, Atticus motions him to be seated. Aristion reaches behind his back for the sword he pushed down his belt, brandishing it high in the air.

Curio makes an involuntary movement backwards but Atticus stops him with a hand at his back. He turns swiftly, apprehension clouding his eyes.

Atticus silences him with a gesture.

The sword slashes the air above the table, clearing the flask and cups from it and, in that same movement, it leaves Aristion's hand and clatters noisily, handle first, towards the Romans.

Atticus nudges Curio forward. *'Your moment.'*

Curio strikes at the hilt as if his arm were an asp. He pulls the sword quickly out of harms way and holds it aloft.

A cheer rises from the ranks of men surrounding the Temple. Curio spins on one heel, flashing the sword so the setting sun reflects like fresh blood across the bronze.

'Athens is mine!'

Cheers resound across the square, falling through the silence of the evening onto lower slopes already fading to shadow, where they nudge awake resting men and prick the ears of horses and mules.

DIEI HORA OCTAVA

Sulla brushes aside the flap of his tent. 'What was that?'

'It can only be from the Temple, General. I know nothing else of import.'

'Then they have him, Marcus. Let us be there and drag him out. I want to make the fool dance to *my* tune, not Curio's.'

'Can you walk, General?'

'Not that far, Marcus. Two horses… and be quick.'

Sulla stamps his numb feet around in the dry earth as they wait, raising dust into the desiccated air that now hangs throughout the camp, attaching to him the worst of the smells created by his siege and the Greek carcasses that rot within the city.

'Gods, what I wouldn't give for a storm. I didn't know I would have to eat so much of Athens in order to conquer it.'

'The horses are here, General.'

'I am lame not blind, Marcus. Where is my mounting stool? Scribe?'

The secretary rushes out with a fabric covered chest. He opens the lid to take out a pair of short leather boots.

'No time, man.' Sulla waves him aside, steps on the chest and swings up onto the horse, snatching the reins from the farrier.

'General, Sir?'

Sulla leans down to the farrier. 'What is it man, we are in need of all speed.'

'Our scouts say a rider has appeared on the road from Delphi. He bears a message from the Pythia.'

Sulla turns the horse around to head up the hill. 'Then let

him give it to the Scribe. I have no time now.'

As he approaches the Acropolis, the western edge of the sky begins to thicken. Storm-heads roil upwards, broad as celestial anvils. The air bears a yellow tinge and the hairs on Sulla's arms spring slowly erect.

A wind arises, shifting eastwards the smell of corruption and devastation, masking it with a salt tang from the peninsular sea.

They crest the slope into the Temple Square to find the central space darkening. It is empty of everything save a canopy, a chair and a table. Wine has spilled across the surface beside them, dried to a stain by the warmth emerging from the stone.

Behind the canopy, a group of soldiers have herded together the remnants of the Greek defenders.

'We are late, Marcus. Curio will have claimed Athens as his.'

Marcus points across to the Temple door. 'There… there was a light. It's gone now.'

Sulla trots his horse across the square. The wind is falling and the air that wraps around him is curiously charged. He feels it upon every part of his body, moving in tendrils beneath his clothes.

Without warning, the clouds disgorge a tremendous lightning strike that excoriates the hill to the East. Rock-hard earth flies high into the air, shattering as it falls on the flat stones around Sulla. In the same instant, copious amounts of water descend upon them. The horses halt in shock.

The last of the light falls with the deluge until Marcus finds himself completely disoriented. Sulla turns his face up to the sky and allows the water to fill his mouth, revelling in the freshness as it purges the bitter dust of the last months.

He nudges his horse forward.

The Temple is a substantively darker element in the

gloom. Dismounting in the shelter of its portico, he finds the door closed firmly against him. From under the sill a chink of pale light flickers and wavers.

He bangs loudly on the door.

'Open up! I am General Sulla.'

Under the sill, the light grows paler until it disappears.

NOCTE HORA NONE

'Sulla is at the door!'

Atticus frowns. 'So soon?'

The acolyte is shaking with fear. The flame of his torch sheds bubbling pitch to the floor, threatening the hem of his robe. At the entrance to the Inner Sanctum, Atticus tries to determine a new path.

A priest pulls him into the room. 'Sulla will kill us all! Close the door. He may not find us.'

Atticus shakes off the bony hand, the skeletal fingers almost audible as they are brushed aside.

'You do not know Sulla.'

The priest hides his hands in shame. 'I know of him.'

'But not as I do. Sulla will know we are here. If we hide he will find us or tear the Temple down trying. There has to be another way… an element of Sulla that I can appeal to… let us hope I find it in time. Send an acolyte to open the door but, before they allow him in, make sure Sulla understands that all within are under the protection of Curio and the Senate. Lead him here only after you have delayed him as much as you dare.'

To Atticus, the Inner Sanctum seems far bigger than can be imagined from outside. Walls and ceiling made distant by the black of a century of torchlight, it occupies the space beneath the central plinth of the shrine to Athena, an area of some fifty feet by forty. One half is stacked with metal-bound chests and large amphorae, some more than half the height of a man.

Under the flare of torches, dark shapes huddle against the far wall, several numbers deep.

Atticus' voice resonates within the stone chamber.

'Listen to me!' He drops to a more sensitive pitch as the figures detach themselves from the wall. 'Sulla is at the door. If you wish to live, obey me now without question.'

He crosses the short distance to the nearest figure and lifts back the dark hood to expose the pale features of a young woman. Her hair is black as night, but dulled from months without care.

'All of you! Remove your hoods.'

The figures swirl like a pool of dark, uncertain water.

'Now!'

With a rustle of heavy cloth, the figures begin to remove their hoods.

Atticus turns to the Priest.

'They are *all* women!' How shall I know which is she?'

He scans the crowded women, each one adorned with the same raven hair as her sister. In the centre, several of them huddle closely. He weaves his arms amongst them, scattering brown-robed figures, peering into their faces before pushing them away. As swiftly as he sends them aside, they return to the centre. He raises his voice in frustration until it crashes around the crevices of the room, echoing and multiplied a hundred times.

They move away from him, stunned by his ferocity.

At the centre of the huddle is a taller figure, still fully robed. He grabs her shoulders and she is made almost weightless by his anger. As her feet leave the floor he sees that they are small and finely boned.

She throws aside the hood. Grey-blue eyes stare back at him in the torchlight. He notices a fleck of green in one iris before the fine, white-blonde hair cascades across her face.

She shakes it clear of her eyes to stare at him openly.

He feels a thrill travel his fingers where he grips her. It passes along his arms until his chest is filled with a strange vibration.

He releases her suddenly. 'You are she.'

She nods briefly. 'If you insist.'

'Sulla must not find you. I do not know how much he knows or is capable of knowing, but he must not find you.'

A small flap is withdrawn in the Temple door.

'Who *are* you?'

'Have I not shouted a hundred times my name? Unlock this door. I have ten good men with me. If you don't open it now we shall lift it from the hinge.'

'I am sent to remind you that I and all within this Temple are under the protection of Curio and the Senate of Rome. You are ordered to commit no harm nor allow any harm to befall…'

'Gods, yes! Open the door, man.'

'Wait…'

There is a sound of many bars being deliberately drawn.

Sulla barges against the door again. This time it swings open easily. A stepladder flies noisily across the floor and an acolyte falls in a huddle at his feet.

Sulla draws his sword and squats beside him. 'Now…'

The acolyte howls in protest as Sulla pokes him, turning the blade to make a slit along the length of an exposed underarm. The bone glows white just beneath the skin. Faint traces of blood congeal instantly around the lip of the wound. '… I shall know what you know. Where is Curio?'

'He is not here.'

Sulla pokes him again in the ribs. This time the sword glances off bone immediately. The acolyte sobs pain into the dark air and curls into a foetal position. The stench from his robes is indescribable. Sulla turns him onto his back and inserts his sword between flesh and bone.

106

The acolyte's screams rend the air in the atrium chamber.

'I tell you! He is not here!'

'Then who is?' Sulla twists the blade. 'I will try not to kill you. After all, you have the protection of Curio and the Senate.'

Gasping for breath, the acolyte turns his head to retch but only green bile issues from his mouth.

'Curio is gone. There is only one other.'

Sulla kneels beside him. 'And who might that be?'

The Acolyte groans loudly. 'It is Atticus. If you allow me to live, I will take you to him.'

'Atticus? You lie. Atticus is in Rome. Marcus… let us find out what's happening.'

'General. This man may indeed be under the protection of the Senate.'

'Then I will insist they pay for a good funeral. Marcus? Your arm…'

A flickering torch leads them amongst the pillars that support the vast roof. At the centre of the Temple is a huge plinth on which stands the statue of Athena. There is an open roof above the plinth and rainwater pours down into the over-flowing impluvium, surrounding it in a solid sheet that is almost impossible to see beyond. At the foot of a broad column, a priest awaits their approach.

'Put away your sword, General.' He steeples his fingers before Sulla. 'I assure you no-one here wishes you harm.'

Sulla returns the gesture with a smile. 'It is my practice to allow my sword to bring me that assurance.'

'Then forgive my lack of modesty, General, but as I and my colleagues were wholly responsible for the relief of the Temple, does that not make me also your instrument?'

Sulla looks around as far as the flickering torch will allow.

Slowly, he returns his sword to its sheath. 'I grant you a moment of trust. Now tell us what is happening here.'

'We are attempting an orderly withdrawal from our Temple. We wish to leave it intact so that we can restore it to order after its occupation by Aristion. Hopefully, with the Grace of Athena, we can then begin to rebuild our city from the ashes you have so gracefully left us.'

An arc of hidden stonework swings aside behind the priest. A figure emerges, stepping into the torchlight.

Sulla reaches for the hilt of his sword.

'Tullius!. How deep is the hand of the Senate plunged? The wrist? The elbow?'

'I fear it is deeper even than that, General. I am sent to ensure the Athens that rises from your ashes will never again be a threat. It will become a city state, governed by its people in covenant with Rome.'

Sulla explodes with laughter. 'Only a true Roman would have the arrogance to return democracy to the Greeks.'

Just as suddenly, his laughter subsides. 'So what are you hiding?'

'I have nothing to hide, General, and my only desire is to see an end to war.'

'We all need a reason to perform for the Gods, Tullius. Do not deny me mine.' Sulla's hand rests on the pommel of his sword. 'Now show me what it is you are hiding.'

'May I remind the General that all persons within this Temple are under the protection of the Senate.'

Sulla catches the senatorial robe in one hand.

'Move aside.'

A soldier enters the torch flare that surrounds them.

'General, sir. I would speak of this only with you. Your Scribe has sent the message from the Pythia of Delphi.'

Atticus draws the Senatorial robes back around himself, rearranging them to keep warm the taut skin of his back.

The priest has withdrawn into the chamber and he is left to face the small group alone. He tries to read Marcus' face but finds him as impassive as any soldier he has ever met.

Without warning, Sulla's sword is at his throat.

'Your name?'

'My name is Atticus.'

'Your name was given to me as Tullius. What purpose lies behind this deception?'

'Please remove your sword, General. Remember that I am under protection.'

Sulla jabs him without breaking skin. 'Atticus, robes do not a Senator make… and may I remind you… while I am in the Temple, that edict also covers me. If I find that your mission is to my detriment, shall I not feel at liberty to protect myself?'

'Our missions are not the same, General. There is no need for conflict. As your mission ends, mine begins. I am to restore order to Athens once your armies have departed.'

'You lie!'

The priest returns from inside the chamber. Marcus and Sulla take an involuntary step back as a rank stench follows him through the door. Atticus raises a hand to Sulla's sword.

'Let us not bring death into the Temple. We all want the same thing.'

Sulla takes a deep breath before entering the Sanctum.

Instantly, the reek makes Marcus beside him gag. There is a strong, ill-earth smell of pitch-fired torches racked along the wall, but an undercurrent of perfumed incense thickens the air until it becomes impossible for Sulla to draw another breath without his own stomach convulsing.

The room is half-filled with amphorae and chests but, aside from these, a huddle of black-cloaked figures swirls away from them in the open space.

Sulla prods Atticus with his sword. 'Throw back their hoods!'

Atticus raises his hand and the women lower their hoods.

Sulla studies them for the sign he has just been given but the women seem identical in the gloom.

He slides the sword back into its sheath and shakes Atticus violently by the elbow. 'Where is she?'

'Who, General?'

'You know very well who.'

Atticus returns his stare with an impassivity to rival that of Marcus. Sulla shakes him again. 'The Priestess with the white hair. Where is she?'

Atticus snatches his arm away. 'She is Curio's prize for allowing the liberation of the Temple without bloodshed. You may have her when he is finished, although from what I hear of Curio, there may be little left.'

'And of what is her importance?'

Atticus shrugs diffidently. 'She has an ability that Curio deems important. I hear it is a certain capacity for futures. Although, I fear…' He glances at the clutter surrounding them. '…it may all be Greek to him.'

Sulla speaks softly, the words falling short of ears other than Atticus'.

'I counsel you, Atticus, do not return to Rome while I live. There are things afoot that I have little time to divine but, be assured, one day I shall know them. In Rome there are few whose lips cannot be prised apart by a coin. When the knowledge is in my possession, make certain you are not.'

Atticus inclines his head. 'General.'

Sulla lifts his feet from the rainwater that has risen inside the chamber. 'Priest. Get your people out of here. This place is flooding.'

'I beg you, General. May we have assistance in this? We are weakened by the siege. We cannot carry our sacraments alone.'

Sulla takes a deep breath in the cleaner air of the outer

Temple.

'Marcus, send to Curio's men for an ox-cart. Anything they have will do. What these people can't salvage they'll have to do without. Use my name. They will waste no time in passing that along to Curio. Let's see how loudly the bars of his cage rattle. Get the women out first.'

The female acolytes assemble in the space before the entrance to the chamber, four carrying between them a small metal-bound chest.

'Leave that.'

The priest takes Marcus' arm. 'Please. Allow us to do what we can. We have a certain dignity to maintain.'

'Take it then. There will soon be a cart by the gate. You may ride in it yourself.'

NOCTE HORA UNDECIMA

Outside the Temple, the stench from the Sanctum is driven from the air by an almost unbreathable volume of rain.

Figures huddle together, extending their hoods for cover in the pitch blackness as water shears down between them, rising up again where it strikes the stone.

In seconds their cloaks are a drab shroud, clinging to bodies gaunt from deprivation. The cart itself is identifiable only as a thing of greater darkness against the backdrop of the square.

Marcus attends to the loading of the priests and their belongings. The chest the women carried is slid in amongst the priests feet.

The cart pulls slowly across to the road that will take them through the shattered gate and down into the city proper. Sulla follows them on horseback, catching up easily with the women trailing in its wake.

Despite the rain, the miasma arising from the wet cloth

attaches to the back of his throat. He rides in front of the cart to bring it to a halt. His purpose seems lost in the constancy of the deluge but gradually the column shuffles to a standstill.

He returns to the cart. 'Your people. Tell them to remove their clothes.'

The priest leans across the rail. 'I cannot do that. They are Priestesses. They have their dignity.'

'How can anyone maintain dignity in the face of such a stench?'

'You will provide a place in your camp where we can be cleansed in a proper manner.'

Sulla lifts his voice above the storm.

'This is your one opportunity. The rain here will cleanse both them and their clothes. We have no standing water in the camp…' He glances up into the deluge. '… and the ground will take all of this at one swallow.'

'I cannot countenance this.'

'I refuse to take pestilence into my camp. Either they disrobe or stay out on the hill. Your choice, but make it now. They will die if left here.'

The priest hesitates for too long a moment.

Sulla barks an order into the darkness.

'Marcus! Gather our men and return to camp. We can reunite these people with Curio tomorrow.'

The priest reaches out to him. 'Wait…'

There is a fear buried in his voice that does not escape Sulla's ear, one far deeper than the consequence of being left out on the hill.

'Order them to disrobe if you must but… ensure their absolute safety amongst your men.'

Sulla lifts the hand from his arm.

Marcus passes amongst the women, lifting hoods and slipping cloaks to the ground.

Rain cascades the length of their bodies, pouring filth onto the flagstones. They huddle for warmth and propriety, bodies skeletal, non-sexual, dark streaks etching their pale features.

Sulla returns to the priest. 'I think you will have little to fear from my men. Marcus? Take them down to the camp. Find them shelter near my own tent where we can keep a watch of them.'

The small caravan disappears into a fog of rain as they descend. Sulla trails by a few paces, an intense feeling of dissatisfaction occupying his mind.

Below him, hooded campfires burn fitfully amongst the shelters, where light is the only thing able to defy the gravity of the descending water.

A sudden reflection catches his eye.

At Sulla's command, Marcus grapples with the ox.

He forces its nose down as far as it will go, hooves sliding as it braces the weight of the cart against the hill.

'Marcus. With me…' Sulla forces his horse through the column.

The priest reaches out as he passes. 'General..?'

Sulla brushes him aside to grasp Marcus' arm.

'Bring her to me.'

The women swirl in the darkness, impeding his passage. Marcus parts them easily although they cling to him, the filth from their limbs attaching to his skin.

He holds her aloft in the light from the distant fires, his sense of triumph turning slowly to one of pity.

Sulla dismounts to study her lean features, the unusual height from which she stands to look down upon him. He reaches up to touch the blonde streaking her hair, wondering how he had missed her before.

A thick streak of heavy lampblack runs across her brow.

He traces the line down the perfect skin of her slender

neck to the dark pool it makes in her collar-bone from where it pours between the cleft of her breasts.

It circumnavigates her navel before continuing into the breech-cloth, where it finally disappears.

'If she isn't what we seek, Marcus, we at least have a prize worthy of any man's salt.'

CHRONICLE

XI

THE EYE OF HORUS

**MARTIUS XV11,
DIES MARTIS**

DIEI HORA DUODECIMA

The air about her is abrasive with imperative voice as amphorae, statues and large chests are hefted across the gap between the boat and the quay.

The shaved elm timbers at her back are hot from the mid-day sun. The pitch between the deck planks has bubbled out and her bare feet stick willingly to it. She tucks in her legs and covers them with her cloak.

A sudden clamour has driven her into this corner against the side rail. Some of the voices she hears are Greek, young men rapidly enslaved after Sulla's coup. Orders are shouted by Roman overseers, who she also understands.

She receives an inadvertent kick as two men struggle past carrying a stone carving. A wooden derrick swings a marble horse statue high over her head until it drops from sight into the dark space of the hold.

Someone takes her arm and lifts her gently to her feet.

The Centurion who brought her to the ship now leads her to a small cabin at the stern. They duck their heads through the door into a room lit by openings in both sides, oiled-cloth blinds rolled tight above them.

A low couch set against the far wall has cloth-of-gold thrown over it. A gimballed lead font stands empty behind the door and the heavy leather chest that has accompanied her travels sits in a corner. He leaves her by a window, her fingers pressed around the sill.

A small bag of auguries hangs around her neck. She

places it on a small table before returning to the window.

Behind the Harbour of Zea, the hill is studded with opulent villas that once belonged to the wealthy traders and ship owners of Piraeus, their households recently displaced by the elite of the Roman army.

Between the villas and the harbour lay the ruins of the town. Smoke rises from it in pockets of still air. Scents of burned wood and flesh assault her but she is compelled to the scene as it flickers in the brilliance of the sun.

The charred hardwood frame of the old market rises above the debris like the ribs of a supine carcass. Framed within it she divines the immediate future of Greece from the blackened bolts of cloth, glowing embers and desolate ash climbing the midday heat spirals.

On the water are many ships similar to the one on which she stands... broad-beamed hollow gourds... converted from grain-carrying to hold the plunder from Athens.

Outside the harbour, a fleet of Roman warships rides at anchor, wind plucking their rigging with the fingers of an invisible archer.

She watches a nearby ship being loaded with chest after chest of parchment. Loose rolls are bundled in the arms of slaves and stacked on deck, careless of sea and weather.

This is the library of Apellicon the Teian, containing works by Aristotle and Theophrastus. It concerns her far more than any amount of jewellery and statues, for when all knowledge is gone, what will Athens have left?

DIEI HORA PRIMA

There is a knock at the door. It opens without her answer and the Centurion re-enters. A youth carrying water follows him into the room to fill the font. The Centurion crosses to the window to stand beside her.

'You have a visitor. Prepare yourself.'

She ignores his words and turns back to the window.

He catches her shoulder with one hand, drawing her away from the scene across the bay to look into his eyes.

They flicker with apprehension.

'Quickly. What do you see?'

'Why do you ask me that?'

'I am told that you can *see*… how that is, I…?'

'It is not a sight that you would wish, nor care to know the meaning of.'

'I have little time, your visitor will be here any moment.'

'I am sorry. I must not do this. Please ask no more.'

He considers her words, realising as he does that to see into a soldier's future she may not have to look too far.

'Do you know your visitor?'

'Yes.'

There is a trouble behind his unsteady, brown-eyed gaze.

She touches his cheek and reads him in the instant that a single trumpet note from the quay reaches them, the tone at once falling sad and dismal across the water.

His flesh trembles beneath her fingers where they touch. The colour fades from his face. Time slows inside him until he is stilled, like a man awaiting the last drop of water through the empty bowl of a *clepsydra*.

Her eyes soften as her vision reaches into him, finding honesty disrupted by circumstance until she discovers an unquestioning soldier's heart.

His face closes against her intrusion, instinctively fearful of what she is doing. His eyes open again… and in them is a new acceptance of fortune.

Withdrawing from her touch, he raises her hood with the tips of his fingers. She is younger than he had first thought. Her hair is now pure blonde, white as the ash of Piraeus borne on the wind. In the shade of the cabin her features are sharpened only by shadow, the skin pale and unmarked.

She lowers her hand. 'Are you to sail with us?'

'Yes.'

She moves into his embrace to whisper her reply.

The door bursts open behind him and she converts the movement into a kiss on the cheek.

Sulla ducks into the room, the fox-like stealth for which he is known pacing suspiciously within his eyes.

'Explain yourself, Marcus.'

'There is nothing to explain, General. I brought water and asked that she prepare herself to meet you.'

The smile remains around Sulla's lips. 'And that warrants a display of affection?'

'I do not know, General'

'Then perhaps I had better ask the lady. Leave us now.'

As the door closes behind Marcus, the Priestess turns her attention to the General, whose agitated complexion breathes life into the Athenian jest that, 'Sulla is a mulberry, sprinkled with meal'.

'I was merely conveying my gratitude, General.'

'To whom?'

'To yourself, General.'

'For what indeed? A pail of fresh water?'

'For such a handsome Centurion.'

She moves to the window, observing the shapes of boats out amongst the water. Some of them appear as shades of inviability… their futures betrayed by her insight. Beneath her feet the deck now seems as insubstantial as smoke rising from the ruins of Piraeus.

Before Sulla arrived, it had been solid, impenetrable.

She considers what it is that sets apart this man who has wrought such change… what dæmons perch his shoulder.

His reputation shows him to be mercurial, as prone to laughter as to slaughter. At fifty-one his intensity of feature lays coarsened by revelry, though his hair, still blonde, weighs upon his head in golden waves as if set there by a storm. His brow is high and has risen noticeably since she first saw him in a dream.

Sulla's strength of voice seems to solidify the air within the cabin. 'The Tuscans tell me this is the end of their Great Year. Is that so?'

She dips her head in mock respect. 'I bow to the wisdom of the Tuscans.'

'I hear that you bow to no man.'

She turns away from the window. She has seen all she needs of the sack of Piraeus. Her own mission exceeds such infinitesimal moments of concern. Athens will recover… in time. She has leafed the pages of history and knows what a small chapter this will become.

'I respect wisdom, General, but am never awed by it. And against power I offer no defence.'

'None whatsoever?'

'That is the best defence of all, for the powerful quickly tire of unresponsive playthings.'

'You would play mouse to my cat?'

'There are few cats, General, compared to the invisible hordes of mice. In that invisibility is their true power.'

'It is said that my own power is derived from that of the Gods. Our sacrifice at Tarentum showed the liver of a sheep in the form of a laurel wreath… with two fillets depending from it.'

She lifts her head into the blaze of sunlight piercing the window. 'The Triumphal Crown.'

The light is a tapestry of gold overlaying her bone structure, her skin an empty palette, allowing the colour to penetrate deep into the flesh beneath.

Sulla is lost in his admiration of her.

'It is a large crown…'

She smiles at his offer, lips wide over white, even teeth.

'No matter how broad a crown may be, General, they never fit easily on more than one head.'

'Then how shall I purchase your wisdom, for I fear that it cannot be bought by wealth alone.'

'What need have you of my wisdom? By your own assertion you have the ear of the Gods. They answered your call for the storm.'

Sulla wipes sweat from his hands on his tunic. 'But I cannot always hear *them*.'

'What would you wish to hear?'

'I wish to hear the things that you hear. See the things that you are reputed to see.'

She shies away from his earnest approach.

'Do not wish that. There seems no end to this panoply of voices, faces, all manner of shapes and shades that loom out of dream and into my waking consciousness. To know that nothing is permanent is a terrible burden.'

'Do not patronise me. I know that men are ephemeral.'

'Ephemeral or not, I see the stricken before the Gods deliver their blow.'

'But with your vision I could deliver to Rome an Empire that will last forever.'

She turns away from him to the window overlooking the harbour. Across the water, boats shift and tilt as the weather drifts around to the north.

'Nothing is forever, General, including myself. Are you prepared to enact the instruction of the Pythia of Delphi?'

The eastern sky above Athens piles high with cloud, the sullen darkness in their bellies threatening and imminent.

Sulla takes a seat on the couch behind the table and flexes his legs. His ague is a constant in his life he would willingly dispel at any price.

'I am not surprised that you know the content of her sooth. I thought you sisters under the skin.'

'Her jealousy is emotion enough to have propagated that message. No other reason.'

'Her jealousy?'

'She weaves a warp-less tapestry of dream that falls apart the moment it leaves her hands. Once in the hands of others it becomes distorted and dystopian. She is blind to this.'

'Lack of a wider vision is not unusual amongst prophets.'

'I am not a prophet, General. This… in the Pythia's vapour-induced *enthusiasmos*… is what she fails to see. I do not make prophesy. I carry the message'

'And what of *her* message that I should seek you out and kill you immediately?'

'General, I have seen your sword sheathed and my blood was not the stain upon it. The first sword to touch my skin will be one that heals and I will ensure that the second shall be the last.'

'Then if I am not allowed to bargain for your life, with what shall I persuade you? Is there nothing that you envy?'

'What about you should I envy?'

'Are Greek women not envious of their men? Your own playwrights say you are 'garlic-smelling barmaids and bakehouse girls', unless I am mistaken?'

From the window, she watches cloud-shadow darken the distant white stone of the Acropolis, the rain in its wake soothing ash from ruined gates and temples.

There is movement in the outer city but all seems still to her, a mere breath of history.

'You study your enemies well, General, but I am not that enemy. I am Cimmerian.'

'And your name is…?'

'I am Priestess of Athena.'

'That I know. Atticus was ordered by Cinna to render you and your… device… unharmed to Rome.'

'Cinna is evil beyond your comprehension.'

'He was once my friend, but he has become my Nemesis and I would know the name of his intended weapon.'

Out to the west, a pale disc is setting early in a singular patch of blue sky. Once the storm passes, the oncoming night will be moonless.

Her eyes flash as she turns away from the window.

'The Tuscans know me as Artume.'

Sulla laughs sardonically.

'The Huntress at bay? Artume… Diana… Artemis… whatever. I am no faun beneath the string of your bow.'

'My real name is unimportant.'

'Let me be the judge of that.'

As she searches the fox in Sulla's eyes, the deck under her feet continues to become less distinct as if at any moment she may fall through into the hold beneath. Every gesture that he now makes pushes her further from safety.

She lifts back the cowl. Once exposed, her hair is white-blonde, as luminous as her skin.

'I shall be known to you as Minerva.'

Sulla stands from the couch, a sudden intoxication of blood bringing him to his feet. She stands above him by three finger-breadths and the power she conveys flows the air between them like an arrow of the Gods.

He is taken aback but holds his ground in order to search for the source of that power.

She has a capacity for beauty, though not by Roman standards. Her face would seem too lean… her features too sharp, though well-oriented… and there is no edge to her… nothing for a man to touch, trace and forgive… no small deflection that would hold a man's heart in thrall forever.

He touches her arm. The material of her sleeve within his fingers is harsh and unforgiving. He allows those fingers to slide to where they touch the exposed skin of her wrist.

In the split second before he is forced to remove his

hand the deck seems to pale and disappear beneath his feet, the shallow water of the Aegean, translucent and green, washing silently below him.

He staggers back a step and solidity returns.

'Then Minerva is how I must know you. Gods have too many names. A woman should have but one.'

She reaches out to return his touch. Sulla flinches but, as her fingers meld into his skin, he feels a calm beckon the fear from him.

Her voice is barely audible against the growing wind outside the window. 'I do not know whether there are many Gods with one name, or one God with many names. But know this… Sulla has no need nor fear of either.'

Sulla is aware of a tiredness rising from the soles of his feet. As it reaches his knees it becomes an acute pain. He falls heavily to the couch. She presses deeper until his pain becomes a negation, an absence of feeling, almost a pain in itself as his limbs refuse to respond.

'Are you a Dæmon?'

She releases her grip on his arm.

'No, General. You are the Dæmon. But a Dæmon with a sense of purpose can be useful to the Gods.'

Sulla knows that his limbs have begun to shake violently without the sensation of her touch but can do nothing to prevent it. 'You have killed me.'

'No, General. I have saved you. As I said, you have a purpose.'

'To live as a cripple? For what ill do I carry this penance?'

Laughing out loud, she resumes the cowl over her hair, an arc of chin looming from the shade like a slip of moon.

'I could say arrogance. But that is endemic in Rome and sets you only alongside many others. No, Time will tell you the story that I am forbidden to.'

She touches his arm again and the tremors subside.

Sulla relaxes into the cushion beneath him. 'Do not leave me like this. I have enemies who would torture me.'

'Would that not be fortune returned in kind?'

'Everything I do is for Rome. I would leave it better than I found it.'

'You will play your part, but Rome is unimportant.'

'How can you say that? An Empire the like of which you and I can create…'

She sits beside him on the couch and strokes his forehead, pushing back the blonde wave that his frustration has tumbled out of place.

'Empires will come and go, General. Each will beat its drum of decadence to the grave.'

'Rome…'

'Is but the latest and, as such, will span less than a moment in time.'

'We could build my State to last forever. Remove from me this witchery!'

'Have patience, General. Your contribution will make it last until the Gods are ready for it to fall.'

'Rome is bigger than the Gods. Damn you all to Hades.'

She laughs brightly at his condemnation. 'Hades realm is very like Rome… except there you *know* who your enemies are.'

'Then beware, Witch, for my Rome is an Idea… and not even the Gods can kill an Idea.'

Driven clouds clear the sky above them as the storm travels around the Harbour of Zea. Over the ruined hills of Athens, the air fills rapidly with black turmoil.

Minerva touches Sulla's forehead with a single finger.

His face relaxes. All signs of struggle die within his eyes as he becomes still, floating at the mercy of her tides, riding the swell of the Gods and dependent on the will of this woman in a way that he never dreamed could be his fate.

He watches her rise and walk to the door.

She grabs the water-boy as he dashes past. 'Where is the Centurion?'

He waves his arm over the harbour. On the quayside, soldiers are drawn up into a loose squad prior to boarding.

'There are many.'

'The one who brought me here.'

He points to a ship berthed the other side of the quay.

She shakes him hard. 'Fetch him.'

DIEI HORA QUARTA

Sulla has given himself into the arms of the damnation that holds him. Minerva sits beside him on the couch and he stares at her impassively.

She touches his arm once and sensation returns to his face. A growing howl of wind from outside floods the silence in his ear. His lips, however, are still held in thrall.

She leans over him to whisper. For a moment, he confuses the urgency in her voice with that of the wind.

'If you heed me now, General, I promise that you will die an old man, fair of favour within Rome. The Gods have one last task of you. In your absence, your old friend has become a dangerous foe and the world is not ready for what he portends.'

She brushes her lips over his. He feels the numbness drop from them but still he struggles to speak.

'You speak of Gaius Marius, the Socialist?'

'Not alone.'

Sensation returns to his neck and upper torso.

He lifts his head. 'Then who, damn you…'

'Cinna.'

'I carry Cinna's pledge. I have his vow to do no damage to my Constitution.'

She touches his brow and his shoulders relax once more

into the soft cushion. 'Under the influence of Gaius Marius, Cinna has already undone many of your reforms.'

'Marius? How many times do I have to defeat him?'

'The Gods will deal with Marius before you can reach Rome.'

'And of Cinna?'

'They shall deal with him also. The people will rise up against his contamination. His legacy shall not prosper if you play your part. These are the dying moments of a Great Age. Your task will be to wrench back the State from the Republic so that it can end its days in a fitting manner.'

'If what you say is true, you had no need of your dæmonic touch. It will be my pleasure.'

'I do not wish it to be a pleasure. Many will die at your hand.'

'That is Rome.'

'That is also the problem.'

She touches his arm and the numbness subsides until only his legs below the knee remain immobile.

There is a rapid knock at the door and Marcus ducks his head below the frame.

Seeing Sulla on the couch, his face clouds. 'General?'

Sulla points to Minerva where she waits by the window, scanning the sky. 'It seems the Witch has plans for us.'

Minerva drops the oiled cloth over the opening, securing it by a thong against the wind.

'Centurion, I need your help. Find a ship, one that will take the General across the straits to Aedepsus so that he may bathe in the healing waters there. Bring it only after nightfall.'

Sulla struggles upright. 'Why don't you use your witchery and remove this damned… whatever it is.'

'My witchery, as you call it, doesn't extend to the cure. I have used your own condition against you. Too much wine, too much flesh, is what ails you. You have luxuriated amongst the ruins of Victory too often.'

'A man should enjoy his conquests.'

'A man should be responsible for them also.'

Sulla is perched on the edge of the couch, rubbing his legs below the knee to little avail.

'How long shall I be at Aedepsus?'

'Take your time, General. The armies that are forming against you are at this moment fragmented and disparate. They fight readily amongst each other.'

'If their numbers are small, they will be easier to defeat.'

Minerva dips her hands in the font and places them over his where they rest on his knees. A coolness flows through him and the numbness in his legs recedes a little, releasing the pain he has been trying to ignore for the last few days.

'Tell me, General, how many battles will you fight to achieve one aim?'

He pushes her hands away. Moisture gleams his skin.

'As many as it takes.'

'What if I told you that one will be enough?'

Sulla dips his head in the briefest gesture. 'Then I bow to your vision. How shall I know when the time is right?'

'I shall tell you in a dream.'

'Are you not already that dream?'

'I am not for your pleasure, Lucius Cornelius Sulla.'

'Then how shall I know the truth of this dream, for having seen you, I may dream of you often.'

'You shall know it by the thunderbolt that I place in your hand. It will be your only guide.'

'To an easier victory than the last, I hope.'

'First it will guide you through fire and flame until you are known by your actions. Then Rome will forget your loose and self-indulgent beginnings and look upon you as a true son.'

'And how shall I repay her?'

'With murder, envy and violence, for that is your way politic.'

DIEI HORA SEPTIMA

'I have found a ship. It will berth alongside after dark.'

'When it arrives, take the General aboard and make your preparations. You must leave before light. If word reaches Rome that he has fallen to sickness, everything may change.'

She reaches out. 'Give me your word.'

Her fingertips make brief contact below the sleeve of the Centurion's tunic.

Marcus' broad arm takes the touch like a blow.

DIEI HORA OCTAVA

Minerva has rolled back the oiled-cloth cover. Evening light glances from the water in the harbour, dappling the hulls that roll on the swell. The sun is a slowly disappearing oblate coin that pierces the cabin window with a lance of deep orange. The carpentry it impales is solid, precise and secure. She waits in silence, anticipating the creak of oars pulling alongside.

The wind has subsided, along with the pain in Sulla's legs and with that has come the return of his curiosity. The chest in the corner absorbs his interest.

'What *is* this, that has cost so many lives?'

'How so?'

'In the fight to reach the Temple.'

'You went to Athens to capture Aristion.'

'Aristion was a rat in a trap… tricked out easily by Curio. Atticus' specific orders were to ensure the safe custody of yourself and this witches cabinet. Perhaps you are not the Adept that I thought. Shall my 'thunderbolt' be nothing more than a whip for a stubborn ox?'

'It will be a gift of great consequence.'

Sulla strokes the scabbard of the short thrusting sword to the left of his tunic.

'If they had heed of consequence, all Generals would stay home and die in bed.'

He sits back as her spark catches the wick in the lamp. A flame flickers into being, tearing the last barb of sunlight from the dark wood.

The leather straps lay unbuckled on the floor. The instrument from the olive-wood box stands before Sulla on the table. The secret door has been unlatched and set wide to catch the light from the lamp. The bright flash of the dial is inscribed with omens and sharply cut jewels.

From under her cloak, Minerva presents a slender metal pencil. It slides through a small hole in one side of the box.

Sulla is fascinated by the movement that it starts. The jewels cut patterns through the flickering light as the dials contra-rotate, settling first in one constellation then another, seemingly without order or design. Around an outer annulus there are thirteen inscriptions in Cyrillic lettering. He stares transfixed as the figures of the sun and moon pirouette eccentrically in a slow elliptic dance.

'I have never seen its like.'

The dials fall still. Minerva returns the corded key around her neck and settles it within the folds of her gown.

'And neither will you again.'

'What value has it, other than as a pretty thing. Does it cant music?'

'Only of the Spheres.' She moves to close the box.

'Wait… I would know more of it.'

'There is nothing more you can know, but I can show

you this.'

On the device are circular dials, divided and sub-divided into regressively small degrees of arc.

'This dial represents the Kalippic Cycle of 76 years. And this one…' She twists the device around to where Sulla can see it clearly. '…represents a cycle of 19 years, rediscovered by Meton of Athens and much favoured by the Babylonians. It is one absolute fourth of the Kalippic cycle… and this…' The dials rotate willingly under her touch. '…is the Saros Eclipse Cycle of 223 years. The outer ring and levers show the nightly dance of the planets while the Zodiac around them describes your destiny. So as you can see, wherever you are in the known world, this device can be your Lodestone to the future.'

She closes the box. Sulla tries to prevent her but has not yet regained his former agility.

She moves it deftly out of his reach, placing it in the bottom of the chest.

'You have nothing more to gain. You are not Adept.'

'By your own word I have the ear of the Gods.'

'This device is not of the Gods. They also fear its power.'

She steps away from him to the window.

There is movement on the wind. Hot air brushes sails and spars… somnolent in their swaying… hypnotic beams of darkness against a paler sky. Above them, the night is studded with smoke-riven stars.

She has borne witness to these bright-silvered omens wheeling frantically, driving the innermost thoughts of men such as this in his search for ambition and perhaps, in his case, a little purpose.

'An Adept can read the machine in a way that may disrupt the power of the Gods… and thereby influence the desires of men.'

'Am I then little more than an object of your design?'

'That may be. But it is not my design.'

'Then I will have nothing of it. Destroy the machine!'

'I cannot do that.' She sees the colour rise in his face and understands the danger that waits behind the decision in his eyes, the devastating combination of fox and lion that has promoted his life to this place. 'There would be little point.'

She takes his arm as his legs give way, easing him back to the couch. 'The design is not open to question. It was there long before either of us and will continue long after we are forgotten. I am only the reader. I have no choice of text.'

She watches his face for the sign that will appear though, in truth, she has no real fear of either.

The fox, silent as a forbidden thought, steals into his eyes. 'There is always choice.'

NOCTE HORA UNDECIMA

She extinguishes the lamp above the table. As darkness palettes the room she pulls aside the blind. A small warship hoves beside them in the water. Its oars at rest are a forest of slender, vertical stems. The rostrum prow is pressed hard against their beam and the Eye of Horus painted above it is observing her closely.

NOCTE HORA DUODECIMA

There is a single drum-beat and the oars fall as one to the water. Stars swirl their eddies as the warship powers out beyond reach of the flaming beacon at the harbour tip.

Once beyond the wall, the drumbeat lifts into a steady pattern. Four stadia out, by a beacon of light glistening the surface, the fleet waits in deep water.

Sulla searches the sky for the constellations he has seen marked on the device. Above him, Ophiuchus wrestles his Eternal Serpent while Argo Navis heels across the horizon as though driven hard by the Celestial Wind.

Despite having studied the stars on many occasions, Sulla has failed consistently to define his own pattern within them. He finds it impossible to believe, even now, that his future is held there by some arcane craft in an interminable pattern.

Through black waters, churning pale phosphorescence in its wake, the bireme drifts on through an opening in the anchorage. Waves ripple the hull as the anchor stone is launched over the side.

Sulla studies the ranks of shipped oars around them.

'You are good at taking orders, Marcus?'

'Yes, General.'

'And if your life depends on it?'

'I am Roman.'

'They tell me you are named Germanicus, and that your father fought against me. Is this not so?'

'Many years ago, General. He was a Gaul, captured by your army while he fought with the Cimbri at Vercellae.'

Sulla smiles into the darkness, remembering the flash of fire and bronze, the echoes of screams battering his senses, shattered trees blackened with blood.

'Your parents were taken as slaves.'

'My father bought his freedom.'

'How so?'

'In the Coliseum.'

'Give me your hand.'

Marcus grasps Sulla's arm and assists him to his feet.

Sulla stands unsteadily. 'Should I then need to watch my back?'

'I was born in Rome, General, three months after my father died. My mother is Antonia, Grecian slave to the wife of Tinnaeus, the Lanista who trained the father whose name I bear. She was taken on an island raid against coastal levies.'

'Then are you not a man torn by allegiance, Marcus

Germanicus?'

In the splash of light from the brazier above the stern of the ship, Sulla sees a look of consternation cross Marcus' face. 'You don't have to answer that.'

'I am Roman.'

'Rome has always clutched vipers to its breast, Marcus. Many more closely than you. But there is one who concerns me more. Send for wine. Let us find a space inside.'

From the darkness around them come the sounds of men and ships… a creak of timber, the bark and shuffle of bound slaves. There are low voices, the ripple of a gentle swell breaking on anchor lines and hulls.

A definable miasma pervades the anchorage… a wash of ordure, unclean skin and the char of spent ash blowing out from the shore.

Sulla takes a deep breath. 'What do your senses say?'

Marcus closes his eyes, distilling the sounds and smells into a single whole from which he can abstract a name.

'Home.'

'And if 'Home' was no more than an Idea?'

'I don't understand the question, General.'

'Then answer me this. Is man created inside of a God's Idea, or are Gods simply Ideas created inside of a man?'

Marcus turns his hands palm up to stare into the lines and calluses. 'Perhaps the Gods gifted us both these and mind, so that we could create either.'

'And how many times have I used those hands to create destruction, Marcus? I had hoped that the Witch would show me an end of that.'

Marcus supports Sulla down the few steps to the mid-section of the deck. Within the small, fortress-like structure the darkness is almost complete. Hard wooden benches are built into the side walls and the archery niches above them are no more than slivers into the night sky.

Westward, a conjunction of Venus and Iovis Noctem outshines all other stars.

Sulla bows his head to what seems the inevitable shape of the Heavens. He breathes in and the sharp taste of home lies heavy on his tongue.

'Wine, Marcus.'

'Your ague… General.'

'I thank you for your concern, but my legs do not drink and my mouth is sore for want of it.'

Against his shoulders the timber walls exhale the latent heat of the day. He stretches his legs to ease them. The sweat of pain stands out on his forehead. He sweeps it dry with the back of a hand.

Marcus returns carrying a wineskin and two cups. The colour of the wine is hidden by the darkness but a scent of black grape and a harsh bite of tannin spill into the air.

Beyond the opened door, a pall of smoke from Piraeus drifts across the sky, obscuring all but the brightest stars.

'Suppose that in this darkness you were the General and I the Centurion, Marcus. What would Rome mean to you then? Speak as a man.'

'Some things are beyond me, General.'

'And you hope they will always be so?'

'I am just a soldier.'

Sulla senses Marcus' concern at the potential of this conversation.

'No, Marcus Germanicus. You are the blocks with which I build Rome. Without your hands I am just a man. And in the night…' Sulla's voice seems suddenly close to Marcus' ear. '…I fumble like the lowliest peasant.'

'Surely…'

'In fact, I fare worse. They at least are used to stumbling around. What do you think it is that makes a General?' Sulla laughs softly. 'Quickly man. What does your heart say?'

Marcus grapples for an original thought.

Sulla responds quietly. 'No... whatever thought you are constructing... it is not that.'

Relieved, Marcus leans back into the safety of the dark.

'The destiny of a General is to find the brightest star and follow it. For both sin and glory, Marcus, I was led to Athens by the cometa that appeared in the skies last spring. Its head was a slip of sun in flight and it bore bright-silvered hair that streamed at length beside it. I watched for many nights until I understood where its path was to lead me. And now I am here, I know why. We have found the daughter of the winged star.'

Sulla stares through a niche to where Venus, fleeing the arms of Iovis Noctem, is leaving him to bring a single point of light above the horizon.

'Yet look... now... in this very moment!'

He points agitatedly through the window.

'West of Hercules... there comes a new star! Its blaze growing brighter than all in the centre of Corona Borealis, my given Birth Sign. The Pythia foretold she would steal my crown, Marcus! I will not allow this. She accepts my offer to share or she must die.'

Marcus leans against him, imprinting the supple leather of the General's bodice with the hard buckle of his breast-plate, but the stars bring no greater understanding.

Sulla stands aside from the niche, allowing Marcus to see more clearly.

'This star has been created for you, Marcus Germanicus. There is no-one of higher import here tonight.'

'And if I would rather follow yours?'

Sulla rounds on him sharply.

'You would be wise to follow your own. The light from mine is diminished by sooth-sayers and witches, false friends and enemies. But take heed, a star such as this one, so quickly shown, can be just as quickly hidden. It is your call to action, not deliberation. Our *praecantrix* in the harbour predicts that Rome shall be no more than ephemeral, not immortal as you and I believe.'

'Then she lies.'

'She says our songs are sung first for us by the stars and that we are merely the chorus.'

'Then I say she is wrong.'

'She says that the device is proof of her words. That mankind cannot be allowed to define his own path. What say you to that, Centurion?'

'Perhaps I wish you had never spoken of it.'

'There are plenty in Rome more than willing to listen. Even now she tells me that Marius will die before I have another chance to kill him and that Cinna is plotting against my return. Well... Cinna can wait. I will return when I am ready. More wine!'

The small chamber is filled now with the scent of their warm flesh and the bitterness of old, sweat-beaten leather.

Marcus shakes the empty wineskin.

Sulla stays him as he begins to rise. 'No matter. I am told that if I abstain my ague will leave me. Although I think I shall find the wait intolerable.'

Marcus holds until he understands that Sulla has finished speaking. 'For what do you wait?'

'For the sign the Witch has promised. You see? Already I cavort to her tune.'

Marcus drains the last of his cup. 'If the knowledge of this device should reach Rome...'

'The knowledge is already in Rome, Marcus. Cinna sent his spy Atticus so that the Witch would be brought directly to him... along with her device.'

'This cannot happen.'

'And we will not allow it. There are two faces to a coin,

Centurion. If Cinna can be made to realise that his role is predetermined, he may lose appetite.'

'And if he doesn't?'

'I can tread this dance of the planets myself.'

Marcus grips his cup tightly in both hands.

'And if this dance itself were no more than the tread of your Destiny?'

'Then I will become a thing of pure History, Marcus. For when Rome herself is no longer the brightest star, where else would a General stand to be noticed?'

DIEI HORA QUINTA

By dawn, the corbita is alive again with sound. In the hold, plundered statues have been stowed vertically. Ropes to secure them thrown carelessly around their necks.

Minerva feels the dull thud of a heavy line thrown onto the foredeck, sensing the freedom of the boat as the spring ties are released from the quay. The corbita begins to rock beneath her.

In the pale light, the clinkered hull shrugs silver from the wave tips as it turns its nose into the slight swell. A small vessel sculls them from the harbour, the tow straining and juddering with every stroke.

Beyond the wall, the tow is slackened and the boat wallows in a long sea while the main antenna is hoisted into position. There is a crack of opening canvas and the hull of the corbita, sluggish under a cargo of two hundred tons in its belly, bears slowly away on the wind.

The gathered storm arises from the hills behind them, raising debris and ash from inside the shattered walls of Athens.

Carrion birds, flocked like driven leaves, seek shelter in the ruins of Piraeus as the westerly Favonian wind swings sharply to south and the black clouds slide the hill to the sea.

Vectoring air drives down behind the boat.

Herded southwards with sails half-furled, their speed becomes incredible for a vessel of such weight.

In ten hours they have covered half the distance to the point of Kythera.

The captain has assured Minerva that the Ionian coast will shelter them as they round the island.

She spends all day within the cabin, studying the device, venturing only briefly on deck.

She slips her key into the side of the box. The cylinder is finely wrought with slots and curves around the narrow circumference. As it fits into the machine, each one engages separately, shifting the internals into a set pattern ready to accept the next section of the key.

As she presses it further home, the outer dials line up in a neutral indication of sun, moon and planets. The next step is her secret alone. The device must first be set against the zodiac as it was at the time of its construction. Without her knowledge of the date at which this baseline is set, the machine is little more than a fancy.

She turns the key to the left fifteen times. The outer annulus spins rapidly under the pressure. She stops and half withdraws the key, turns it again, this time to the right until the required number of months slip by, moving the numbers against the rotation of the moon etched into the inner dial.

She withdraws the key, slips onto it a small silver collar taken from her purse of auguries and reinserts it. Fourteen turns bring the dials into a familiar conjunction. She removes the collar from the key and inserts it again. This time it slips the whole way in without resistance.

Turning the box into what small light trickles from the window, she studies the position of the symbols. Rotating the outer annulus one click, she watches the sun and moon dance around the inner dial, their indicators pointing to one jewel after another.

From memory she enters the birth date of General Lucius Cornelius Sulla, then moves the device forward fifty-one years. She relaxes, allowing the meaning of the dials to settle in her mind.

It is exactly as she had thought.

NOCTE HORA TERTIA

Through the window, the rapidly driven sky is cloudless. Minor stars fall into existence from the corner of her eye as she seeks out one in particular, the new star that beckons bright in the midst of Corona Borealis.

The box is safely in the chest. The key is returned to her neck. The silver collar is amongst her bag of auguries. She has done all she can. She holds tightly to a rail as the deck bucks beneath her feet.

At the stern of the boat, a brazier flares high above the men straining at the steering oar, sparks flying across them in the churning winds.

She waits until the darkness of night is complete before returning to the couch, but sleep escapes further from her each time she closes her eyes.

They have slipped unwillingly past the northern tip of the island of Kythera at speed. The storm has propelled them beyond the channel which leads to the Ionian Sea but there is another, between the island and its smaller sister, Antikythera. As the wind fades, the captain forces the boat south-westward to meet it.

NOCTE HORA QUINTA

Barely half the night has passed before she hears the faint staccato of a drum. As it becomes louder, she lifts the cover from the window. At some small distance, the low, sleek hull of a warship stands off their beam. Lit only by the flickering of the brazier across the water, its hoisted mainsail is hauling them abreast of the cargo vessel.

From its prow, the Eye of Horus glares back at her as the ship slides to tie alongside the corbita.

Marcus enters her cabin without announcement.

'Am I not to expect General Sulla himself?'

'No, My Lady. He has taken ship to Aedepsus.'

'Then you have taken it upon yourself to follow me? I am flattered.' She motions him to the couch with a low sweep of her arm. 'At least let us be comfortable.'

Marcus Germanicus will not meet her gaze. He braces his feet against the wallow of the deck and continues to stare at the joint between the wall and ceiling.

'I would sooner stand.'

She reaches out. He flinches and moves rapidly aside.

She lifts back her cowl, noticing how his eyes are drawn immediately to the pure white-blonde of her hair.

'Then you had better give me your orders. They are from Sulla, I assume.'

'Yes, My Lady.'

'And…?'

'The General insists that you are to surrender yourself and the device to my care… and that you avow your willingness to operate it for his advantage alone.'

'Or else?'

'There is no or else, My Lady.'

'No threat?'

'No, My Lady. Just my orders.'

'And they are?'

Marcus shifts uneasily, hoping it will be misunderstood for a sudden movement of the deck.

'My orders, My Lady.'

Minerva touches him before he can move away. Her fingertips press into his bare skin and Marcus feels the sensation spread from there to the rest of his body, travelling along nerves like fire.

She moves aside her bag of auguries to pull him gently down beside her. 'Sit with me.'

Marcus holds himself rigid, resisting the power flowing through him but she has practised the words she needs to say.

'Sulla has no need of the device. His fortune is assured.'

'My Lady, I have my orders.'

'Then you must carry them out, for I have no intention of surrendering myself or the device to Sulla. Nor to anyone else.'

He places a hand over hers. 'You have no idea…'

She lifts a finger to his lips. 'I know exactly what your orders are.'

She brushes her hand across his face, feeling salt on his skin, aware that he has stood alone for hours in the prow searching for the flicker of her ship's brazier.

'When you first came to me, you asked for a service.'

'I no longer wish to know what my future holds.'

She places a hand each side of his face to stare into his eyes. 'Perhaps not… but I do.'

The restraints of the room cease to exist as she falls into the vortex of his life. She swims along the edge of the current before allowing it to sweep her to his core. She is whirled around, stretched, waters closing over her head as she sees into him.

She releases him with a start. Her vision snaps back to the cabin and the stilled shadows across the wall.

Marcus sees joy and concern flash across her face in equal measure. 'Tell me what you see…'

'I see an unusual man… a soldier with time for both conscience and consequence.'

He is amused. 'It seems neither are fit requirements.'

'Yet in your life there is time for two gifts to Destiny.'

'But little time to give?'

She touches his cheek to search the heat that now resides under his skin. 'You do not need me to divine a soldier's fate.'

'Then what two gifts are these?'

'The simplest essences of Life.'

Keeping her back to the lamp, she shrugs the gown from her shoulders. She is bound in a white linen sash across her breasts. Another forms a pale triangle around her waist. In shadow, her skin glows as if the lamplight passes through her slender frame.

She untucks the bindings until she stands naked.

Her eyes carry no great desire for him, just an irresistible earnestness. 'I will take the first of your gifts now.'

She lifts him to his feet with a single finger beneath his chin.

Freed from doubt his hands strip belt and sword, armour and tunic until they scatter at his feet.

Her fingers close around him and his manhood leaps between them like a spark. Her hands are bowls of ecstatic fire that surround his flesh.

She reaches a hand behind his head, pulling him to her, while a slender fingernail traces an irregular shape at the nape of his neck. The skin there flashes with a deep fire. He shakes his head free but the fire remains.

'What have you done ?'

'Roman or not, you are now a true son of Aegila. All her true sons will take the mark of the city with them wherever they go.'

The whites of her eyes gleam blindly in the flickering lamplight as she offers herself.

He lowers her gently to the floor of the cabin as her knees rise and she opens to take him, her hands in constant motion across his body. Wherever they touch they twist and shape him, gathering him above her as a cloud that aches to burst. His ears fill with the storm of her breath. He feels her rage approaching and wonders at his ability to survive as she writhes beneath him, smothering him, tongue entwining his again and again until her visions have become his.

Floating free in Time, insignificant as a mote, he watches the pages of history ripple behind his eyes. Fanned by the rapid movement of her body, terrible images sway around him, erupting in explosions of light, each existing for an instant, surpassed only by the brutality of the next. He sees the stars themselves set free in the sky but… himself… as trapped by fortune as a wasp in amber.

Torn free from all conscience by her visions, he pours down inside her like a free rain. As it falls, it cleanses away the last of her voices and portends.

She closes her body around him to drain him complete.

Her hands slide the muscles of his back, fingers deep into his flesh as she continues to absorb him.

Marcus finds himself aroused again by the tension that still resides in her.

'Was that one of the gifts?'

'Yes. That was a gift for Destiny.'

She begins to move beneath him, wave-like, coaxing his body to rise inside her again. 'This time is for me.'

NOCTE HORA GALLICINIUM

There is a warmth beneath his cheek and in the distance a drumbeat that quickens rapidly as he listens. His eye opens to the pink bud of her breast… and he understands that it is her heart he hears. He closes his eyes to wish that the sound would never have to stop.

He hears her breath draw swiftly as her legs wrap to the small of his back, urging him further in. Eyes closed, she searches his face with her fingers, exploring his eyes, lips, ears and nose as if to commit them all to a future memory.

He tries to lift but finds himself inside her still... still totally erect.

This time, as her movement begins, it is for him.

NOCTE HORA DULUCULUM

She awakes alone. By the faint light of dawn trickling the window she can see that his armour, sword and tunic have been stolen away as she slept. Her skin is cold and she drags the cloak from the table to wrap around her.

Something metallic drops to the floor.

She feels for it under the table until her fingers close around the blade of a dagger. The touch makes her smile.

He has misunderstood, but that is of little consequence now. There is nothing she can do to alter events that no longer attach themselves to her skin. She has considered the consequences of this moment often, and many times she has been afraid of that irrevocable act but now, elation spills through her, ecstatic and pure.

She turns her hands upon herself and feels only flesh without portend. She holds them to her face to inhale the sharp tang of her blood, the softer, musty scent of his seed and the salt, ammoniac taste of her own waters.

No longer informed by destiny, she begins to understand the vessel she has become.

She is no longer the reader.

She is the message.

Foetal on the hard floor, she struggles the cloak around her to wait for the light.

HORA PRIMA

The dawn fret is a white blanket that dulls the waves, that throbs with sound, that glistens in the flickering light of a brazier.

Banked oars chatter as the warship is swung around the Point of Glyphadia to chase Minerva's beacon.

Her heart resonates to the hollow sound of the drum as it begins again, quickening perceptibly as the oars pour back into the water.

Eye of Horus aglare in the light from the corbita's fire, the warship looms rapidly from the mist.

The drumbeat stops.

The corbita's timbers splinter as the warship's rostrum prow shatters the hull beneath Minerva's feet.

The deck lists as the statuary are slid towards the impact.

The horned head of the ram presses on through shores and bulwarks, scattering stacked marble and amphorae.

Oil and sea water swirl in the bilges of the ship.

A revived drum beat begins, a rhythm huge enough to fracture the air with sound.

Oarsmen pound the water.

The warship begins to withdraw.

Loose rope is caught in the horns of the ram.

Statues are dragged across the hold.

Marble tilts and tips.

The ship rolls as if broached by a vicious wind.

Water cascades into the breach.

The air fills with the frantic beat of the drum and the crack of whips urging men to perform an impossible feat.

The cargo vessel rotates.

Statues fall into the deluge.

The ram of the warship is dragged beneath the surface.

Soldiers in full armour are washed overboard.

Men, chained to their benches, are screaming.

Blocks are struck free.

Chains rattle out through iron deck hoops.

Slaves leap into the water.

Shackled as they are, they disappear beneath the waves.

The remainder sit resignedly along the rails as the ships groan into destruction, waiting for two hundred tons of marble to take them down.

Minerva experiences this solely through the movement of the ship and the vibrations of the air, for once revelling in her lack of other senses.

Without warning, the deck beneath her splits as the hull is tortured open.

She is pitched down into the blackness of the hold.

The chest slides the floor of the cabin to follow her.

Its weight pins her against the side of the ship.

The water rises rapidly around her, filling the chest through handholds in the leather.

Minerva forces her head into an upright position. Above her, the underside of the main deck forms a pocket where the edge of the hatch timbers project downwards.

Beyond sight of anyone above she tries to move but the chest is jammed by the arm of an alabaster statue whose fingers reach out, beckoning her into death.

The cargo vessel is sinking rapidly.

She slows her heartbeat.

This has come as no surprise.

With the mist closing over its final rotation, the corbita snaps the prow from the warship, setting it free.

The warship lunges astern, water shipping rapidly over

the aft rail.

The shattered bow rears clear of the waves.

Men spill from its open mouth in a necklace of chain.

It slams down upon them, the ruined Eye of Horus glaring through the mist as the warship slips beneath the sea.

The shock of water on Marcus' skin is all the more for it being warm. He knows he must be close to a stony beach. His ears are filled with the screams of drowning men and bursts of escaping air as the ships wrestle each other into the calm below the surface, but beyond this comes the sound of surf on shingle.

The cargo ship has settled in the water with the tip of its mast several feet above the surface.

He swims towards it. Around him, men are hanging on to broken spars and deck gratings, too shocked to do any other than hold fast until the chains call them under. He searches the water for sight of her hair, calling her name into the mist.

He reaches the masthead and clings to it for support. Under his hands it twitches violently, shaking him free. It settles another two feet lower. On impulse he takes a deep breath and follows the timber, hand over hand into the water, until he can reach the shattered deck. It is broken upwards and twisted so that the hold is exposed, but the water is dark and he cannot see down into it. He returns quickly to the surface, drifting upwards with a sudden burst of air.

Above Minerva's head is a faintly silvered surface in the water. The shard of decking between wale and hatch that hides her contains a pocket of air. She struggles herself upright until her face reaches it. Greedily, she gulps air into her lungs, feeling it warm on her lips and in her nostrils. She slumps back into the water where the light from the surface filters down into the hold.

The chest has pinned her legs against the side of the ship and the statue fallen across it is immovable.

In the struggle, her cowl drifts from her head and allows her hair to float free.

She lifts her face back into the air pocket to find that it has receded. This time, her nose touches the underside of the deck before she finds it. She breathes steadily until she feels her strength return.

Marcus surfaces to find the mast tip has disappeared below the waves. He gulps air rapidly then drives down along its length.

The cargo ship is impaled on a rock overhanging the abyss. As he scans the water for sign of her, there is a flash of pale, blonde light below the hatch.

He swims towards it, grasping at an edge of broken deck to pull himself into the gloom of the hold.

She is trapped by the corner of the chest. He thinks at first that she is dead, but when her eyes flash open he almost loses his breath with shock.

Her right leg is directly beneath a corner of the chest, supporting its weight across two deck spars. He tries to pull her free but a marble statue is pressing directly on the lid.

He spins around in the water, feeling the rising panic of breathlessness begin in his chest. There are no levers within sight. His soldier's instinct decides for him.

He puts his hand firmly over her mouth to prevent her losing her last breath in a gasp of pain.

Through the sole of his sandal he feels the bones snap.

He reaches down with one hand and tugs hard.

Her leg distorts into the space between the spars and he pulls it free.

She hangs in the water, her breath slipping the edges of her mouth in a bright stream of bubbles.

A part of the huge shelf on which the ship has been

hanging snaps loose. The rock descends to the sea floor, obliterating the warship completely.

Marcus' hands climb her body until they reach the cowl. With his last breath he fills it with the air from his lungs.

He takes her waist in both hands and sends her spiralling upwards with a push. As she rises into the light, he returns to the chest.

The ship rolls slightly as it begins its final slide.

The statue rocks away into a more upright position. He lifts the lid and rummages swiftly inside, feeling for the device.

His hands lock around it.

The hull catches a small outcrop.

The corbita spins violently on its axis.

The statue behind him tilts.

The outstretched finger of the philosopher impales him inescapably against the side of the cabin. The device drops into the jumble of debris at his feet.

His eyes are open, even though the marble is penetrating his heart. Before they fade, he sees her shadow break the surface.

The dawn fret has cleared. Minerva floats unconscious in the clear blue of a calm Aegean, buoyed by the air trapped in her cloak. The fine weave is leaking slowly and her own body, dense as pure bone from months of deprivation in the Acropolis, will not sustain her at the surface.

She begins a slow slide into the water.

Her feet slip the layer of cloak as she begins her turn to vertical.

Three feet down her heels hit shingle.

It anchors her. The slight wash to shore spins her around until her head is toward the beach. From there, hands catch her gently under the arms and slide her onto the land.

The air is cooler than the sea. It passes over her, chilling the water held in the weave. The sun is still low and she shivers involuntarily before giving in to sleep.

Close to hand as she wakes is the crackle and spit of timber bursting into flame.

She opens her eyes… and immediately wishes she hadn't.

A hand takes her legs to curl her body around the fire, ignoring her screams.

Beside her is a giant of a man. His skin is pale, with pockmarks showing through a torso covered in coarse black hair. Through his belt is a roman pugio, ten inches of steel blackened by recent blood.

He draws out the sword and holds its tip into the fire. When he withdraws it, the end of the blade glows readily.

He turns towards her.

Unable to defend herself, Minerva's eyes roll up into her skull. The lids descend across the whites, shutting out all vision.

DIEI HORA SEXTA

There is a warmth surrounding her that flows like silk over her face. The cloak under her fingers as she wakes is solidly dry. The sun is directly above and it dazzles her eyes as they flash open. She turns her face away towards the fire.

The man has gone. The sticks are down to embers but the heat is a tangible force as the gathering wind picks up the effort, fanning it towards her.

She reaches out in her mind to experience the phantom limb where the man has removed the lower part of her leg.

She finds nothing, but this may be part of the thing she has just accomplished, this denial of her powers so that, through her line, Marcus can achieve the immortality she has seen for him.

She tries to sit up but her leg will not bend. She flicks back the cloak and sunlight shows both her legs, though the right has timber strapped tightly to it. Her meagre flesh is squeezed from under the leather where it has been tightened by pieces of kindling twisted into the knots.

There is no sensation below the first binding. The flesh four inches above her ankle is swollen and inflamed. There is a deep wound where the metal-bound chest had fallen across it but this has been healed by the edge of a hot blade.

Close beside the scar is a mark made by Marcus' sandal.

She forces herself to look again, beyond the fire, across the beach.

It has been cleared.

While she slept the bodies have been removed… the half-drowned soldiers she had seen with their slit throats gaping at the open sky… the slaves with amputated hands and feet… the shed chains that had littered the dark, volcanic pebble.

Smoke is arising from a place behind the Point. The wind takes it across the earth, bowling it around shrubs and rocks, imprinting the land with a smell of burning flesh.

There are footsteps in the shingle behind her. She turns as the man speaks to her in Greek.

'I have done what I know how to do.'

'Then I must be grateful.'

'Do not be anything. I have not saved you for yourself.'

'Then for whom?'

She is gathered in his arms and lifted from the shingle as if she were no weight at all.

His arms are strong and secure, and in the pulsing of his blood there is a peace that envelops their slow movement over the headland towards Potamos Bay. He shifts her in his arms, bracing her more tightly against him and begins the slow climb up the track.

Aegila is a sound that brushes her ears from a distance… a scent that travels the winding slope… educating her of those things that await the traversing of the ridge, the entry through the gated wall… until she understands the place again before she arrives.

Silence falls around them as they push on through the crowded market. People make way for them, opening like a wave… silent questions hanging in their wake.

She looks up into his face.

His eyes are clear… impassive… his jaw is set… his chest expands and retreats against her, showing little sign of the effort of carrying her up the hill.

The city that surrounds her has been expanded greatly, fuelled by an inveterate piracy and a policy of political indifference.

The walls have been rebuilt since she had skinned her knees on them as a child. They now form two bulwarks. The inner one encircles the centre of the city… the gates streaming with people visiting the market at its heart… the outer one is now a buttressed stronghold, rolling with the dips and lofts of the topography overlooking Xiropotamos Bay.

At the highest point of the land between the two walls stands a house.

Once, this house had stood outside the city wall… a position that encouraged its occupants to adopt an over-whelming arrogance… an image firmly emphasised by the visible patronage of its vast window openings… the demure, lowered eyelashes of their sunshades fluttering in the wind with a false humility.

She knows this house only too well… but perhaps not so well as it knows her.

His strong arms settle her body against the fabric of a chaise. He arranges her broken leg on a stool and stands back… arms folded.

In this room, the windows shed slippery light into the corners… displaying an air of neglect apparent in the webbed reaches where hands rarely venture. A tapestry in the corner shivers in the breeze through an open door.

She stares outside to where her readjusted eyes blend the walls, the sunlight and the people milling far below into a maelstrom of blinding colour.

The sound of dust underfoot comes from behind her.

She resists the urge to turn.

'Hello, Father. It has been a long time.'

DIEI HORA SECUNDA

The air that flows the hill above Aedepsus is sharp and clear. Small clouds rag the summit, high above the villa. It has been a long time since Sulla felt this enervated, although his impatience has increased in direct proportion to the length of his convalescence.

The villa is dry of alcohol and although the water from the stream is crystal and pure, Sulla is disturbed by the lack.

The ague in his lower limbs has receded to manageable proportions and flesh no longer protrudes angrily between the straps of his sandals.

To his regret, there are no women here at the villa. Not even a slave girl. With no outlet for his rediscovered energy his time is spent in a daily round of devotions and ablutions.

The spring that rises immediately beneath the bath house is high in phosphates and lime and an hour's soak leaves his skin encrusted with a fine, drying powder. Once brushed away, the skin beneath has never felt softer. Even the more extreme florid patches have feathered their edges into the paler spaces between.

The mountain air wakes him repeatedly, its sharp edge piercing the open windows of the bedchamber. Each time he awakes he hopes that this time it will be her promised dream, but his short periods of sleep have remained silent and colourless.

Weeks have passed and although he has been starved of news he has convinced himself that the mission on which he sent Marcus Germanicus must have succeeded.

He rises from the warm seat of stone he has found on the slope high above the villa. A few days before, he had seen shepherds occupying this same spot and now he finds himself understanding how it must feel to exist within meagre needs and desires.

A small herd of goats have coalesced around him as if they are seeking out his presence for security. As he rises to his feet they scatter across the stones, rudimentary bells around their necks dulling the air with thudding, off-key tones.

Sulla smiles darkly, recalling how often he has seen men behave in similar fashion. He places a small coin on the stone before descending the slope.

The goats gather like a small, ragged cloud on a ledge above him.

Eyes fixed to ensure the safety of his own footing, he doesn't notice the way they descend behind him.

JUNIUS V111
DIES SATURNI

NOCTE HORA GALLICINIUM

Sulla swings out of bed to find the floor cold beneath his feet. The last of the pain in his legs drains swiftly into the chill of the marble and for the first time in memory he is entirely free of it.

In the darkness of the bay below, the brazier of an incoming ship flickers bitterly against the night and above the villa the darkness remains almost total, broken only by a shatter of dislocated stars yet, just outside his window, the earth is achingly bright.

Within this pool of light a herd of goats stand watching. The light around them has an exhaustive clarity. The soft sheaths around their horns are disconcertingly apparent... their short manes and pendant beards harsh and grey... eyes an impenetrable black.

Between their cloven hooves the tended grass grows thick and luxuriant, fed in the cool of the night by waste water from the villa... but their mouths are for once thin-lipped and tight.

They continue to stare at him as if waiting... but for what he does not know.

He turns away from the window to find that a figure occupies the bed from which he has just risen. The figure is wrapped tightly in cloth as though its sleep has been angry and disturbed, rolling ever tighter into the mesh.

He peers closely at the blonde hair, before pulling aside the sheet to note the fractured complexion.

He stands back to allow his breathing to calm and settle.

'I have waited, as you said. Although I thought you dead.'

Her voice comes from beyond the window.

'And so you should.'

In the centre of the silent herd is a figure, taller than himself yet more than slender inside a robe so similar in colour to the pelt of the goats that he wonders if, in his confusion, he might have missed her.

She extends an empty hand towards him.

'I would be dead. Were it not for Marcus Germanicus.'

'He persuaded you? I never thought he could.'

'Not in the way you assume. His very presence persuaded me that Rome was not capable of containing the potential of the device. It would allow foreknowledge to become fuel for further violent expansion.'

'Then why did you allow yourself to be captured in the Temple?'

'I had little choice in the matter. But in my efforts I have tried to preserve our discovery against a future generation, perhaps one more able to withstand the pressure of greed.'

Sulla issues a short, barking laugh.

'And you think that possible?'

'There are many possibilities, and many places where the history of man will hang upon a cross. Each one brings a new portend for the future.'

'Did you not try to convince me that our future was mapped and incontrovertible?'

'The device remains the best indicator of the most advantageous possibilities.'

'To whom?'

'To the holder of the device... and its Adept.'

'Then how could you not know that I would kill you?'

'I knew this.'

'Yet you intimate you are still alive.'

'But I am no longer Adept. Your choice formed a crucial point.'

'Would I make that choice again had I known?'

'Inevitably.'

Sulla sits down on the edge of the bed, contemptuously pushing aside his own inert body. The figure rolls away from him, tightening the sheet.

He ignores it as the past rivers quicksilver through his memory. 'Marcus Germanicus...'

'You gave him that most dangerous gift of the Gods.'

'I find all God-given gifts potentially so.'

'But none so as free will.'

The walls of the villa fade as Minerva walks through the outline of stones, the dark cracks of mortar, until she stands within Sulla's reach.

He notices that she stands unevenly, hip canted to the left, favouring a disposition. In her eyes there is a small pain that he recognises.

'You are hurting. Your leg...'

'It is a small price. Marcus paid far more.'

'For what?'

'For my life.'

Sulla rises from the bed. The figure lying there rotates violently, screwing itself into an increasing bundle.

He walks around her where she stands.

She appears dimensionless. Wherever his viewpoint, the eyes beneath the cowl never leave his progress.

He indicates the figure on the bed. 'Why do I sleep in this fashion, yet remember nothing of it when I wake?'

'Asleep, you are the plaything of the Gods. How else would they practice the calumnies with which they trouble the soul of man? Without the use of dream to sharpen their wit they would have killed us all long ago. Then what would they play with?'

'I care not for things beyond my comprehension. You say you are no longer Adept?'

'This is true. I bear the gift that has set me free from that tyranny.'

'Then where is the device?'

'Beyond reach.'

'There is little beyond the reach of man.'

'Ultimately yes, but this is far enough to defeat even yourself, General. And I was the last known Adept.'

'Then Rome is safe.'

She laughs at his contention. 'Nowhere is safe.'

'Then what of your promise?'

'I have not forgotten.'

Her hands reach inside her robe. She withdraws a small, flat parcel, bound tightly in white kid.

She holds it out before her.

Sulla lifts it delicately from her hands.

'This seems thunderously silent for a lightning bolt.'

'It has all the power you need, General. There is little in

this moment that is stronger.'

Sulla holds the gift in both hands, for the first time in his life, uncertain. 'Will you return?'

'You do not need me… and I am a message that will take over two millennia to arrive.'

She reaches a hand to touch his forehead.

'Marcus told me of your search for the brightest star so, from now on, your history shall bear the name *Epaphroditos*, Beloved of Venus. The Stars shall be your shelter and the Storm will carry your feet but your Soul will forever be poised between. Use your gift wisely and you will prevail.'

Dawn light falls into the room as her figure fades from Sulla's sight.

He sits on edge of the bed, the parcel on his knees, despairing of the tremor in his fingers as he unwraps the binding.

He peels away the last of the skin until his hands caress an oval of smooth, dark wood… no larger than his own spread hand.

On impulse, he turns it over.

There is a sudden flash of polished, reflected light.

The figure on the bed behind him erupts in laughter.

CHRONICLE

XII

THE 13th. SIGN

2006

JUNE 7th.
WEDNESDAY

9:22 A.M.

Fabrienne is standing quite still, arms braced against the sides of the stone box.

André comes to stand beside her. She twitches visibly but continues to stare blankly. He speaks softly… aware of how fragile she appears standing this way.

'What have you found?'

'I don't know.'

'What did you expect to find?'

'Alec would say a 'Red Herring', but as we are in the Aegean, perhaps that should be a 'Red Mullet'.'

Beneath her bare feet, the bottom of the box is covered in newly-exposed, well-fitted, flat stones. Their surface has a fractured, shale-like appearance.

Fabrienne traces the edges with the point of her trowel.

She digs the tip under one.

André bends to pick it out of the box. In the sun, tiny shards of mica glint hypnotically.

'I don't know this stone. Not in these islands. Where do you think it might be from?'

Fabrienne takes it from him. Smoothing it between her palms to remove the dust from it, she holds it so that it glitters in the light.

'I don't know. But I do know a man who might.'

'If I didn't know better, I'd say it was 'M' type granite. But there isn't any on the island that I am aware of. This is what we call 'two mica' granite, seventy percent silica.'

Alec rinses the flat stone in the filtering water. Its surface dries in the sun almost immediately. The shards of crystal blink back at him.

'The rock on this island is finer and softer. It allows the water percolation that provided the shower you had with Manon.'

'You were watching?'

'No such luck. I was washing fragments while you two were having fun. Manon talks in her sleep.'

'I have not heard her.'

'Perhaps when she is snuggled up to you she has no need to.'

Fabrienne withdraws the stone as if it had been an undeserved present. 'Manon and I do not 'snuggle up'.

Alec laughs at the frown on her face. 'Don't get a complex about it. You do as you please for me. Look, there are three of us here who would willingly share your tent. Manon gets to win… this time.'

'Three?'

'And you can leave Veronique out of *that* equation.' Alec gets up to see to his filters. 'And as for your rock, I don't know how that got here. I sometimes wonder how *you* did.'

The sun plays amongst the crystalline structure of the stone in Fabrienne's hand. She calls across the camp to him.

'Ok. Best guess. Where might it have come from?'

'The last time I saw schist like this was in Lentekhi.'

'Nice name. What were you doing there?'

'Skiing and climbing. The slopes on Mount Elbrus are

easy enough for an Englishman.'

'Isn't that in Russia?'

'Yes. We sneaked in from Georgia. Had to sneak out that way too… and quickly. Russians don't take kindly to digging without a very expensive licence. The one thing they do well is bureaucracy. But the area has a history, too.'

Fabrienne comes over to stand beside him, watching his fingers sift earth from shards of broken pot.

'What kind of a history?'

Alec shakes his hands dry on the warm air.

'To the south was an area called Urartu. Part Turkey, part Armenia, and part Iran. They relied for their success on a wild tribe of outsiders that settled the region. Any dig there brings up an amazing mixture of cultures. Their tribe were the Gymrri. But you would perhaps know them better as Cimerrians.'

Fabrienne's heart feels as though it has stopped. A vast space has opened inside her that swells with the recognisable notes of a flute.

The day rushes back in as Alec speaks to her.

'André wants us to catalogue the week's finds.' He stares into the blankness of her expression. 'But you'd better find yourself first by the look of you.'

'That's what I came here for.'

Alec hands her the pad and pencil.

'Then I only hope I'm here when you do.'

11:30 A.M.

The dirt under the stones is soft, like dry cement bound by a coarse black fibre.

André takes some from the blade of Fabrienne's trowel.

'Goat hair. Not untypical.' He sifts some of it through his fingertips. 'I'm amazed Alec stopped at the arrowhead.'

'I think he was supposed to stop there.'

'Then why did you make such a fuss about which direction it was pointing in?'

'I think it's significant… and then there was the stone.'

Manon is perched on a corner of the box, changing a roll of film in the camera. 'What about the stone? Who would go to all this trouble?'

'Tradition. If an important person could not be returned to their homeland, then a piece of the land was brought to them. Refugees would carry a jar of home soil to be sprinkled in their coffin.'

Manon leans further in to clear away the dry dirt. 'Like Dracuulaaarr… but look here… there are tiles underneath. You can see the lines where they fit.'

She hands the camera to Fabrienne. 'Here… you may as well have your name on the photographs too.'

Fabrienne passes the camera over to Veronique.

'I don't care about that. It's just important we found it.'

Veronique rattles off the film until she is nudged out of the way.

André leans into the box with the old magnifying glass he keeps in his shirt pocket but at the right focal length the sun always seems to find the lens.

He puts it away, reluctant to burn a scar into the newly exposed surface. 'I think we need to shield these, but let's see what we have here first… Alec?'

'Looks like a varnish but under that the colours show a degree of sophistication I've seen before. Reminds me of Qalaichi Tepe.'

Veronique takes one long look before stepping back with a shudder.

She pushes the camera towards Fabrienne and nods to where André stands absorbed by the find. 'Now you have it all. I'll go and fetch the canvas.'

André watches her go for a moment, then returns his attention to the find.

'Manon. Top of your head… what do you see?'

'Here…' Manon points into the box. 'I can't be sure in this light… symbols of some kind… animals? And a series of black studs.'

'Yes, the black studs. They seem to form a pattern… but not one I'm familiar with. Fabrienne, an opinion?? After all, you found it.'

'No. We all found it.' She hands the camera to André and takes a drawing pad from her bag. 'But I may find an answer. If you will all leave me alone for a few minutes I will draw this and we can discuss it back at camp.'

André shoulders the camera. 'Alec? How about lunch?'

'It'll be out of a tin.'

'That will be fine. Just… no ketchup.'

Manon looks up from studying the box.

'I'm going for a shower. Anyone else coming?'

She glances from André to Fabrienne. 'Ah well…'

André watches her climb across the circular dig walls.

'I'll collect the cover from Veronique. She'll be on her way back by now. I'll probably catch her halfway down.'

'No. You go on up.' Fabrienne rests her pad on the top of the box. 'Let her bring it.'

Fabrienne is sitting on one end of the stone box, legs wide apart, heels braced on the two long sides, her hands making quick, careful strokes with the pencil.

Veronique drops the cover and stakes beside the box.

'If I had not been coming back with the canvas, André would still be here. No?'

Fabrienne lifts her knees to allow air to circulate between her skin and the heated stone.

'No. I sent him away.'

She works steadily on, the pencil tip reproducing on the paper exactly what she sees in the bottom of the box.

Veronique rolls the canvas parcel across the ground.

'You will forgive me if I do not believe you.' She points to the way Fabrienne straddles the wall. 'Is that how he likes you?'

Fabrienne ignores the remark.

Veronique unknots the bundle of snarled guy ropes.

'And Manon, too. I can bet that is how *she* likes you…'

Fabrienne continues to work. 'You forgot Alec.'

'It is easy to forget Alec.'

Fabrienne stows the pad in her pack. 'Veronique, have you not noticed the way André looks at you?'

'How should I? I have seen him look nowhere but you since you arrived. Why did you have to come here? I was…'

'You were doing nothing.' Fabrienne slides off the wall and picks up a stake. 'No matter how many nights you spend talking in his tent there is a barrier around André that you could never penetrate.'

'And you can?'

'No-one can. He must find his own way around it.'

'And when he does?'

'Then I may not be here, Veronique… but you might.'

Veronique grabs the other end of the stake and pulls hard. It slides through Fabrienne's hand, a splinter tearing skin. Blood flows across her palm to drip from the end of her fingers.

Veronique stares at the flesh she has damaged, her voice softening with shame. 'I'm sorry. I didn't mean to do that but you make me so mad. You do nothing, you say nothing and everyone falls in love with you. You find the only thing of importance we have discovered here and you are the only one who is not excited by it. What are you?'

Fabrienne holds up her palm. It streams with blood from the gash that runs the length of her lifeline.

'Doesn't this tell you what I am?'

'It doesn't tell me *why* you are.'

Fabrienne wipes the blood onto her tee shirt.

'I am only just beginning to find that out for myself.'

She catches Veronique's hand as if by accident and senses the barely-constrained anger flowing the veins under her fingertips.

She applies a little more pressure before letting go.

Veronique sits down abruptly in the dirt. She lifts her hands to her face but the tears find their way through the spaces between her fingers.

'What did you just do? There were things you made me remember that I never wanted…'

Fabrienne reaches down to her. 'Don't ask me. I don't know myself.'

Veronique jumps away as if she has been stung.

Fabrienne catches her and lifts her easily to her feet.

Veronique stares at the hands that grip her arms, an expression of quick surprise on her face.

'I am alright now.'

'Then help me with this. Hold it while I fasten the ropes.'

Fabrienne drives in a second peg.

'Are you sure you're alright?'

Veronique nods blindly, stunned in the aftermath of the kaleidoscopic revelation that has lanced through her.

'I don't know how I feel. I thought I knew… but now it's different. It's all mixed up.'

Fabrienne pegs the last of the ropes. 'Say nothing of it.'

'But Fabrienne… with such a gift…'

'I mean it. Back at the camp… say nothing of it.'

1:33 P.M.

The back seat of the car has been discarded in the dust.

André tugs at an exposed loom, snipping cleanly through a wire to draw a length free.

Alec pokes around under the bonnet. 'This one here. It's burnt black.'

André hands him the wire. 'Reminds me of your food. Wind this end around the terminal on the coil… and if I attach the other end… here.' He reaches around the back of the engine. 'That should do it. Oh, wait…'

He replaces a damaged headlight cable with one snipped from the horn relay.

'Now jump in. I will push.'

Alec stands back. 'No, *you* jump in. This thing is lethal.'

The engine fires immediately and runs with a familiar clatter. André lurches the car around until the rear wheels come up against a small rock. He leaves the engine running to charge the battery.

Manon is putting finishing touches to the midday meal.

'André? Do we have to have that contraption running? It stinks.'

'I'll get Alec to put some ketchup on it.'

He holds out his plate. 'Is this the last of the vegetables?'

Manon nods. André picks at it with a fork. 'Hmm… good.'

'You sound surprised.'

'No… no. I didn't mean that. I mean it's good I got the car going. The boat from Piraeus calls this evening and I want to go down and get some fresh things. Anyone want to come?'

The others remain silent, staring pointedly at the car as they eat. André's eyes settle on Fabrienne.

She puts down her plate and fork. 'Why don't you take Veronique?'

Veronique flashes her a look. André shrugs away the implication. 'I… no reason. I didn't think she wanted to.'

Fabrienne takes her things over to the wash table. 'I have things I need to do this evening before it gets dark.'

André looks up as she takes his plate. 'Can I see your sketches?'

'Not until I have discussed them with Alec. Then I might know what we have.'

'Why discuss them with Alec?'

'You didn't think you were the sole subject of my home-work, did you? I'd call that arrogant.'

André catches her arm. 'Take your hands out of that water.'

He turns her left hand palm up, unwinding the strip of old tee shirt wrapped over it. 'Come over to my tent. I have some bandages and stuff.'

2:54 P.M.

She watches his fingers gently unwind the rag, stopping only when he reaches the last of the binding, finding it stiff with dried blood. '…and stuff?'

He pours clean water over the hard layer to soften it, wincing as he peels it away.

'Why did you suggest I take Veronique?'

'I know how she feels about you.'

Blood oozes again from Fabrienne's hand.

'Can you not feel that? Your hand…?'

'Of course I can.'

'Then why do I sometimes think you are not human like the rest of us?'

'Only *some* things are worth crying for.'

'I wish I had your objectivity.'

He taps antiseptic powder along the line of the cut then binds her hand with a clean, narrow bandage. 'How did you do this?'

'It was an accident. Accidents happen, you know…'

She holds down the end with her finger while he knots the bandage.

'… to all of us.'

JUNE 9th.
FRIDAY

11:15 A.M.

Fabrienne pushes herself beneath the surface of the water. The borrowed wetsuit is far too large and the warm sea flows through the gap in the neck to pool against her crotch. She pauses a moment to pressurise her ears.

Six feet away, Jorgé bends his finger and thumb into a familiar 'OK' ring. He follows her down, away from the light, admiring the ease with which she controls the fins.

He checks his depth gauge and begins to power after her, but she has already paused to pressurise again. He steadies himself on her shoulder, scanning the settings on her tanks. He taps her head and makes a sign. She checks his, making a fine adjustment. He tips his head down into the gloom where a rock overhang casts a wavering shadow.

The water sleeks the lines of Jorgé's body into a singular teardrop. His image ripples in the convection currents from a patch of sun-warmed rock over to their left. He is a seal at play... elemental in the one place on earth that he knows who, what and where he is. Fabrienne follows him down, envious of his certainty.

He is hanging by one hand from an encrusted limb of stone when she catches him, pointing into the shadow cast below.

There is little she can see in the shade but Jorgé indicates an area with a spread of his hands, sweeping his arm to her left and down.

The sunlight is moving, slowly spreading into the gloom below them. Gradually, shapes are becoming more distinct, hard edges sharpening their ancient outlines.

She pauses to pressurise, checking the depth on her wrist gauge and the tank capacity where it hangs over her shoulder on a tethered tube.

At this depth she has less than five minutes of activity.

Beyond her focus, Jorgé accelerates past.

Without thought she follows as he makes the last feet in one effort.

Fabrienne hangs in the water as Jorgé swims the line of the wreck, defining length and breadth with movements of his arms.

There is little enough that is recognisable, yet she tries to rebuild in her mind the sweep of the hull, searching for the jut of the prow. At one end would have been a small cabin, hopelessly lost in the slow persistence of decay.

She glides along ten feet above the outreach of the timbers, turning at the end to look back. Her hand moves each way with a flowing action.

Jorgé points to the near end of the wreck. He sits upright in the water, sculling an imaginary oar, his long black hair flowing around him in the movement of water.

The water inside her suit is cooling as she explores the part of the wreck that extends beneath the overhang, but finds herself not caring. There is an old diver's remedy for a cold suit but the pressure inhibits her bladder.

She rolls and twists in the water, ecstatic in the way it plays with her senses, the ease with which it teases her understanding of gravity until she neither knows nor cares which way is up.

She moves deeper under the overhang, experiencing an acceleration of heat from her inner organs out towards her skin until she begins to radiate.

Under the rock the world is calm, dark and still.

She hangs horizontally in the water, staring upwards into

the looming stone until she believes she can see stars tapering above her. Her vision narrows to the confines of her mask, blurring the constellations into unfamiliar shapes. If she takes it off, just for a moment, perhaps she can fly up there to bathe in them, wash them along her skin like a healing shower of silver milk.

Jorgé clasps her firmly to him and drags her out into the light. She fights him but he holds tight and kicks upward. By the time he checks his gauge and pauses to decompress, she has fallen limp against him.

At the last decompression stage, a bare twenty feet below the surface, she wakes suddenly. Her eyes bulge inside the mask as she struggles to unearth the memory of where she is. She spits out the mouthpiece as if it has turned foul against her teeth.

Jorgé feels her chest heave in panic as she prepares to take a breath of seawater. He clamps his hand over her mouth and holds her tight until the distress leaves her eyes.

Her fingers relax their grip on him. Blood flows in the water where her nails have pierced his skin.

He scoops the mouthpiece and rams it between her lips.

Fabrienne grasps it with both hands to suck greedily at the air. She lifts the bottom of her mask to blow out the water that her panic has allowed in.

Jorgé places a hand each side of her ribs to guide her towards the half-mirror of the surface. For the first time since leaving the wreck, he notices a second hull suspended above.

11:45 A.M.

Fabrienne breaches the surface between the boats.

Hands reach down to drag her over the side.

She is stretched on the slatted duckboards as the tank buckles are released.

Rolled onto her back, the sun is overwhelmingly bright.

She holds up a hand for shade. Someone brushes it aside to remove her mask, untangling it from her hair. She rolls away from the sunlight, hearing the start of an outboard motor.

The movement of the boat perpetuates the sensation of free-fall. She empties the contents of her stomach into the slats beneath her face. Her throat racks until it is sore.

She opens her eyes to a familiar pair of boots.

'André?'

André is on the side bench; hand on the tiller of the outboard. He leans over to see around the side of the small cabin that obscures his view forward.

'Don't talk to me. Don't even *think* of talking to me.'

His hand twists the throttle and they shoot forward, each cresting wave spraying over the gunwale into the boat.

As they slide into the mooring where Fernando's rib had been, he drops the anchor and leaps ashore with a bow line.

'You can get up now.'

Fabrienne turns lazily. She tries to get her feet under her then retches loudly again.

André holds out his hand. 'Come on. You're not going to die. Jorgé told me he'd decompressed you properly. I don't know whether to thank him or kill him.'

He drags her from the boat onto the quayside. 'I asked you not to dive with anyone else. Now look at the state of you. Will you listen? No! Do you ever do anything other than whatever Fabrienne in her infinite wisdom wants to do? No!'

She stares up at him defiantly. 'That's what you told me.'

His hands push through his hair in the gesture she was waiting for. 'What did I tell you? I'm doing my best to protect you…'

'When I asked you to dive the wreck with me that's what

you told me… *No.*'

'I said no because…'

'Yes… because?'

'Because it's too deep.'

'And you are too scared.'

'It needs a special air mixture.'

'And you are too scared.'

'Too damn right I'm scared. Look at the mess you are in. You had the Narks.'

'And Jorgé?'

'He knows what happens. That's why it's hard to forgive him. Fernando I would expect this from.'

With one hand he drags her to her feet.

She stands shakily but with a growing confidence.

He withdraws out of reach of her touch, pointing to the edge of the ferry landing. 'The car is there. Get in it.'

The rib's engine burbles softly as Jorgé manoeuvres it into the space. André makes fast the line as Jorgé steps onto the shore.

Jorgé holds up his hands. '*Lo siento, mi amigo.* But she is safe, no?'

'Drop the *Hispaniola* crap, Ramirez, your French is better than mine. Reassure me about the decompression.'

'Every stage, my friend, like I was at my mother's breast. The Narks will pass. It hit her more quickly than I thought. By the time I realise, it is nearly too late.'

André's hand snaps back… then up until it connects.

Jorgé's head whips backwards, his balance shifting, until he tips full length into the water beside the rib.

JUNE 12TH..
MONDAY

4:28 P.M.

For three days André's silence reigns over the camp.

Veronique hovers, keeping André in visual range without crossing the fine line drawn between him and Fabrienne.

Alec finds somewhere else to be each time he invades the space near the tents.

André has moved Fabrienne to a dig lower down the eastern slope, forbidding any further exploration of the box until he has made an executive decision on it.

Manon moves cheerfully between them, taking samples to the camp, bringing fresh water to the digs and all the while bearing a lopsided grin.

She catches Fabrienne in silent contemplation of a piece of rock in her hand.

'Special?'

The rock falls from Fabrienne's hand into the dust where it is almost indistinguishable from many others at her feet.

'Not especially.'

'I thought from the way that…'

'No. I was just thinking.'

'Then it *was* special.'

'It was a rock.'

Manon dips both hands into the bucket she has brought and bathes Fabrienne's face with cool water, using the hem of her own tee shirt to pat it dry.

She applies sun cream liberally to Fabrienne's forehead.

'You should be more careful for someone who burns as bright as you do.'

'I'll be alright.'

'I didn't mean in the sun.'

Manon rubs the remainder of the cream into Fabrienne's forearms. 'You think you are the only one who knows things. Don't you? I wish *I* could be that certain.'

'Manon, where is this going?'

'Look… you think you're special, and I can tell you from where I'm sat that I think you are too.'

'Ah. Now I see.'

'I said I'd take no for an answer on that, but how anyone so special can throw away a perfectly good thinking stone escapes me.'

'A what?'

'A thinking stone. See, you thought you knew everything. That's what makes you such a smartass.'

Manon retrieves the stone and hands it back to her.

Fabrienne closes her eyes, her fingers searching around the rock to maximise the contact.

Manon slides her hands into Fabrienne's hair. 'Now tell me what you see.'

'It's hard to tell. You are so good with your fingers.'

Manon's hands move down to Fabrienne's shoulders.

'Ok. I'll start you off. How long are you and André going to keep up this fight?'

'I wasn't aware that we were fighting.'

'If you want to see the collateral damage, just look around you.'

'I'm sorry if I've hurt you. I wouldn't want to.'

Manon disregards the apology. 'And where are your other clothes? How come he drags you back here naked inside someone else's rubber suit?'

Fabrienne smiles, still keeping her eyes closed. 'Didn't think you would mind that.'

'That doesn't answer my question.'

'And he didn't *drag me back*, as you so quaintly put it.'

'Listen, when André drags you back to camp looking like a drowned walrus, you'd better learn to enjoy it or you'll have Veronique to answer to. So what's the story?'

'I was diving with Jorgé.'

'Oh. Fernando there, too?'

'No. We were alone. I dived with the club at Uni and Jorgé is the best there is.'

'That's not safe. You should always have someone in the boat.'

'Jorgé said that Fernando was still in bed. They'd been in the bar the night before.'

Fabrienne allows the exploration of her skin, even to the point of enjoying it. Manon slides her hands the length of Fabrienne's spine, her fingertips slipping gently over the breadth of the scar.

'Then how come Jorgé wasn't hung over too?'

'We arranged it.'

'Now I begin to see…' Manon flattens herself against the small of Fabrienne's back, feeling the heat pulsing out into her own skin. 'Around two hours after you left to go on your 'walk to the port', Fernando arrived in the borrowed waste truck. We thought André would explode when he saw him up at the camp but he just went quiet. Fernando drove off in a cloud of dust but when André went to the car it wouldn't start. He dragged Alec from halfway down a cliff to help him.'

She rubs more cream into the back of Fabrienne's neck.

'You know the rest of it better than we do.'

The sun-cream cools Fabrienne's skin like the salt water surrounding the wreck. She opens her eyes, expecting the world to ripple with shadow. The sunlight bites so hard she jumps.

'Manon, there are many things you know better. I think I may have spent my entire life with my eyes closed.'

Manon slips the tube of cream into a back pocket.

'I know that it's your turn to make dinner… and the can opener is in Alec's tent.'

'Can you find it for me?'

'Sure… as long as he isn't in there.'

5:32 P.M.

Fabrienne allows her eyes to adjust to the dim light of her tent, searching around inside her pack and finding loose clothes, pocket knife, a torch with dud batteries… all things that should be there… except…

Manon's voice filters in from outside. 'I got it.'

'Give me a minute…'

'I'll get the fire ready. I'm out of matches. Got any?'

Fabrienne's fingers search for the cheap, plastic lighter from her emergency kit. It is missing.

'No.'

She unpacks the device to examine it.

It appears undamaged. The small door in the side is fastened tight, but there is an indefinable air within the tent.

She wraps the device into her pillow roll before leaving.

'So… what are we not cooking?'

Manon has assembled a loose pile of kindling in the centre of the hearth. 'Whatever's left. The cans are just inside Alec's tent.'

Fabrienne grimaces. 'Why can't we have fresh food? All I can taste is tin.'

'The boat is due tomorrow but today you get to choose which flavour of tin we are eating.'

Fabrienne reaches in the flap of Alec's tent to sort the tins. They are covered by a discarded tee shirt. She stops, immediately realising what it was she had noticed in her tent.

Grabbing at the cans, she throws three of them on the ground by the fire.

Manon opens them all. 'Right… do we have the custard with the steak and mushroom or the chilli-con-carne?'

'Qalaichi Tepe?'

'You probably know it better as Boukan. By now the town must have spread up to the dig.'

Fabrienne slides a couple more plates into the trestle bowl. Alec makes a quick pretence of cleaning them before passing them back.

'It's about 90K southeast of the salt lake at Urmia.'

'Iran, right? Don't tell me you've been there too.' She throws the dishcloth at him. 'I know they don't have skiing in Iran.'

'You think you know so much. Of course they ski in Iran.'

'What on? Sand?'

Alec throws the dishcloth back at her. 'In case you've forgotten, they have mountains in Iran. Where did you think Noah's Ark ended up?'

'Mount Ararat. Isn't that in Turkey?'

Alec tips the washing up water into the earth toilet behind the tents.

'Is now… wasn't then. *Mannaea… Cimmeria… Urartu…* take your pick.'

'What does that make the tiles we found?'

'Probably Cimmerian…' He stashes the trestle between the rocks at the base of the tower. '…with a dash of Mannaean and Urartuan. The whole area was dynamic in the latter centuries BC.'

Fabrienne unties the branches Manon has carried up. She leans some of them against a stone to smash them into kindling.

'Then why do you say Cimmerian?'

'Because they had something of a catacomb culture and the tiles explain that and the arrowhead I found. They used arrows as an offering to Ishtar, their Goddess of War and Sex. I'd forgotten…'

'*You'd* forgotten?'

'I didn't make the connection until we'd unearthed the tiles.'

'Then why didn't you say something?'

Alec pads up his jacket to sit on. 'How many egos do you count on this trip?' He shakes his head. 'Perhaps you need to have one to be able to see them. Take Veronique… desperate to be Alpha Female… but hasn't a clue how to go about it except to attach herself to the nearest Alpha Male.'

'That's not fair.' Fabrienne drags over more timber. 'She's in love with him.'

'She's lost, then. She's looking for something that no longer exists.'

'Aren't we all?'

Alec nods to where André's tent twitches in the breeze that circles the tower. 'Take more than an Archaeology First to unearth that one. He only exists on what remains of his academic laurels. He doesn't dare look at anything else.'

'Isn't that *his* problem?'

'No. It's our problem. Whatever you discover here, how much of it do you think will get past his filter? You'll get a by-line at the bottom of the page that says… *André Barnard was accompanied on the dig by several others…*'

'Then why are you telling this to me?'

'Because you don't have an ego and you won't steal from me.'

'I already did.'

'What?'

'Hope… remember?'

Alec holds out his hand for the pad on which Fabrienne

has drawn the tiles. 'Let's see what you did.'

'They were a little hasty.'

Alec lifts them up to the fading sun. 'I'd like to see what you could do with a little more time.'

'Photographs are quicker.'

'But not better.'

'Qalaichi?'

He pulls a pack of cigarettes from his shirt.

Fabrienne brushes away the offer and lifts her eyes to where a dark line marches across the eastern sea. 'They'll be back from the boat soon. Along with their egos…'

Alec sits upright. 'Alright then, Qalaichi. The arrowhead should have clinched it for me… but until we found the tiles… there's just so much archaeological debris kicking around here that I didn't think.'

'I think we were meant to notice the direction it was pointing. How accurate would you say the line was that we drew on the map?'

'As accurate as my memory.'

'We'll rely on coincidence then. So tell me about the tiles.'

The temperature is dropping significantly. Alec wraps his arms around his knees and hugs them closer.

'In the eighties there was a hugely illegal dig near Boukan in North-west Iran. It was rescued in eighty-five by a team of professionals… but not before a lot of the tiles had made their way into private collections. There are a few samples in Japan but the rest have been taken for study in Tehran.'

'You think these are similar?'

'I'm not sure until I can see under that brown coating. According to André, Antikythera had a large city but, for the sake of historical record, the inhabitants of this city, 'Aegila', welcomed pirate traders. The straits between the islands were the gateway to the Adriatic so anything passing through here was fair game. Greek, Roman, Venetian, Meroites…'

'Meroites?'

'Southern Egypt… Nubia… or Ghana as it was called back then. They traded cattle across the Med to broaden their pool of breeding stock.'

'Those ships must have been worth the taking.'

'Yep. Their cholesterol levels must have been through the roof for a week or two.'

Fabrienne attempts to reassert his focus, his reluctance making her wonder which side of the dig he'd been on.

'Qalaichi?'

'May I?' He makes as if to tear the drawings from the book.

'No matter. I can easily do more.'

'I noticed. Do you do everything that well?'

She puts down the look in his eye. 'Only those things that I choose to do.'

'You've done that all your life, haven't you.' Alec arranges the drawings on the ground, anchoring them with small stones. 'Here… help me out with this. Do you remember how they went?'

'Of course I do.'

He pushes two drawings towards her. 'Then where did these go…'

On her knees, Fabrienne sifts the pieces of the drawing as if they are a child's puzzle. Alec sits back to watch the quick certainty of her hands.

'There.' She sits back alongside him. 'Now what?'

'Now we read them…'

'It's not a glyph.'

'Nor Cuneiform or Runic.' Alec studies them intently. 'They are not language at all.'

'Then what are they?'

'Art.'

'Then how do you propose to read them.'

'Have you ever heard the aphorism that goes... every picture tells a story?'

'Have you ever seen a Pollock? Or a Mondrian?'

'Art is not made for anybody and is, at the same time, for everybody.'

'Who said that?'

'Piet Mondrian. Pollock said, *the painting has a life of its own.'*

'Is there anything...?'

'...that I know nothing about? There must be. I'm working on it.'

'Then look no further, Alec... its name is *Modesty.'*

10:41 P.M.

The car rolls quietly to a halt against the base of the tower. André rolls a stone behind the front wheel, avoiding Fabrienne's stare as Veronique and Manon scramble out of the rear seat.

Manon flashes a smile from the other side of the fire. She rubs her hands together in the glow and whispers across the embers.

'I think he wanted to see whose tent you climbed out of.'

'Then he will be disappointed.'

Manon sits beside her. 'I think not.'

The rear door of the car is wide open. André hoists out boxes of cans and packets of dried food. Veronique stacks them together outside Alec's tent. On top, she balances a full carton of cigarettes.

André looks around, unsure what to do with his hands now that the car is unloaded. He checks the flat, dark rim of the horizon.

'I think I will go to bed.'

He disappears from the firelight into the space behind the tower.

Veronique stumbles through the tents, hands on hips in a gesture of resignation. A shudder makes its way through her body as she vomits loudly into the latrine.

Manon leans heavily against Fabrienne.

'There was so much tension between them in the bar… if I could have wound it up it would have got us back here without the motor.' She pushes harder with her shoulder. 'Can I share your tent tonight?'

'Why? Are you cold? You aren't upset. I can see you're enjoying this.'

Veronique is still bent over the latrine.

Manon pushes harder still. 'No, I am not cold.'

Her eyes close and she rubs both hands over her face.

'But I am too drunk to be left on my own.'

JUNE 13th.
TUESDAY

8:30 A.M.

Alec makes his way carefully across the hillside, a large plastic bottle of water clutched in both arms, hair wilder than ever and eyes no more than half open in the glare.

Below him, Fabrienne has already raised the sun screen over the stone box.

She hears the slide of his boots in the scree as he spins around. An extra spade hangs down his back. His trouser pockets are stuffed with trowels and brushes.

Fabrienne unhooks the spade. 'You took your time.'

'The donkey is never as quick as its master.'

'Nor as intelligent.'

Alec drops the water bottle at her feet and empties his pockets into a small mound beside it. He reaches down to pick something from the pile.

'Here…' He hands her a throwaway lighter. 'I stole this from your tent. Mine got wet. Any clearer about what this box means?'

Fabrienne pockets the lighter. 'Not yet.'

He places one foot inside the box before Fabrienne drags him back. 'You are not going in there with your boots on. What are you thinking?'

'I wasn't. Sorry.'

Fabrienne sorts through the things he has brought. 'And you forgot your gloves.' She snatches the pair hanging from his trouser pocket. 'These are mine. Your hands are going to be sore. And don't bother undoing your boots, dig here.'

'Yes, Oh Master. And what am I looking for?'

'The bottom of the box.'

'Look inside. You can see it already.'

Fabrienne climbs in barefoot, carrying a small dustpan and brush. 'Just dig.'

The night air has shed a layer of fine dust, obscuring the surface of the tiles. Fabrienne removes it slowly. There are joints between them, barely thick enough to accept the blade of her trowel.

Outside the box, Alec has settled into a rhythm, ensuring each spadeful is deposited into a pile that can be filtered later.

'Move along the edge…'

Alec pauses. 'Don't you think it would be better if I just dug in one spot until I found the base before moving along?'

'I have my reasons. Put some of the water into the bottle in my toolbag.'

Fabrienne teases the fibres of the brush into the gaps between the tiles to ease the dust out onto the surface. With a piece of soft towelling, she collects it into the centre of each tile. The tiles measure around thirty centimetres per side. They are three across in number by seven down the length of the box. She can only admire the precision with which they have been laid.

Alec stops for a moment to wipe the sweat from his eyes.

'Hope you're not knocking yourself out in there?'

Fabrienne places her hands against the cleaned surfaces and closes her eyes to concentrate.

Alec peers beneath the sunshade. 'You okay in there?'

'Just dig.'

Alec returns to the spade. Fabrienne sits back suddenly.

'I'm sorry. I didn't mean to sound like that. What have you found?'

'Nothing. No bottom edge. No foundation. Nothing at all yet, except…'

'Except what?'

'Pigmentation. I think this stone was painted white, but the end slab I would swear shows traces of pink.'

Fabrienne climbs out of the box. 'Take a break. I think you've already found what I wanted.'

Alec has created a pile of finely disturbed soil a yard away from the box. 'How'd you work that out?'

She stands the spade in the bottom of the hole he's dug.

The handle falls well short of the box rim.

'I'd say you're down the length of the spade plus a good half metre, wouldn't you?'

Alec stands the spade carefully on the tiles inside the box. The handle protrudes from the top by a good six inches. 'That makes at least two feet beneath the tiles until we find the bottom. What's in there?'

Fabrienne climbs back into the box. 'Not what. Who. Let's find out, shall we?'

'Hold on…' Alec catches her arm. 'André?'

'What about André?'

'He's in charge here.'

'Of what?'

Alec persists. 'We have to clear this with him. Out of courtesy…' He notices the look still inhabiting Fabrienne's face. '…if nothing else?'

'What time is it?'

He scans the sky. 'I don't know… ten… maybe?'

Fabrienne swings her feet clear of the box. 'Okay. They should have recovered by now.'

10:17 A.M.

'Who gave you the right to begin excavations without clearing it through me? How do I maintain rigour without notes… details… pictures?'

'You were still in bed.' Fabrienne reaches into the tent and throws the hand-drawn pages at André.

They scatter into the dirt by his feet. He scoops them up and hands them back. 'That is no excuse.'

Alec scrapes the remains from his breakfast plate into a rubbish bag. 'Look… we did a little digging and Fabrienne cleaned the tiles. That's all.'

'Without my permission or knowledge… that is quite enough.'

Fabrienne jumps up, fists on hips, knuckles white.

'So I spend the whole morning at the camp just waiting around because you have a hangover?'

'Yes. I have a headache…' André glares back. '…and it doesn't seem to want to go away.'

'Then when you have recovered, you may accompany Alec and myself back down to the dig.'

André holds up his hands in mock surrender. 'Then there is no time like the present. I would hate to think that this dig lacked discipline…'

10:47 A.M.

André tilts the canopy further against the lifting sun.

'So… suggestions as to how we propose to get the tiles out?'

Fabrienne brushes sweat from her eyes. 'Not until we have understood what they represent.'

'Manon?' André moves aside to allow her through. 'Is there any film in the camera?'

'A fresh roll.'

'Ok. Shoot from this side so you cast no shadow. Alec, have you found the bottom edge yet?'

Alec twists on the spade handle. 'No, Boss.'

'How deep are you?'

'About three feet.'

Alec lays the spade on the ground. 'Think about the logistics of this. How on earth did they carry this thing all the way up here?'

Fabrienne sorts a trowel with a worn, narrow blade from the tools beside her feet.

'"Why?'… is the real question. 'How'… depends on the number of fools that will fit on the handle of a spade.'

She passes the trowel to Alec. 'Use this. You must be close now.'

Alec works the blade easily alongside the stone slab until it stops dead. He trims away earth with his fingers.

'Something here… it's a plinth… four or five inches wider than the box. Clean edge. Fine joint as far as I can see.'

André passes him the loose end of a tape measure.

'That's okay. Stop digging. Hold that on the plinth.' He draws out the roll until it reaches the top of the box.

'One point nine four metres.'

'How much is that in Pounds Sterling?'

'More than you can afford after you've paid me for the cigarettes.'

Fabrienne lowers the end of the tape into the box.

'Ninety four centimetres. There is exactly a metre below the tiles.' She brushes the dirt from her feet and climbs into the box. She places her hands against the surface of the tiles and leans down until she touches them with her forehead.

'There is someone in here.'

André smiles at her naiveté. 'What makes you say that? I'm not saying it is impossible… look at the box alone… but this is deep for a burial in this type of soil.'

Manon moves around the box to where Fabrienne kneels towards her as if in prayer. She lifts the camera to take the shot she knows she will always keep for herself.

She closes her eyes to the shutter's click. Her decision is becoming clearer as the days pass… and the thought of making it brings a curious smile to her lips.

'I'm only surprised Fabrienne doesn't know their name.'

11:16 A.M.

André helps Fabrienne out of the box. He passes her boots but she shakes her head.

'I need reminding of who I am.'

'Perhaps one day you will let the rest of us in on the secret.' He leans into the box, trying not to obscure what light there is. 'I wish I could understand the significance of the black dots.'

Fabrienne is intent on deciphering the shapes. 'I think I know what this is…'

Manon clips a new roll of film into the camera. 'How can you say that? We have only just seen it.'

'I have seen this blackness before.'

Manon returns the camera to its carry-case and slings it

over her shoulder. 'Where?'

'That would take too long to explain.'

Fabrienne catches Alec by the wrist. 'Go back to camp and fetch your ketchup.'

With a little of the ketchup smeared onto a corner of rag, Fabrienne works on one of the larger black dots. She allows it to soak into the surface for a minute, then buffs it clean. The dot gleams back at her in bright silver. An hour later she has removed the oxide from them all.

André motions her to one side as she climbs out of the box. 'Good work… unorthodox… but still good. Manon, get some photos in case the silver tarnishes again. Everyone move aside.'

Manon circles the box, the camera a cricket voice in the midday heat. 'I think that's about all I can do. I have it from every angle.'

'Ok.' André allows them to approach the box. 'Now let's see what we have. Is it any clearer to anyone?'

'It's a star map.'

'Yes, Alec, I think that has become obvious… but of what?'

'Stars?' Alec screws the lid back on his ketchup. 'This looks familiar but different… if that makes sense.' He leans under the sunscreen, tracing lines between the silver studs with his finger. 'I'm still trying to work out what it is that's familiar. Wait… look here…'

With his fingernail he flakes an edge of brown glaze beside a star. It flicks away to reveal a slice of bright blue.

'The ketchup… it has lifted the coating too… look…' he flicks again at another piece, exposing more of a bright, sea-turquoise.

André pulls him away from the box. 'Stop that. We might

cause irreparable damage…'

Alec shakes himself loose. 'It's the acetic acid in the ketchup. That's why it cleaned the silver. This coating must be an organic alkali.'

'But the acid might also destroy the glaze.'

'The blue is the same as I've seen before. If this has a glaze like the tiles from Qalaichi, you'll find it impervious to most things.'

'Then *I* will try it.'

'Ok, Boss. It's your dig.'

At full stretch André's reach is ineffective.

Fabrienne snatches the rag from him and climbs into the box. 'It needs a woman's touch.'

12:02 P.M.

As Fabrienne works at the tiles, a clearer picture begins to emerge.

A vast serpent stretches its coils between the stars. It writhes in green scales around a blue-clad human torso, the outlines of their bodies defined against a pastel ground by the silver studs.

Veronique shudders visibly and backs away outside the canopy, counting ten deep breaths on her fingers.

Fabrienne passes the empty ketchup bottle to Alec.

'So… are these similar to the ones at Qalaichi?'

'Different patterns but the pigments are unmistakable.'

'Then how did they end up here?'

Alec grins across the box at her. 'You forget yourself… *Why*… is always your real question.'

'You're wrong today. *Who*… would be my first question.'

Alec grabs the bucket. 'So why don't we ask them? After all, they are still here. And invite them to lunch. I'm starving.'

André flicks through the pages of Alec's Star Chart.

'Why do you have this?'

'The nearest light pollution spots are Chania in the south east and the Peloponnese to the north west. This is a dead spot in the middle. The night sky here is brilliant, as you know. Thought I might catch up on some neglected study.'

'So where should I be looking?'

Alec riffles the pages slowly. 'Here… this one.'

'Ophiuchus?'

'Also known as the 13th. Sign of the Zodiac. At this time of year you'll find it rising in the west.'

'Then I should have seen it many times since I have been here.'

Alec spreads the book on the floor between them.

'I think you had something in your eye.'

André touches the stars visible on the page. 'I always waited for the sun… Oh…'

'Hang on. Fabrienne? Those drawings you made?'

Alec spreads them on the floor beside the book. 'I think there's something here…' He shuffles them around. His fingers touch star after star, repeating the progress on the page. 'Here. This one is missing from the chart. It's on your drawing as a large star but it's only a dot and a number on the page.'

André turns the book toward himself. 'Perhaps the drawing is inaccurate. We shall see when we go back to the dig.'

'You are accusing *Mademoiselle Parfait* of inaccuracy?' Alec opens the book to the catalogue at the back. 'Be very sure of your ground.'

His fingers slide through the columns. 'Now I see.' He

follows the link to a further page and scans the notes. 'How very not surprising.'

'What have you found?'

Alec hands him the book. 'You.'

'Me?'

'Here... in the catalogue at the back... stars in Ophiuchus... non-visible...'

Alec flicks the page over for him. André runs a finger down the lists.

'What am I looking for?'

'V2500 Ophiuchi... or Proxima Ophiuchi... or... better still... *Barnard's Star.*'

'I didn't know there was a star with my name.'

'You're in good company. Ever read Hitchhikers Guide to The Galaxy?'

André shakes his head.

Alec chuckles. 'Sorry... no offence... but you've never exactly lifted your gaze above the ground, have you.'

'None taken.'

Alec returns the book to its plastic folder.

'Ever hear of Project Daedalus? In the mid-seventies, the British Interplanetary Society designed an atomic-powered, unmanned, interstellar spacecraft. Their intended target was Barnard's Star. Perturbations in its orbit meant that it had at least one companion. Problem was, only a planet the size of Jupiter could cause that much perturbation.

'So how come it has my name? I would be surprised if we were related.'

'I wouldn't.' Alec throws the plastic folder into the tent behind him. 'It's an ageing star. Much of its energy has been dissipated and it's a wanderer... also known as a runaway star.'

André puts a single step of distance between them.

'What do you mean by that?'

'I'm sorry if that sounds like a cheap shot, but it's moving faster than anything around it, possibly as a result of a close partner going… supernova…'

André's expression is visibly rigid but his awareness of Alec's discomfort is palpable.

'Then why is it just a dot in your book?'

'The 'V' stands for 'Variable Star'. Also known as a 'Flare Star'. Needs a good telescope to see it usually but it displays unpredictable moments of brilliance.'

'Then I will accept the relationship.'

'There is one more thing you should know. It is blue-shifted.'

'And you mean by that?'

'I mean it's coming towards us at a fair rate of knots. Around 140k per second.'

'When does it get here?'

Alec does the rough calculation in his head. 'Nine thousand seven hundred AD. Give or take a century… or two.'

André glances up at the sky. The sun is beyond zenith and the shade will need to be moved again to prevent bleaching of the tiles.

'Then let's try to get this dig finished before my star arrives.'

2:33 P.M.

'I cannot go near it.' Veronique keeps several feet between herself and the box.

Fabrienne struggles with the poles at one end of the screen. 'Veronique, help me out here.'

Veronique shakes her head violently. 'I…I…'

Alec catches her from behind as she backs away.

'What is it?'

She twists away from his touch, then back again as her

priorities begin to shift. 'I am afraid of snakes.'

Manon laughs out loud. 'Good grief… it's only a picture.'

André silences her with a glance. 'If you feel so strongly about it, Veronique, perhaps you should return to the camp. There are things you could be doing with the notes?'

Veronique tears herself free from Alec to make the climb back to the tents.

'Leave her alone.' André calls their attention back to the box. 'It is better that we deal with our phobias in our own way.'

'That's as may be.' Alec reinserts the sharp end of a pole into the earth. 'But have you any idea what hers is called?'

'No, but I will take ideas on how we lift these without causing any damage.' André shifts around to the shaded side. 'Fabrienne… get out of the box until I have agreement on what we are doing.'

Fabrienne tucks the thin-bladed trowel into the back pocket of her shorts. 'It's just an idea… but maybe we can 'float' them out.'

'I see…' André climbs to his feet. '…but if we soften the bed won't the water be a problem to whatever is underneath the tiles?'

'That's your call.'

'Alec? What was under the tiles at Qalaichi?'

'Nothing much. A bed of dry mortar… just earth under that.'

'No voids or cavities?'

'Not that I know of, but if you were to ask me, I would suspect that under these there is a lid.'

André tilts the shade to hide the sun. 'That seems obvious if this is what we think it is. Fabrienne?'

'There is someone important in here. Important enough to ship these things from so many miles away. I think it goes without saying they would protect the remains. Perhaps even revere them.'

André rearranges his hair then stops. They are all watching him. 'I am thinking.'

'Ignore them, Boss. We always know when you are thinking… but the clever part is we never know what. That's why you're the Boss.'

'Thank you for the vote of confidence, Alec. That means if we screw this up my name will be on it.'

'And if we don't..?'

'Then I think it may well be yours and Fabrienne's.'

Sunlight lifts a ridge across Fabrienne's brow. 'And if I don't want it?'

André stares blankly into the box. 'You must have this if we succeed.' An overwhelming sense of loneliness overtakes him, the way it does when he listens to the voices on the night wind. 'It will make your career.'

'Give it to Alec.'

'Uh-uh. This is yours. I'd given up on it, remember?'

André steps in. 'Let's see what we have first. We can swap egos later. Fabrienne? Get back over here with your tools.'

He balances the bottle on the edge of the stone.

'How much water do you think we'll need?'

Fabrienne nudges Alec. 'How thick were the tiles at Qalaichi?'

'Oh… an inch or so.'

'And the mortar bed?'

'How should I know?'

Fabrienne nudges him again.

'Ok… no more than an inch.'

'Then empty the bottle in. It may take a while.'

She roots around in the canvas bag for a hammer.

Finding a small one with a long, inlaid shaft, she inserts it through the looped handles and swings the bag over her shoulder.

Alec watches her with a quiet amusement.

'Who taught you to do that?'

Fabrienne smiles enigmatically.

'The love of my *Grand-mère's* life.'

10:12 A.M.

'What is *what* called?'

'Don't be so English, Alec… Veronique's phobia.'

Veronique forms a triangle with them across the open hearth. 'It's called Ophiophobia. A fear of all things serpent-like.'

André drains his coffee cup into the ash. 'That would explain your reaction to the tiles.'

She glances quickly at Alec. 'It also explains why I am sitting over here.'

Fabrienne is leaning in through the passenger side of the car. Veronique finds something in the embers to become absorbed by as André crosses the fire to talk to her.

He taps his fingers against the roof.

'What are you looking for?'

Fabrienne continues to rummage through the depths of the parcel shelf, under the seats and the debris scattered between. 'If I find it I'll let you know.'

'In that case, I'll see you back down at the dig.'

TO SKÁPSIMO
GALANIÁNA

10:33 A.M.

'The water has all gone.'

'Not quite, Manon. The surface is still wet.' Alec tests the tiles with the tip of his finger. He rocks it across the surface.

'I still think we'll have to prise them out.'

'Perhaps not...'

Fabrienne pulls a mirror from her pocket. Attached to it is the sucker that had once held it to the windscreen.

André takes it from her hand. 'Forgotten it had one...'

She takes it back and presses the sucker firmly to the centre of a tile. 'Pass me something soft but heavy.'

Manon laughs. 'Jorgé isn't here.'

Alec passes the rubber mallet from Fabrienne's toolbag.

She taps at the tile, travelling minute blows around the perimeter until a rocking motion begins. She grips the mirror with both hands and lifts.

André takes the tile as it comes free.

Alec scratches the earth with his foot until he has a flat patch in the shade from the canvas. 'Here...'

They lay it on the ground and peel back the sucker.

Fabrienne slides the trowel blade under the next tile.

'I'm working clockwise from the middle, so be careful how you lay them...'

'Fabrienne... there's a picture on them.'

'I know.'

'Well, so do we... just keep them coming.'

2:16 P.M.

Fabrienne scratches carefully away at the exposed mortar until she strikes something hard.

210

'It's a dome… well, dome-shaped at least, but it feels like metal… a soft metal.'

'Then don't go back in…'

They turn to stare at Alec. 'What?'

'Lead. It's consistent with the apparent age of this thing. The Romans had been using it forever. This looks like a sarcophagus, so unless you want to become intimately involved with whoever is in there, don't put your weight on it.'

4:22P.M.

Manon climbs onto the edge of the box. In an hour she has removed the last of the mortar. Beneath it is a leaden-grey, highly arched cover, with the occasional nick showing bright where it has been scuffed by Fabrienne's trowel.

Set into the lid near each end are two large decorative bosses, each pierced by a circular bronze ring.

Worked into the lead between them is an inscription:

Lucius Cornelius Sisenna

André motions everyone back. 'Photographs please.'

Fabrienne jerks suddenly aware. Her eyes open against the bright, wavering landscape that surrounds her. The slope of the hill on which she stands is all too familiar but a short distance away, a group of people are gathered around a large stone box set deep into the earth.

She recognises most of them immediately.

Veronique… sitting on top of the water carrier at a respectable distance… Manon, camera in hand… Alec, slight to the point of concavity… André, fingers poised in his hair as he waits for the photographs to be taken… but there is a fifth that she does not immediately recognise.

She rubs at her eyes. The air between herself and the

group is thick with tremors.

The sound of goat bells arises behind her, growing closer yet, as Fabrienne has found, goats rarely graze this side of the island.

She turns slowly. A woman is approaching.

Fabrienne shields her eyes against sunlight that reflects like molten gold from the hair escaping her hood.

'Daughter… do not be afraid of me.'

Fabrienne flashes a glance to the group by the box and back again… a question in her eyes.

'That *is* you over there. We rarely recognise ourselves.'

Fabrienne reaches out a hand to the woman's cloak. The dark fabric is rough and warm to the touch. 'You seem real.'

'Yes, I am real. But only as real as you.'

Fabrienne releases the edge of the cloak from where her fingers are unconsciously stroking the material.

'Then how…?'

The woman holds out her hand for Fabrienne to take.

'Walk with me.'

5:16 P.M.

Fabrienne is led away from the group and up the path to the ridge. Goats follow them, drowning the silence with the dull knock of their bells.

The woman stops beside the stone where André spends his evening vigil.

'Sit.'

The stone is hot from the sun. Fabrienne lowers herself gently against it. The woman sits beside her. With a quick gesture she waves the flock away to meander a short distance into the shrub.

'Who am I… will be your first question.'

Fabrienne denies her. 'Who am *I*… is always my first question.'

'Then you are truly my daughter.'

The woman faces Fabrienne, pushing aside her hood.

'Tell me what you see.'

Fabrienne studies the fine features that have remained half-hidden since the woman appeared. Her eyes are clear… grey-blue with a light green fleck in the left iris… the lines around them finely drawn by exposure to the sun though her skin remains translucent.

There are soft creases around her mouth as she smiles at the look of recognition on Fabrienne's face.

'*Grande Maman*? But you cannot be… you are little older than I.'

'How old is a dream?' The woman remains unflinching under Fabrienne's scrutiny. 'An entire life can be lived in a dream of no more than a few seconds.'

Fabrienne hugs her knees to her chest, the way she does when she finds herself close and alone with André.

'Am *I* a dream?'

'No, daughter. You are the culmination of one. Though be aware, my line has a predisposition to tragedy.'

'Then who are *you* to dare such a dream?'

'I am Minerva… and, in *my* dream, I was Priestess of Athena.'

5:28P.M.

'Fabrienne, get up. I can't see this thing if you're going to lay all over it.'

Fabrienne remains impervious to Alec's touch.

His fingers turn around her wrist and lift her so that he can see her face. Her eyes are closed. A look of confident serenity has settled across her features.

He shakes her lightly, then searches the faces of the others. 'André?'

André pushes him aside. 'Fabrienne?'

He repeats Alec's gesture then scoops her into his arms. Her head rolls to rest against his shirt. 'Drop the canopy!'

Veronique rips the poles from the ground and spreads the canopy beside the box.

André lays Fabrienne down on it.

'Here…' Manon slips off her own tee shirt and folds it into a pad. 'Put that under her head.'

Alec takes it from her without a glance. He pushes the pad into place and takes up Fabrienne's wrist.

'There is a pulse…' He waits a moment, counting.

'… seems steady.'

He leans forwards to catch a scent of her breath.

André pushes him away. 'What are you doing?'

'Ketones… you have heard of Ketones?'

'No…'

Alec sits back on his haunches. 'Oh… I get it. *You* thought I was… '

'You don't know what I thought.'

Alec returns his attention to Fabrienne, sweeping the others aside with a gesture of his arm.

Veronique splashes water from the carrier into the small

tool bucket and hands it across.

'What is the matter with her?'

Alec wets his hands and applies them gently to Fabrienne's face.

'I was about to find out…' He glances up at André. 'May I?' He leans over Fabrienne, his nose and mouth close to hers as André watches him intently. He closes his eyes to concentrate. 'No… no Ketosis.'

Manon hunkers down beside him. 'Is that good?'

Alec examines the inside of Fabrienne's arms then lifts the hem of her shorts.

'What *are* you doing?' André casts a shadow that fits the whole of Fabrienne where she lies on the canvas.

Alec rocks back on his heels. 'Do you know how many diabetics never disclose it? Not even to their friends… and especially not to anyone allowing them on a dig like this. The liability alone…'

'Well… is she… or isn't she?'

'Veronique, there are many ways to disguise the condition… and many places to hide the injection marks.'

Without warning, Alec lifts Fabrienne's tee shirt. The smooth edges of a vivid scar wrap around towards her stomach. He slides a hand beneath and rolls her slightly to one side. 'Dear God…'

'Is she safe to move?' André has come around beside him. Alec's eyes lack focus. 'What? Yes… I suppose so.'

André lifts her from the canvas and settles her head against his shoulder.

Half way up the hill he checks his watch. 'What day is it?'

Manon's tee shirt is slung shamelessly over one shoulder. 'It's Wednesday. Why?'

'There's a boat heading for Chania… in fifteen minutes.'

André picks up his pace, following the meander of the track up the hillside, his boots searching for grip amongst the scree.

'Manon, run up and rip the back seats out of the car. Alec, go with her and get it started. Veronique? Get behind me and push, my feet are slipping.'

6:18 P.M.

'Manon, move over. I will drive.'

'No, André. Get in the back with Fabrienne and Alec. You will be more use there than I would.'

'But you don't drive…'

'And you only aim it. Shut up and get in.'

Manon closes her eyes and throws the car into first gear, the way she has seen André do it.

The car lurches forward until it hits a rock. A wheel rolls over it, gaining enough momentum for Manon to throw it into second gear. Her foot hits the floor and stays there until the engine screams.

As they approach the place where André sits in the evenings, Fabrienne's body stirs slightly. The two in the back bend over her, searching in vain for any further sign of awareness.

VRÁCHOS GALANIÁNA

At the sound of a racing engine, Fabrienne stares back along the track. André's car is a huge cloud of dust, hurtling in their direction. Growing in plain sight, the face behind the wheel is Manon's, set in a grimace of fear.

Veronique's arm is out of the window, holding the door closed. Alec and André are thrown sideways in the area behind the seats, ignoring the road. The car roars around the first bend, beginning the fall to the sea without slowing.

Minerva's hand falls on her arm. 'Have no fear for them.'

6:27 P.M.

Manon throws the car around one bend after another, front wheels sliding then gripping, rolling them impossibly beyond gravity. In front of her is the last straight drop into the port. The heel of her hand thumps uselessly on the disconnected horn.

A blast from the ship's klaxon rebounds from the pale bowl of the natural harbour. Along the jetty, sailors have unhitched the moorings. Water begins to churn around the stern of the ferry. The wash hits the moorings of small boats, pitching them skywards off the dock side.

Manon keeps her foot hard on the accelerator.

She is close to the ship now, its huge maw still open.

Steel plate extends towards her like a serrated tongue.

The ship's klaxon sounds again as it begins to withdraw.

The car engine stalls as it hits the ship, wheels caught hard by the rising metal plates.

Around them, the hydraulics of the upper section hiss as it lowers. Below them, the ramp begins to lift and the car roof comes down to meet Manon where she sits.

The fold begins between the front and rear seats, separating herself and Veronique from the three in the back.

There is loud screaming as Veronique's arm is trapped in the crushed window. The rear door is forced open. André braces his feet against the rear wheel arches, holding tight to the inert form of Fabrienne.

Alec is slid across the floor as the whole car tilts, arms and legs jamming into the aperture to prevent their fall to the sea.

Alarm bells ring loudly all around them.

With a shudder, the ship regains ground on concrete.

6:35 P.M.

'There is nothing you can do.'

'My friends are down there…'

Minerva's hand steals into hers, fingers entwining. 'Can you be sure of that?'

Fabrienne slides her fingers free. 'I saw their faces. What right have you to frighten them this way?'

Minerva draws the cloak more tightly around herself.

'I have no right to frighten them… but I do have a duty.'

'Is this why you have waited so long?'

Minerva clicks her fingers. The goats cease to forage and draw closer around them. 'If you know who I am, why ask?'

'Because I know who you are does not mean that I know *what* you are.'

'Then who am I?'

'You are the woman in the stone box.'

'Walk with me…' Minerva paces slowly along the road towards the hill that overlooks the harbour.

Fabrienne remains standing by the stone, lit sharp by the golden light.

Minerva stops. 'Come…'

'Why should I?'

'Because it pleases me.'

Minerva continues on to the summit of the road. Within her sight, the island scoops Potamos to the safety of its wide arms. She feels the presence of Fabrienne close behind her… hears the shallow-drawn breath of her uncertainty.

Fabrienne points to the ship, where it hankers for the shore, nose tight to the jetty, ship lights ablaze around the wreckage of André's car.

'There had to be an easier way to get my attention.'

Minerva's hair swings aside to reveal age settling over her

skin in a fine shower of ashen lines.

'It is not your attention I need.'

'Have you always been so enigmatic?'

Minerva laughs quietly in return. 'It appears I am not alone in that regard. Perhaps that too is my fault... along with your impatience.'

'I am *not* impatient.'

'I wait two thousand years for the privilege to walk this road in your company and you ask why.'

'I question everything.'

'Then that is your curse... for you shall never be satisfied with the answer.'

Around Fabrienne's feet, shadows are fleeing into darker blue. 'Then I have need to be careful of which questions I ask.'

'And of whom you ask them.'

'I choose my friends carefully.'

'Is that why you have so few?'

Fabrienne points to the harbour.

Minerva reaches up to knock down her hand. 'Before you begin to count... down there you have friends, lovers and enemies. It is up to you to work out which is which.'

'That should not be so hard.'

'You think not? What if a lover and an enemy share the same body?'

'It is not possible to hide a wish for harm from me.'

'She who knows everything knows nothing, *ma vie*. Keep a little ignorance in hand.' Minerva turns her face away. 'If you choose to see only that for which you wish, the reality of love will escape you... as it did me. There is a very thin line between love and duty. Choose wisely.'

'And how well did you choose?'

'You are here.'

CHRONICLE

XIII

ANDRÉ

JUNE 14th.
WEDNESDAY

6:42 P.M.

'Do you have a Doctor on board?'

'Your arm is only bruised.'

Veronique supports her arm across her chest and steps away from the ships officer. 'It is not for me. It is for this one.'

Fabrienne is laid between Alec and André, her head supported in André's lap.

'What is wrong with her… the accident?'

Manon drags herself free from the broken driving seat.

'That was no accident. I was trying to get your attention.'

The officer unclips a radio from his belt and nods to the damaged deck section. 'Now that you have it, you may find it expensive.'

Manon shrugs. 'A drop of paint…'

'And a check of the hydraulics before we sail.'

'Look…' André's voice carries from the rear of the wrecked car. 'Get your Paramedic here… now! This girl is in a coma. Do you think this is a game?'

The officer bends to examine Fabrienne, taking the excuse to speak quietly with André.

'It is no game.' He indicates the ship with a roll of his eyes. 'She is my responsibility…'

'And *she* is *mine*… Paramedic… *now.*'

6:53 P.M.

'Put her in here… no… wait… I will pull down the upper bunk.' The Paramedic locks it in place and hangs the short ladder. He offers a hand to Veronique.

'Up there. Lie quietly. I will examine your arm in a few minutes.' He shuffles into the small space of the shower to make room for André to pass.

'Put your friend on the bunk. What can you tell me about her?'

'Not as much as I once thought. You would be better asking Alec.'

He moves into the corridor outside the cabin. 'Manon? Give them some space…'

Manon steps out into the corridor to join André. He pushes a bundle of soft cloth into her hand. 'Take your tee shirt and go down to see if we left anything we might need in the car.'

André leans over the rail, watching water convulse in the margin between the quay and the side of the ship. A shoal of silver fish is making its way through the undulating gap, their movements as turbulent as the thoughts in his head.

The car lies in a mangled heap across the loading apron, steam escaping the layer of foam that the deck crew have sprayed. He recognises the finality of it and looks away.

The Paramedic taps his arm. '*Professeur?*'

André turns around… visibly struggling to refocus from the bright reflections to the dark interior of the ship.

'What?'

'Sorry. I didn't mean to startle you. Your friends told me who you are.'

André rubs away the glare of reflection. 'You know me?'

'*Of* you. I have heard of your search for my city.'

'*Your* city?'

'I was born here. In the room behind the bar. We have always known there was a great civilisation here. My *mitéra* says it will rise from the ashes of the past. She also says you are the man who will do this.'

'*Aegila…*' André leans against the rail, shaken by a sudden vision of bleached ochre soil under thousands of milling feet. 'If only I had her faith in me.'

He pushes himself away from the rail. 'Fabrienne. How is she?'

'As far as I can tell she is fast asleep.'

'Asleep? She collapsed right in front of our eyes.'

'She responds to all the usual tests… pupil dilation, heart rate and blood pressure are fine. If I prick her with a needle she stirs and makes noises like a child.'

'Then what can you do?'

'Not a thing. I think she will wake up when she is good and ready. But if you would like to accompany her, we can take her to the hospital in Chania. There is, however, the small matter of making sure the ship is seaworthy again.'

The Paramedic points to where Manon is slipping the tee shirt over her head down by the wreckage.

'My driver should look like that… but if she drove like that I would be my own best customer. Why don't you go in and see your friend.'

'Can I?'

'Of course. It may make *you* feel better. My *mitéra* says you are like a man in love with a long sandwich but don't know which end to begin. She says also that you like ouzo… maybe one time too much… and that your friend in there likes fresh oranges.'

'Ah. Now I understand. What else did your mother tell you?'

'That you tip well. Go and see your friend. She will know you are there.'

7:02 P.M.

'There has been no change?'

Alec jerks his thumb towards the top bunk. 'Only up

there.'

André reaches over the edge of the bed. Veronique's arm is tightly strapped with bandage. Her skin is warm and her pulse is obviously racing. 'How are you?'

'I have a headache.'

'I thought your arm…?'

'I sat up quickly…' She points to the ceiling two feet above her head. '…when *she* laughed out loud.'

'Did she wake up?'

'No. She just gave the most self-satisfied laugh I have ever heard.'

'Veronique… you mustn't… she is ill.'

'She is not the only one. I am sick of it *all*.'

André ignores her to sit beside the lower bunk.

Fabrienne is in foetal position under a white blanket.

He hesitates… then caresses her forehead with the backs of his fingers. She is cool and still.

She jumps at his touch then settles back into sleep.

He sits a while, hardly daring to resume the touch, until his fingers take him where his thoughts dare not go.

This time she remains still. A smile flickers to life on her face and he wonders what she is dreaming.

The cabin door crashes inwards to rebound from the shower room wall.

'How many more women you kill?'

André has no need to look up to know who has entered.

1997

**MARCH 1st.
TUESDAY**

10:16 A.M.

Paula Barnard drifts in and out between black smokers. The tidal flow that swings through the Lubang Fault spreads the surface discolouration wide into the surrounding sea.

Between the fumaroles the water is clean, although heat ripples bend the pale light into strange refractions.

Small fish dart between the fingers of her grapple as she collects samples of the bacterial colonies on which they feed, snatching at dislodged chunks of lichen that swirl in the micro currents.

She floats within a cage of six black columns, moving between them with the skill of a dancer, ever one step away from the searing heat. At the base of each column the earth has opened, raw red light pouring into the surrounding water before turning into the liquid, black, smoke-like plasma that gives them their name.

She unclips another bag from her waistband and fills it from a colony of tendrils that billow with movement. Yellow dye from the clusters at their heads is staining her fingers as she packs them into the clear plastic.

She catches sight of André beyond the circling pillars. He hangs in the water, rig tuned to negative buoyancy, a spear gun held across his chest. Inside the mask his eyes are wide, unblinking. Despite his insistence, there is little danger here. The big fish have no reason to inhabit this area of the sea. The fish that live around the smokers are small and dangerous to catch.

She waves, but his gaze is occupied elsewhere, beyond the intense clouds streaking to the surface. She unclips another bag and returns her attention to a yellow sheen that coats a small outcrop of volcanic rock.

It is a shade she has seen before, but only from the camera of a remote submersible. To find the precipitate of lobed cocci this close to the surface was once thought impossible, but perhaps no more so than the pressures and temperatures in which the world's most extreme organism is normally found.

This is her reason for being here. To sequence the DNA from these bacilli could open up our vision to colonising star systems and planets previously thought untenable. Perhaps to finding a way of re-sequencing our own genes to meet the dictates of a changing planet.

The genus is already known as *Pyrolobus…* her eyes smile shyly inside the mask… but maybe this strain will now be… *Barnardii.*

André feels the tremor through the water. Not a sound, more a swift strobing of pressure waves.

He looks up quickly, expecting to see a large ship, tanker-sized at the very least, changing course above him, but the surface mirrors distant daylight back to him, spoiled only by the teardrop shape of his yacht's hull.

Around the mouthpiece, his lips draw into a facsimile of a smile, imagining her face when she surfaces to finds the Renault 4 he's had delivered for her birthday. By now it will be waiting on the Tingloy dockside, complete with pink ribbon.

Paula experiences the same vibration on every inch of her skin. She spins rapidly, ever mindful of the columns containing her. A lazy kick brings André within visual range.

She watches him go through the motions of looking all about him, head rocking, sun-blonded hair in fluid motion, eyes wide inside the mask, his spear gun swinging up again to rest in the crook of his arm.

She returns to her study of the yellow film, expecting to brush away the pursuing small fish.

They are gone.

She turns slowly around.

The water is clear and the bacilli colours shout even more loudly without their usual living shroud. She unclips a fresh bag and heads for one she hadn't noticed before.

Below her, a crack ruptures the sea bed. The rock tears open like a wound. A ray of heat lances upwards and a swift, new column of plasma roars towards the surface.

The water above it boils out of existence in an explosion of live steam and the sea rushes in to resolve that displaced.

It catches Paula in a violent hand that shakes her into the rising column.

The concussion hits André in that same second.

His ears implode as the shockwave passes through him like a hammer blow.

He loses all orientation, only regaining it by sight of the new fumarole pounding its way to the surface.

He can only watch as Paula is flung in and out of it, her body flayed by the searing heat, mouthpiece torn away and melted, a look of shock and horror in her eyes.

Halfway to the surface her tank explodes, blowing her remains clear of the column. Pieces of flesh spin through the water, caught and tossed aside by the other smokers in a descending arc.

With his last remaining spark of lucidity, André dumps his ballast.

Within seconds, the big fish arrive.

2006

JUNE 14th.
WEDNESDAY

7:05 P.M.

For André, time has ceased.

His eyes are open. Fabrienne is beside him on the bunk. Fernando is framed against the light from the gangway.

He lifts his head to answer Fernando's anger but no words arise. He has nothing he can use to defend himself from the sadness and guilt that fills him.

He reaches out to touch Fabrienne's skin. His fingers caress her brow until suddenly he reels away from her, his emotions emptied... hollowed out from inside.

There is movement in the doorway as Fernando reaches for him, but when André searches for a response he finds his limbs are useless hollow shells where sadness had previously provided him with strength.

Strong fingers grip him by the throat and lift him into the air as a vision of the man he might once have been rushes in to fill the emptiness inside him.

His hands tear the fingers from his throat. An insatiable anger propels him forward, pushing back hard at someone who has made him their haven for a blame that lacks reason.

His fists ball and punch. Fernando flails backwards in shock, stumbling over the doorway to sprawl in the corridor outside. Beneath them, the ship shudders and lurches as the engines drag it free of the concrete. André throws himself from the cabin, pouring a storm of blows on Fernando's head.

Fernando grabs his wrists and holds them, straining. André's fingers are inches from his face, stretching out for his eyes.

Fernando's knee comes up between them. André gasps with pain and is pushed aside. As his eyes clear, he sees Fabrienne running blindly along the gangway.

Fernando drags him from the floor as if he were weightless and throws him after her. 'You catch… *¡Ahora!*'

André sets off at a limping run.

Fernando grins at his disappearing back. 'Now we see what you made of.'

'Fabrienne… wait.'

André grimaces in pain, attempting to grasp a shoulder that is always three steps beyond his reach.

'Please…'

Fabrienne slows to a walk but still doesn't turn. She steps through an open bulkhead door onto the car deck. Around her, the steel plates of the ship rise like an unassailable bulwark. She moves on, heading for the iron stairs that will take her up to another level.

André follows, unable for the moment to overtake her, his hands falling short between them.

At the head of the stairs she turns along the side of the ship. Her body weaves around ventilators and life rafts until she finds a clear space beyond the rail.

She steps over.

André thrusts out a hand to catch her arm.

'Fabrienne… wait.'

Running on pure instinct, Fabrienne presses her face into the wind from the shore. Arms raised, she dives forty feet into the sea.

André watches from the rail for her reappearance.

Suddenly her head bobs in the foam beside the blank steel side. The nose of the ship is approaching the arc of the harbour point, where he knows the pilot will engage the bow thrusters, dragging her down into the churning blades.

She is ten feet away as he surfaces, the steel side of the ship nudging her towards him. She is swimming blindly but the ship is turning more quickly than she can escape.

He kicks hard towards her, the pain in his groin is an animal sensation he has to reach to ignore.

His fingers close on hers and she fights him with all of her strength.

They sink into the water, the curve of the ship pressing them deeper as it begins its march eastward.

Between the vibration of metal, the violence of her struggles and the air escaping wildly from her mouth, he hears the hard clunk of a gear as it engages.

JUNE 14th.
WEDNESDAY

7:05 P.M.

The thoughts given to Fabrienne by Minerva are now imprinted on her mind like ancient memories.

'How do I use this knowledge?'

'You will know when the time arrives.'

'Can you not be a little more pragmatic?'

'Why should I?'

'You take me on a journey of two thousand years…'

Minerva laughs out loud, drawing the cloak around her.

'You are too much like me.'

'Then how will I recognise my *true* future?'

'Truth is not in what you believe, daughter. Truth lives in incontrovertible fact. Truth is the foundation. The search for it is the purpose of Life itself.'

Fabrienne steps to the edge of the roadway, peering down into the bay. The car has been dragged out of the ship where it remains on the dock as a mangled heap. Hawsers have been shipped and the ramp is rising to its final position.

'What about my friends?'

'They think you are asleep.'

'But they are leaving…'

'And if they take your body with them this part of you, your soul, will cease to exist.'

'Then I can't stay here with you?'

'Time will not allow that.'

'Then what must I do?'

Minerva clicks her fingers. Goats appear from nowhere to gather around her feet. 'I own no more answers. I only laid the foundation.'

'But how does it work?'

'I have held this door open for two millennia. Only you can see what lies beyond it. Those futures are now yours.'

Fabrienne turns away from the scene below.

'And if I have not yet learned how to look?'

Minerva raises her arm in farewell.

'Then enjoy the lonely walk.'

The air closes silently around her, folding her from view.

Fabrienne is jolted alert by an echo of the ship's klaxon bellowing around the bay. Her feet find the tarmac at the top of the hill and begin to fly down it at great speed.

The hill unfolds below her as if in a dream. She reaches the first bend and skims across it, alighting on the roadway below in a single bound.

Her ankles flex. She spreads her arms wide like wings, soaring over the roofs of houses and down into the bay.

The water cloaks her in a violence of sound.

She watches from a distance, breathless, as André takes her arms and wrestles her panicking form into submission.

She hangs silently beside them in the water, movement mirrored by her own body as he shifts his grip. Her arms float freely from her sides as he catches her head in his hands, her feet pointing straight down as if she has sprung from the sea floor. She slides into herself, becoming one again under his hands.

André pulls her to him, covering her nose with his cheek as he pushes the last of his own air hard into her lungs. He pushes her to the surface as a current begins around him, dragging him down towards the bow thruster blades.

A dark shadow appears in the water beside him.

His lungs are aflame with the desire to breathe.

He knows it can only be seconds before he finds that instinct impossible to deny.

With that knowledge, a curtain of calm descends around

him. He finds a space in his mind that exists beyond his mortality. There he finds the strength that he has hidden for the last twelve years. With one remaining effort he begins to push away from the current swirling into the turbine… but the pull is irresistible… urging him towards its spinning core.

The shadow in the water looms around him, grabbing his arms and pushing him in the direction of the thruster.

The sound it makes in the water is incredible… then suddenly they are beneath it… skin tearing on the underside of the ship before entering a current that pushes them away and up to the bright mirror of the surface.

Fernando hauls him above the water with one hand, feet treading violently below. 'Breathe… *bastardo*… breathe!'

André's stomach convulses. He retches violently until he is emptied and gasping for air. Fernando turns him onto his back, floating him on the surface as the ship draws away from them. He cups André's chin with his palm.

'I think for one minute I lose you there, brother-in-law.'

André coughs as water splashes into his mouth from a cresting wake. 'Where is…'

'I am here.'

Fabrienne's hands reach down to help him into Jorgé's rib.

The ridged deck is digging into his torn skin… but this is happening in that other space he has found… the dark place that is threatening to open up again, expecting to be filled with sadness.

Fabrienne touches his arm.

Inside him, a door slams shut.

He cries out as the pain returns… until she places a finger on his lips. 'If I keep my finger there, will you promise not to speak?'

André nods as the last of the pain ebbs from his body.

'Then close your eyes.'

JUNE 16th.
FRIDAY

9:10 P.M.

'Jorgé and I will sleep in the truck.'

'But it stinks in there.'

'*Gracias*, Veronique. I take that as an offer?'

Veronique shrinks away. 'Why don't you go back to the bar? I am sure your money will be welcome there.'

Fernando reaches into the pocket of his shorts and pulls out the lining. '*Por que no aqui?*'

Jorgé steps between them. 'You know we are not welcome here, amigo, we'll take the truck back to the dock.'

Fernando brushes him aside. 'No, I want to see what they do this side of the island. I know André. Whatever else… he do not waste time.'

Alec climbs out of his tent and casts a withering glance at Veronique. 'Look… sleep in the truck or wherever you want. Most of us don't care. Thanks to you we still have a job, a boss and a friend.'

Fernando looks him up and down. 'In this order, eh?'

'At the moment, Fernando, we are very grateful. Don't push it.'

9:20 P.M.

André is laid face down on top of his sleeping bag.

Fabrienne has wedged a rolled towel under his forehead so he can breathe more easily.

Her hands are calm and certain as she unpacks the small medikit. 'I hope there is enough left of the salve.'

'Show me your hand.'

Fabrienne pushes her hand into the lamplight, turning it

palm open. There is no visible scar.

'It worked on you. Must be good stuff.'

'I only used it the once.'

'It was my healing touch, then. See if you can repay the favour. How much skin have I lost?'

She dips her fingers into the smooth paste. 'Not much… considering how thin it is…'

She applies salve to the area of his back where Fernando had dragged him under the nose of the ferry.

Her fingers pause a moment as she pushes the hair away from his neckline. Hidden beneath it is a livid birthmark in the shape of this island. She spans it with her fingers, closing her eyes, absorbing an emotion she has not found in him before.

'What are you doing?'

'Finding another piece of the André Barnard puzzle.'

His thoughts, searching for memories lost within the flicker of a lamp, find only an echo from the bell of time.

Grateful for the simple darkness behind his closed eyes, he relaxes under her touch. 'Then you had better use it to heal me.'

Fabrienne wipes her hands on his tee shirt, inhaling the scent of aloe from the salve.

'I think you have done that yourself.'

JUNE 17th.
SATURDAY

9:03 A.M.

'How are you, Boss?'

'Fine, thank you Alec.'

André stretches in the bright air of morning. The truck has been parked where he usually leaves the car. Inside, Fernando is laid across the whole of the seat, still asleep.

'He's okay. Found some raki in the glovebox.' Alec tugs the stray hair from his forehead. 'Good stuff too. Hope we didn't keep you awake.'

'Doing what?'

'Arguing.'

André looks him over. 'Hope it didn't get…?'

'No. Veronique insulted him with such middle-eastern aplomb all he could do was laugh.' Alec averts his eyes, scuffing at the dirt with his boot. 'How's Fabrienne this morning?'

André spins around to stare at the tent, as if expecting to find her there in the doorway. 'I don't know. I haven't seen her. She left my tent before I fell asleep. Isn't she with Manon?'

'No. Jorgé is in there.'

'With Manon?'

'Even though she will never admit it, she was so rattled by her 'driving' experience that she didn't want to sleep alone. Veronique wouldn't… Fernando and I both offered.'

A sudden realisation makes André smile. 'Get your boots on. I think I know where she is.'

Unconsciously, he slips a hand into his pocket, searching for the keys to Paula's car. The one he'd had for himself had been worn completely smooth, the other one, *hers*, still pristine, unused, the serrations sharp and waiting for her return. He pushes the memory deep into the empty lining.

9:13 A.M.

They hear the truck door slam behind them as they set off down the incline. The sea sparkles so brilliantly they are glad to turn away at the sound of a voice.

'*Hola*, brother-in-law. Since that I found you again, do not think you get away so *rapido*.' Fernando slithers in trainers across the scree until he catches up with them on the path. 'Where are we go? Where is *cosita bonita*? You lose her again?'

André ignores him and strides along the path. As they turn across the hillside, the lower slopes open up in front of them. Down below they can see the box beneath its shroud of canvas. There is no sign of Fabrienne.

'Looks like you were wrong, Boss.'

'Not yet, Alec.'

Fernando stops a moment. The circles of the dig spread out in ripples, overlapping with precision like the wheels of a clock. 'This you do, brother-in-law?'

Alec nudges him forward. 'Impressed…aren't you.'

Fernando picks up the pace. 'It looks too… too…'

'Intelligent?'

'No… *trabajo duro*… too much like hard work.'

9:21 A.M.

André lifts the edge of the canvas, expecting to find Fabrienne curled up underneath, but only the exposed metal of the lid is there.

Folded into a pad at one end is an old tee shirt of his. He lifts it out and runs the cloth through his fingers. It is cold.

He straightens up and spins around, searching for her across the landscape.

'Bet *I* know where she is…'

'Ok, Alec… seems I was wrong.'

'She'll be at the spring. We might not be welcome if she's showering.'

'Go back and send Manon down.'

'Veronique is awake…'

'No. Wake Manon. Make sure she is the one that goes.'

André lifts the tee shirt to his nose. It smells of himself under a strong scent of Aloe Vera. He lifts it again… there is something else in there that makes his heart race.

He turns away from the box to begin the climb back to camp. Fernando catches him by the arm. 'André.'

From half a step up the hill, he stares Fernando directly in the eye. '*André?*'

'*Si.*' Fernando allows his hand to slide the length of André's arm until he grips the hand firmly. 'Past is past. We let it slip away, no?'

André returns the firm shake. 'Okay, brother-in-law, but I think the past is about to catch up with *us.*'

Fernando indicates the sarcophagus under its canvas shade. 'What is this?'

André tugs hard on Fernando's hand, drawing him up onto the path beside him. 'I don't know yet. But I know a woman who thinks she does.'

9:42 A.M.

'She is not at the shower, André. I looked everywhere around there.'

'Thanks, Manon. There is only one place left she can be.'

Jorgé pokes the ashes around under the coffee pot, resettling it in the hottest embers.

'I have to take back the truck. If she is down at the dock I will bring her back first. You can come with us if you like, André, but there are only two seats inside.'

The back of the truck is scattered with filth and debris.

'Where did you put me last night?'

'In the lap of the Angels, *mi amigo.* I think you owe Manon and the *cosita bonita* a new set of clothes.'

André throws his coffee into the embers.

'Thanks for the offer, but stay here and have breakfast. I need to find her myself. I have questions.'

10:06 A.M.

Fabrienne hears his footsteps approaching long before she herself will become visible from the road. She moves around to the other side of the rock where she is more confident that he won't see her.

The footsteps stop.

André sits by the rock, careful not to lean his damaged back against the warm stone. The stored energy radiates into his skin through the shirt, liquefying the salve into a sluggish rivulet down the curve of his spine.

'Of course… I can only imagine how it must have felt. My own injury is nothing by comparison.'

Fabrienne remains silent, watching from the corner of her eye for the cormorant that inhabits the rocks below. It appears not to be there today. Or perhaps it is so still that it has become invisible.

By André's feet, tiny ants form a continuous stream around the soles of his boots, all but a brave few shying away from actual contact.

'If Fabrienne doesn't wish to speak to me, perhaps I can understand that. But just in case I am *not* sat here talking to myself… I have to add that she owes me nothing.'

The sun lifts over the rock behind him and sets alight the sparse bushes with a cacophony of cricket voices.

'Of course, I would like to know where she is. If only to thank her for the opportunity she gave me to find myself.'

'And the pain?'

At the sound of her voice, André relaxes. Eyes closing, his feet push an unconscious swathe through the rushing ants. 'Pain is a funny thing. It appears that it only hurts when she is not touching me.'

Her voice seems closer now. 'And if she had a choice…

what should she do about that?'

'She should do only whatever she chooses.'

'Do you think she is so wise?'

'No.' He feels her hand caress his shoulder. 'At least I hope not. If she were so wise she would see right through me.'

'And if she was not afraid of what she saw… what should she do then?'

His eyes are still closed, the skin on his back is drying… contracting in the heat. 'I cannot imagine this person ever being afraid again. I have seen…' His chest heaves the way it did as Fernando plucked him from the water.

Fabrienne confronts him, knees either side of his outstretched legs, her face so close to his he feels invaded.

'What did you see?'

'On the ship… your scars. I am sorry. I didn't know.'

'Manon never said?'

'Manon?'

'No matter.'

He opens his eyes. Hers are an unflinching grey-blue but there is a small fleck in the left iris, similar to the one he remembers of his own *Grandmère*.

He finds himself reflected there… his own eyes are his father's… dark brown… hiding from the sun under sharp-ridged brows.

'Who did *you* find to heal your scars?'

She presses him slowly to the ground. 'No-one. I didn't know I had them until yesterday.'

He cries out as small flints make their mark in his wound. She touches her lips lightly against his to stifle the sound but, unlike the night before, André can still feel the stone digging into his consciousness.

She lifts her lips from his. 'I need you awake, but I promise to be worth the pain.'

JUNE 20th.
MONDAY

11:32 A.M.

'You are not so strong.'

A sense of relief washes visibly across Veronique's face as Fernando lifts the timber out of her hands.

'Jorgé? Take the other end.'

André and Alec take up the strain of the other log. The ropes they have slung through the lifting rings on the sarcophagus lid creak into tension.

The lid begins to rise within the stone walls.

With the men at full stretch, the edge of the lid hovers above the stone, wavering as they strain for another inch.

André shuffles his feet more firmly into the dust. 'I can't hold this much longer. It feels like my back is tearing apart.'

The strain is shifted to Alec at the other end. Fabrienne feels something click into place inside him… another gear that no-one would have suspected could exist in that slight frame. The metal lifts fully clear.

Fabrienne inserts her branch cleanly through the gap. Manon catches it from the other side.

'Ok, guys. Let her down again.'

André spreads his legs and sways his mid-section until he feels a shift in his lumbar vertebrae. From beneath the lid comes a scent that he struggles to identify.

Then he recalls it. 'Clover.'

'Clover, Boss?'

'Never mind, Alec. Look at the thickness of this metal. Someone measure it while we catch our breath.'

'Fifteen millimetres.' Fabrienne has a calliper from the

toolbag in her hand.

'Jesus. No wonder my nuts are like melons.'

'Thank you for the scientific assessment, Alec.'

They rotate the lid across the stone walls.

'Flashlight!' André holds out a hand behind him as his eyes attempt to pierce the gloom inside.

Manon presses a torch into his hand. Fabrienne snatches it away before his fingers can affirm their grip. She leans in beside him and switches on the light.

The beam slices the darkness inside the stone walls. Light is caught and blurred by layers of hard translucent granules, but where it penetrates the surface, there is form.

André reaches into the box to lift out a handful. He examines it in the light. 'These are sugar crystals.' He hands some of the grains to Alec. 'How have they stayed so sharp-edged over all this time?'

Alec tosses them lightly in his palm. 'Re-crystallisation? I don't know until we examine more of them. Perhaps they have dissolved every winter with the ground moisture.'

'I don't think so… look…' André holds out the granules in his hand. Already, the angular freshness is disappearing as they swell and shift in the heat from his skin.

Alec takes the flashlight and pulls Fabrienne out of the way. He follows the edge of the box with the beam.

'There is lead here, too.' He leans in and probes amongst the softening granules with his fingers. 'Same thickness… all around the sides.' He flicks a shard of loose material from the top surface, finding a layer of the same on the underside of the lid. 'This thing was hermetically sealed.'

André turns over the hardened layers of sealant. 'What is it? Some kind of gum?'

'At this stage… wait…' Alec places a few of the granules in his mouth. His eyes close.

André watches the contraction of his throat as saliva

builds rapidly on Alec's tongue.

'Alec!'

Alec's eyes flick open to the sunlight. 'You were right, Boss… clover.'

'You're sure?'

'Makes the best honey.'

'Don't ever do that again. We have no medication here. What if…'

'Hold on, Boss. There is no better medication. It's what kept the ancient world alive. They also believed that anyone drowned in honey could be revived.'

'To what purpose?'

Fabrienne is leaning in so far that Manon has rushed to hold her legs. 'Perhaps so that you could find her…'

'Fab…? What are you doing?'

Inside the box the granules are swelling as they absorb warmth and humidity from the air.

Fabrienne's fingers are clearing the area around the face she has seen. The moisture in her breath is softening the hard grains and they move sluggishly aside as she pushes them, releasing them from the skin they have adhered to for two thousand years. She clears it reverently until the whole of the face comes free.

Fabrienne takes a deep breath and holds it, then allows it to whisper between the corners of a smile.

'Hello again, *Grande Maman.*'

She scrambles clear of the box, inviting André to bring the torch.

The face below André is incredibly human.

Pale skin reflects his light but set within it are eyes that stare up at him. Their implacable gaze enters his mind with force. He jerks backwards until Fabrienne catches his arm and pulls him back to the box.

'Don't be afraid. She just wants to know what you are.'

André feels the grey-blue eyes stealing his every thought.

He switches off the torch, aware that if he leaves it on he will not be able to pull himself away until the battery runs out. In the bright sunlight, he pushes his fingers through his thick blonde hair, shaking the heat from it.

'Who is she?'

'A distant relative.'

A few feet away, the rest of the group are removing the granules from the sarcophagus.

André watches them with a growing interest. 'That's not enough. I believe you know more.'

'If I told you what I know, you would believe that I am mad.'

'Fabrienne… you are many things… but you are not mad.'

'What makes you such an expert on insanity?'

'It's a land I've visited often. A few days ago I thought I'd left it behind. Now I find that it has never left me.'

'Was it something I said?'

André's laugh is, brief, sardonic. 'I will not push you. You will tell me when you are ready.'

He walks off across the hillside, his steps working in the loose scree until he reaches the simpler security of the path.

12:30 P.M.

Both buckets filled with granules, Alec hefts one in each hand. Fabrienne grabs a handle. 'I will take one.'

'Thanks, Fabrienne, but with two I am balanced.'

Something in his face has changed. It is hard for her to decipher but then she sees it… the man showing through the boy he wears each day as a cover… the way Raoul hid himself. She snatches a bucket from him. 'You will not be the only unbalanced person around here.'

The camp is silent as they approach the ridge. The tents

are swaying in a slight breeze. There is a symmetry in their movement that will disappear as soon as the others arrive.

Alec tips the buckets into the sieve and rummages with his fingers in the coagulating swirl, separating hard granules out and allowing liquid to drip through the mesh.

'Fabrienne?'

She is ignoring him. Beside the remains of the old tower, the earth is scored with tyre marks that the breeze has not yet obliterated. André's footprints cross them at right-angles.

She counts the steps she can see, waiting for them to make the veer towards his tent, invisible from this position, but they carry straight on.

'You left your tent flaps open, Fabrienne. You'll be sharing it with more than Manon tonight.'

'No, I didn't.'

Behind her, the tent flaps are moving independently, the tie ropes cracking as they whip. She ignores them and strides off, stepping into André's prints with each fall of her bare foot. The headland tapers down before her, shortening the visible horizon. Eventually she notices the top of his head, fingers deep into his thick, flowing hair. He must be aware of her presence yet he gives no sign. Slowing her pace, she moves around into his peripheral vision. Still he ignores her.

She sits beside him on the rock where she had played Artus' flute to the goats that first morning.

He clutches something to him and turns away, hiding it from view.

She touches his shoulder.

He turns his face towards her, cheeks stained with dust and tears.

Without ever taking her eyes from his, she reaches into his lap to take back her linen jacket.

André shifts his gaze far out to sea where there is no horizon… where the blues blend perfectly to infinity at the edge of vision.

Fabrienne folds the jacket over her arm, smoothing out the creases. 'When I wear this, what do you see?'

André drops his face to rest on cupped hands. His shoulders remain widely set and rigid, his breathing tightly controlled.

She waits for an end to his silence.

The prevailing easterly whips salt scents from the shore below as she waits. It catches in her throat, forcing a sharp sound from her.

'Then it seems I have no choice but to tell you. You see a ghost.'

André turns to face her.

'I am no longer afraid of ghosts.'

'Then tell me what you do see.'

'I now see only empty rooms.'

His eyes have dried and shadowed.

Fabrienne is intensely aware of his fear of the past and hopes she can contain it.

'Am I not in your rooms?'

'And if you were, what should I see? I can't see in ultra-violet... or infrared... and you are somewhere outside of the spectrum. I only know you are there because I feel the heat as you pass and the burn after you've gone.'

'And three days ago... up at the rock... what did you feel then?'

'Used.'

1:50 P.M.

Alec sifts honey across the mesh, the coarse weave taking the liquid until only hard, sharp crystals remain. He takes a handful, allowing them to drift through his fingers... until he finds a small woven bag, drawn by a cord and perfectly preserved by the honey.

He opens the neck to allow the contents to ooze out onto his hand. The first of them he recognises as the middle section of a human finger.

He rinses it carefully. The carvings on it show black with age against the preserved white bone. If his memory serves him, there should be another twelve like this…

He pours the contents slowly into the sieve. After a few minutes, he has found and cleaned another eleven.

He drops the bones into his pocket. There will be time to search for the last one tomorrow.

He bangs the sieve against the top of the tank to remove the liquid clogging the fabric and a small, blackened ring leaps into the air.

He catches it with one hand, rinses it clean then slips it into his pocket to nestle amongst the bones.

2:06 P.M.

'Manon?'

'Sorry, Alec. It's not my week for self-flagellation.'

'Well don't be afraid to ask if you need a hand. Where's Veronique?'

'Down by the shower. She could be a while.'

Alec spins on one heel, staring around the camp for inspiration. Beside his tent are the last four tins he's opened, all of them custard.

'Why don't you ask Fabrienne to walk down to the port with you? I hear she has a way with Jorgé.'

'I only need to borrow a truck, not Jacques Cousteau and his gang.'

'You might find them difficult to separate.'

'Ok. Where is she?'

Manon points to Fabrienne's tent. 'She's been in there for the last two hours. No… don't ask.'

Fabrienne takes the time to reset the device carefully,

gauging the approaching footsteps in time to hang the key around her neck. She wraps the box in her pillow roll as Alec twitches the guy rope beside the door flap.

'Fabrienne?'

'Yes? This is Madame Third Choice. What do you want?'

'I need some company.'

'A perennial quest…'

2:27 P.M.

The rock by the turn in the road seems strangely deserted. Alec pauses to lean on it and light a cigarette.

Fabrienne circles it before sitting down, reading the signs she'd left in the dust before, some of them now obscured… she couldn't help but feel deliberately… by the more recent tracks of André's boots.

Alec grinds out a stub in the exact spot where she'd carefully laid *his* head… where *his* hair had swept the soil.

She wipes her palms on her denims. They are clean. She wipes them again, and again. The sensation of dust clings to her the way it did that night in Raoul's workshop.

She stifles the rising tide of her grief with a shudder.

Alec is at the crown of the bend, beckoning to her.

'Come on. It's all downhill from here.'

2:52 P.M.

'*Buenos Dias*, Jorgé. Is Fernando around?'

'*Hola*, Alec. You I did not expect.'

Fabrienne slides around the table to sit beside him. He flinches slightly as if a shock has passed between them.

'Fernando is with the boat. Why do you want him?'

'I don't… really. But he knows a guy who knows a guy. I need to borrow the truck to take some food back to camp.'

A small boy comes out from the bar carrying a plate with a freshly segmented orange and places it in front of Fabrienne. He scampers away laughing before she can thank him. He returns with three small beers.

This time she grabs and holds him.

He smiles up at her, milk-tooth gaps vivid in the small mouth. He nods and pulls away, lisping Greek words over his shoulder, the smile never faltering on his lips.

'So what is it, Fabrienne?'

'So what is what, Alec?'

'Don't tell me you don't know the effect you have on the whole male population. Look at Jorgé. He's scared spitless in case you get any closer.'

Fabrienne moves closer to Jorgé who shifts slightly in his seat. 'Is that an advantage?'

Alec pulls hard on his beer. 'From where I sit it's positively Darwinian.'

'And Manon?'

'She's the exception that proves the rule.'

The small boy is at Alec's elbow, tugging on the sleeve of his tee shirt for him to follow.

'Okay. *Entáxei…*'

The boy drags him through the bar flap and into the room behind, where he swings open a large door set in the wall.

Inside is a deep larder stacked with jars and tins. An old woman draped in black appears from the kitchen. She nods to him, ushering him with both hands to help himself.

Alec deliberates slowly, choosing only tins with pictures printed on, or jars where the glass is clear and the contents readily visible while the boy loads them into a cardboard box at his feet.

Alec feels in his trousers for his wallet. It is missing.

The boy taps his shoe on the floor for attention.

'She say an more day.'

'*Parakalo.*' Alec hefts the box to his shoulder.

Outside, the table is empty apart from his own glass.

As he picks up the remains of the beer the truck arrives, dust squeezing from under the bald tyres.

Jorgé is in the driving seat, Fabrienne peering round from within his shadow. Alec glances down at the box, then back up at the truck. No-one moves. He shoulders the box onto the flatbed, climbing on alongside it, settling his back against the metal.

The driver misses a change on the second hairpin and has to stop. The truck rolls backwards until it finds a rock.

They lurch off again.

Alec turns to glance through the rear window of the cab.

Jorgé is in the passenger seat.

JUNE 24th.
SATURDAY

11:40 A.M.

'I think we should leave her where she is.'

'But… Boss… you would never have to work again.'

'Some of us enjoy it, Alec. I know as an Englishman you may find that hard to understand.'

'How long before she begins to deteriorate?'

'I don't know. I only know that I won't allow that to happen. Whatever it takes.'

'According to Fabrienne she has spent two thousand and ninety years in solitary. That should be enough for anyone. I think she has something to teach us all.'

'If only that certain things should be left alone.'

'And that is your considered contribution, Fabrienne?'

There is movement in the air beyond the tent lines.

'There is only one person to whom this really matters. I suggest we ask her.'

André spins around. A circular array of goats are holding position outside the camp. They stare back at him, their black eyes dissolving the distance between them.

Fabrienne's hand slips into his as Minerva steps from nowhere to stand beside her.

'I think that now is your chance.'

'*Bonjour, ma vie.*'

'*Bonjour* again, *Grande Maman*. André has a question to ask you.'

Minerva walks around, pointing to each of them with an extended forefinger. 'Since you are here it no longer matters what happens to me. I want to know if you have decided *their* fate.'

'Stop that, *Grande Maman*. They are each all three… given different times and circumstance.'

'And what of this one? I know he carries my signs.'

Alec reaches into his jeans pocket. He holds out a cluster of carved, segmented bones.

'They are twelve. Where is the thirteenth?' Minerva turns around, searching the empty spaces inside the circle.

'And where is the Ophiuccan?'

Alec's fingers sift amongst the bones. 'I recovered twelve of these from the honey. The last thing I found was a silver ring. I thought they were safe in my tent but there were times when Veronique was alone at the camp.'

Minerva folds his hand around the bones and pushes them away with contempt. 'You must find it. Without that ring, Fabrienne is no more than an empty amphora.'

'*Grande Maman*… your amphora is no longer empty.'

Minerva swirls around to face André.

'You would interfere with my plan?'

Fabrienne turns her away. 'It was not André. It was I, *Grande Maman*. The choice was mine.' She reaches out, placing Minerva's spread fingers over her own stomach.

'I am not the one. Your wait is not over.'

'Then destroy your Device. There has been enough strife with one. With two abroad the world will become untenable.'

'*Grande Maman*, the other Device is imperfect, as you well know. That was always in your plan.'

'Then imagine the implications of the Device that Raoul made. If mankind can see the future plain, they will fail to create one for themselves.'

'But in the right hands…'

'And whose are the right hands? Yours? Theirs? For once, daughter, do as I command. A thing such as this must be returned to the past.'

André is glancing between Fabrienne and Minerva. The

likeness is growing stronger by the moment. As the sun reaches to touch them, each shadow falls exact, each line… but in Fabrienne's skin it is a waxing, a telling of the story to come while in this woman's it is a lessening… a fading of age.

Minerva takes his hand. Her skin is cool and inert. There is no penetration in the way Fabrienne's touch seems to, but still there is movement. It flows out to him from the earnest grey-blue of her eyes and, this close, he notices the fleck in the left iris… her scent of honey… undertones of sweet clover in her breath as she speaks to him.

'Fabrienne tells me you have considered my line in your every thought. For that I remain in your debt and yet… there is one more thing I should like to ask of you.'

André allows the fingers that are searching the creases of his palm. They track his lines… *Life… Head… Heart… Fate…* before finally caressing the Mount of Venus.

'If it is within my power…'

'I wish to remain undisturbed until my wait is truly over.'

'I have already made that decision. And… if you are as indebted as you say… I should like to know about your city.'

Minerva folds her legs gracefully beneath her to sit by the hearth. 'Given time… all the knowledge of Aegila shall be yours.'

'And if it does not grant me the right?'

'Those of whom I speak are long gone, but you will earn their inheritance.'

Despite her apparent solidity, the sun strikes through Minerva with a fierce heat. She places a hand on André's bare forearm and is rewarded by a swift jolt of muscle while the touch of his skin reminds her heart of a fullness she had thought forever lost to the waters of the bay.

'Yes. Aegila was my city. But it can be yours, if I show you how to look.'

CHRONICLE

XIV

AEGILA

67 B.C.

HEKATOMBION
HEMERA KHRONU

NYMPHÊ

André's eyes close and a brush of wind fills his ears with the sound of his nights alone… the harsh bark of spattered language he hears around the edges of the camp while the rest are asleep.

A sense of well-being enters him and his eyes flash open.

He is alone, but set into a wall before him is a gate whose timbers are solid, sun-seasoned and wedged hard into rough-hewn volcanic stone.

The gate is open.

And beyond it lies a living city.

He steps through into Aegila.

He glances behind him. The wall is there but the gate is now obscured. He turns back to face the city.

In the near distance, bright colours flap against the blue of the sea. The harbour below is heavy with the timbers of ships… sails bound tight against trimmed antennae… the odd lateen rig triangulating the spaces between.

The air is abrupt with a sharp hum of commerce, echoing his staccato night-voices. People in vivid robes roam between market stalls where kaleidoscopic canopies thrum the breeze.

The faces around him are a microcosm of the whole Mediterranean… skins so black they shine with a blue light… browns of infinite variety… others who flit like bleached patches across the tapestry.

They ignore André's own face. Instead, their eyes focus on his clothes. He glances at the robes surrounding him. His clothes are very different… and different is something he cannot afford to be.

A young man reaches out to finger the sweat-stained and dusty patch-pocket shirt André has worn for over a week.

He tries to push away the fingers but they catch in the edge of his pocket and he allows himself to be towed away between the rows. A short few metres brings him to a stall stacked high with bolts of cloth, their ends forming a rainbow across the plinth. Behind a screen against the sun, an old woman sits on a collection of roll-ends. In contrast to her surroundings, she is dressed totally in black.

She reaches up, grabs André's belt and pulls him down to sit beside her. She wipes a terracotta cup on the hem of her dress and hands it to him.

Under the edge of the stall is a small amphora of ouzo. André holds the cup in both hands as she fills it.

She takes it from him and turns the cup in her hands three times before taking a drink. She hands it back. He hesitates… then does the same. She smiles at him across the cup… gums pink and toothless… eyes alive with knowledge and mischief.

She stares briefly at the brown of his eyes before her hands reach under the stall for a robe from the pile.

The fabric is a deep, rich purple. He recognises the dye immediately. Roman Imperial… from the predatory sea-snail, Murex Brandaris. In this time, its gland alone will be worth its weight in silver.

There is an organic energy within the cloth that writhes around André's fingers and he wonders how many lives were spent as the price for this probably stolen shipment.

She snatches it away and he is glad as the touch leaves

him. She pushes another at him. This one is blue as the sky before dawn. The cloth is a coarse weave. He breaks it over a finger… the weft is lighter, more open-spun. Gentle-soft hairs arise to fill his touch with a sense of luxury. He slips it over his head and tucks away the collar of his shirt.

The young man kicks over a pair of stained leather sandals and André swaps them for his boots.

'*Tóra échete na moiázei me.*'

The youth's Koine Greek sounds coarse to André's ear but the message is still clear.

He replies in the Greek he studied at Uni. 'So I look like you now, do I?'

The young man grins back, a smile igniting deep within his brown eyes. '*Ne.*'

He tugs on the robe, holding out an open palm.

André slips his hand through a slit in the side of the robe and finds only an empty trouser pocket. In the other is a set of car keys that he is still unwilling to be parted from. In the patch pocket of his shirt is a magnifying glass with an ivory handle. He has nothing else. Perhaps he can earn this back.

He presses it into the young man's fingers with a sudden flash of his own thirteenth birthday… his father's Will being read… the empathetic smile of the solicitor… and in his hand, carefully wrapped inside an ancient, olive-wood box, the only thing of any value.

'*Aftó aníke ston patéra mou.*'

The young man turns it over against his palm, reading life-lines already set. He holds it up, studying André with one eye close to the lens.

'Your *patéra*… he must be very old to give you this.'

'Unfortunately, my *patéra* never reached the age that I am now.'

'He is younger than you? I do not understand.'

André tips back his head as if to study the blue of the

sky. Close to the horizon it becomes a reflection of the robe he is wearing. 'I'm not sure I understand, either.'

He smiles down at the young man. 'What year would you call this?'

'*Giagiá mou* says it is year of Athens 173.'

'Then he's not yet born. Now there's a puzzle you can study with your glass.'

The old woman snatches the glass from the youth's fingers and examines the lines of her own hand, turning it over into the light. A porcelain bowl beside her holds a scattering of coins. She holds one under the glass… then throws it into the dust at her feet. The next one she returns to the bowl. After a few seconds there are several coins in the dust.

She waves the glass at André and nods her gratitude.

'*Ne… ne… efcharistó polý.*'

The young man sweeps the coins from the dust in one movement and puts them into a small leather pouch at his waist. 'You want food?'

André stops at the question. His instincts have been replaced by the sights, sounds and smells of the market… but this can't be real… no more than can the young man at his feet picking up coins. Yet his hunger is more than real.

He reaches out…. the youth's hair is soft to the touch… there is a truth in it… one he had better accept quickly while he has the chance.

'*Ne.*'

As basically human as it is possible to be, he hopes the act of eating will help him merge his thoughts with the situation.

Minerva has brought… taken?… sent?… him here. And in that there must be a purpose… higher than the education of a mediocre Professor of Archaeology.

The young man is tugging his sleeve. '*to ónomá sas?*'

'I am *Kathigitis… oche…*' He shakes his head, changing his mind. 'No… my name is André. *Kai eseís?*'

There is a clarity in the young man's smile as he points upwards. 'Strátos… like heavens.'

MESEMBRIA

On a wooden table at the centre of the market are chicken carcasses, roughly seared in a stone oven at the feet of a shabbily-dressed old man. His beard is silver over a chalk-white face. He looks up, startled, as they arrive. The surfaces of his corneas are scarred with healed ulcers. The pupil of his right eye is milky-blue and André can see the aqueous flare of cataract already descending across the other.

The young man pokes around with the carcasses until the man slaps his hand.

'Do you buy today, Strátos… or do you come to annoy my chickens?'

'I think they have been annoyed enough, Decimus. Did you remember today to kill them before you put them in the oven?'

'I promise I shall not kill you before I put your head in there. Now buy or go away. You are scaring away my customers.'

Strátos makes a pretence of looking around for buyers. He knows, as well does Decimus, that he will be unlucky today. A new gyros stall has opened and the scent of roasting goat is everywhere.

'You are a man of Gaul…'

The statement comes from nowhere. Decimus isn't even looking at André as he speaks. '…and as such you will have much experience of the Roman.' He holds a silver Denarius out to André. 'So tell me whose face this coin bears.'

André turns the coin into the light. Its surface is well-rubbed and the edges uneven but all ancient coins were hand minted and never lacked originality.

'I don't know. It's familiar but...'

'It is Metellus. This face has been my Nemesis. When he had driven out the pirates from Corinth he ordered slaves who had fought with them to be decimated. I stumbled away and hid.' He chuckles into his beard. 'With a name like Decimus, what would you have done? When I was found I used Metellus' face against him. I bought my life from a Centurion blinded by the flash of silver. I thought I had found peace from war here... but I fear you are it's Herald.'

'I am no-one's herald.'

'That may be... but you are a presager... I see a Fury by your shoulder and it's one I no longer have the strength to run from.'

Strátos clears a space by throwing a chicken back into the oven at their feet.

André sits on the edge of the stall. 'You have no need to fear me. I am here only to learn.'

'Wisdom is a Fool's pursuit. Harness the wind, there is more power in it.'

'Then should I hang you out for my canvas?'

'My soul would add little to your speed.'

'But with such a spread?'

'You will gather the coming storm.'

Decimus falls silent. Dragging Strátos towards him with one hand he empties the leather pouch of its coins.

Strátos smiles at this deception. He snatches a chicken from the oven onto a flat wooden platter and nudges André away from the stall.

Decimus is sifting the fake coins into an orderly pile.

'Go. You are a cloud before the sun and I have seen enough of you.'

The old woman rips the chicken apart as soon as they

arrive back at the stall. Her hands are so quick that André has no time to admire their surgical efficiency before a chicken leg is pushed at him. The meat runs with pink juices.

'*Efcharistó polý.*'

The flesh is undercooked but tender and full-flavoured.

The old woman picks up the magnifying glass to study the grain in the breast she has torn from the chicken. She chuckles and puts the glass aside, tearing a long sliver of meat which she inserts slowly between her gums.

André looks for somewhere to put the chicken bone.

Strátos takes it from him and throws it on the floor. An old tortoiseshell cat approaches warily, settling his narrow withers into the dirt. He lowers his head towards the bone.

A lithe, golden-coated female arrows through the space, picking it up from under his nose. The tortoiseshell looks up expectantly. André tears a piece of skin from the chicken and lowers it to the floor.

The cat snarls and spits at his fingers.

'Be quiet, *paliá gáta.* I won't take your bones, for I too am an old cat.'

SPONDE

A drum begins, carried on the up-draught from the harbour. A wave of excitement rides the sound across the market. The man with the gyros has a crowd but even they break apart to point out to sea. André shields his eyes.

A ship is slipping around the headland that shelters Xiropotamos beach. In minutes it will be in the bay but, even at this distance, André can see that it is high in the water and all but empty. The oars are a shamble of half-shipped, dragging timbers but its sail remains filled... driving it at speed towards the anchorage.

A small boat swings around its bow, grappling it with hook-ended ropes. Its oars plough deep troughs in the water but the south-westerly drives the sail on into the mooring.

Oars are pushed out from the berthed ships to fend them off and the sound of cracking timber kindles the air as they are shredded into the harbour.

André attempts to lift Strátos' fingers from his robe. 'I'm going down there.'

Strátos holds on tight. 'Without me you are lost.'

'I know this road as well as you do. But you'd better come.' He grins at the question on Strátos' face. 'We may need another chicken.'

The crowd that had rushed to the quay has turned and is now fleeing up the hill. André and Strátos brush their way through them in silence until they reach the harbour.

The surface of the sea is littered with the remains of splintered timber. The sail is still set on the drifted ship and the wind is pressing it hard against the moored vessels, grinding them into the dock until the rock beats the faces of their hulls.

A giant, shirtless man in breeches leaps from the stones, crossing empty decks until he reaches the drifting ship. With a short sword he prods the limbs of men scattered on its deck, peering into lidded eyes, severing arteries and searching for warmth in the bodies. Salt-water spray is lifting the blood from the timbers and swilling it into an even coating that congeals in the drying breeze.

He shouts at André's approach. 'Come no further. There is a sickness.'

André moves Strátos aside. 'Go back.'

The man on the ship ignores André's approach in his pursuit to find someone still alive, the short stabbing sword dispatching those too far gone.

'Can I help?'

The man looks up. 'Only if you are a God.'

André climbs across the shifting decks.

'There is a sickness amongst the dead?'

'These are coastal levies. They fought with the Cretans against Metellus. This is all that he left of their fleet. If the Gods were sound of mind they would have swept this harbinger beyond the bay.'

He rolls a corpse with the toe of his sandal. On the exposed chest there are a number of lesions… small oval puckers with pus-filled mouths in the centre.

'*Mikró stomá*… I have no sword against this ague. The plague of Antoninus gives little favour.'

'And does it always have these lesions?'

'*Ne*…' The man turns his back to André.

His skin is impressed with small scars, embraced by the coarse dark hairs that cover his torso.

'Then you do have a sword against it.'

'I know when the wings of death ride my shoulder.'

'And now they seek another.' André points to the shore where Strátos creeps ever closer to the harbour's edge. 'One such as him, and we must protect him from them.'

'They call me Doktor but I have only my sword.'

'But we both have a shield. Mine was scratched into my skin twenty years ago. This ague will not ride you or I again. We can stop it here.'

André climbs over the gunwale to untie the ropes of the sail. The canvas flaps across the deck, driving salt crystals against his skin. The grinding noise stops abruptly and the ship, freed from the wind, bounds out into the harbour.

'You are a brave man or a fool. Shall I have time to discover which?'

'It seems I'm here to find that out for myself, Doktor. I will let you know.'

Strátos is halfway along the hill between the people of the market and the dock, torn between safety in the crowd and a new loyalty he has found.

A small boat warps the ship out of the harbour, grapple-hooked to its bow. The grapple is cast off and the ship enters the airstream that surges around the cape.

Backtracking up the hill to keep them in sight, Strátos sees the sail reset and the steering oar swung against the wind.

ELETE

'Where do you take us?'

The Doktor is so close beside André he can feel the heat from his skin, but his thoughts are with the crowd on the hill to the harbour. At the stern he watches Potamos slip away behind them.

'We need to head South.'

'South?'

'*Signómi.*' André raises a hand to bisect the arc of the sun. '*Nótos* …that way. Follow the coast around the island.'

'And what shall we find there?'

'There is a freshwater spring…'

'That will not fill our bellies.'

'There will be goats… and wild mountain greens. There should also be *agelades.*'

He casts a glance across the horizon, searching for the source of the wind that fills their sail. 'I know she will send me agelades.'

'She?'

'I don't know how to explain.'

The boat beats its way around the southernmost tip of the island. Kápa Apolytáres slips away to starboard and the sail is hauled against the southerly-deflected coastal air. Their wake is now tangent to their direction of travel. Both men hang on the steering oar, keeping wind in the sail and the hull from the jagged rocks barely feet below the surface.

André searches the hills for a familiar rock formation.

There should be rainbows above it at this time of day as the sun settles westward, but he finds no rainbows. The vegetation is dense here… more dense than André has ever seen it. An elongated crescent of tree-line rises from what can only be the cleft he remembers.

He needs to listen. 'I'm dropping the sail.'

Immediately, a coiling backdraught from the ridge grips the hull, sliding them in towards the rocky shoreline.

The Doktor prods him. 'We have to move the ship. There are rocks.'

'Quiet…' André strains to hear the fall of the spring, but the trees soak up any sound there may be.

They are at the mouth of a shallow bay. This must be the cleft he remembers… but the shapes are subtly different. He shakes his head at his own foolishness. Time exacts a toll of all things. Behind a small rocky bar is the anchorage he is hoping for.

As they approach, the sound of fresh water gushing into the sea becomes apparent.

'Drop the anchor stone here.'

'And now we are here… what do we do? Wait to die?'

'Not yet.'

DYSIS

Fresh fire crackles on the shingle beach, born of sparks struck from the Doktor's flint. The swim from ship to shore had been a short one and mercifully warm. There had been no food left on board, except for a full round of hard cheese.

The Doktor burns his sword clean in the flame and the cheese gives off a harsh scent of thyme as the hot blade cuts through. He carves a slice for André.

'How you can know we will not die here?'

The cheese is hard and old and there is no telling how far

it has travelled. André takes a bite. A familiar amine reaction burns his lips. He works a stick through it, holding it into the fire until fat is coaxed from the pores and it sizzles in the flames.

'I am… or was…' He stares through the flames into the darkness above where stars are real, brighter and as hard as the cheese, but more distant in time. '…or perhaps I will be… *Kathigitis.*'

'You have studied in Athens?'

'No, but I have studied Athens.'

The Doktor offers him another slice.

'Then you are *Kathigitis* of Contradiction. It is a long time since Athens knew what it was.'

The scent of thyme sings in André's nostrils.

'Knowledge is what Athens will leave to the world.'

The Doktor's laughter penetrates across the smoke.

'Then the world will never know when to eat, sleep, drink, or wake up and make love. Athens lives in the fire of the moment.'

'Knowledge is a slow fire.'

'And what will you leave to the world?'

André shrugs away an answer. 'How can I know that?'

The Doktor points his sword to the night sky, describing an arc where stars are now a brilliant, white-hot spelter.

'Look, Argo Navis rises on the sea… there stands Malus, the mast… Vela the sail is set upon him proud and there is deep water under Carina, his keel… and where am I? I also was born on the rise. The promise of the stars was that I would become a Captain.'

He laughs. A sharp sound, brittle as a burst of flame in the kindling. 'Of what, I would ask my mother… should she still draw breath.'

André lays back beside the fire, a small pillow of brushwood pushing sharp fingers through his hair.

'We all have only the one ship. I am trying to be satisfied with that.'

'And the wind that brought yours here?'

'I fear has yet to blow.'

AUGE

Sunlight primes the far horizon. André opens his eyes to blue dawn shades. The east of the island will be punched into sharp relief by the low sun and he wonders if Fabrienne has taken her flute down the hillside below his tent. His back has taken the uneven form of the ground and he groans himself upright.

A low fret rimes the rocks beside him… a thin, smooth blanket extending across the sluggish morning water.

The Doktor stirs slowly, turning over.

André pokes him with a stick. 'Wake up.'

The Doktor sits up too quickly. One hand holds his head, the other strays to the flesh of his throat.

'At least the ague has left us our lives.'

ANATOLÊ

Hauling up the anchor stone, they tack the ship out then swim back to shore. As the ship enters the wind that surges around the cape, a sudden flare of pitch-soaked straw from the brazier roars across the deck.

Dragged out into the cross-current under a burning sail, the ship carousels, fanning smoke in all directions.

NYMPHÊ

The cleft down which the water pours is far narrower than André remembers and the stream has an urgency that he doesn't recognise. His sandals slip on the stones that slick the bottom but the bushes afford handholds that will not be there in later times. When he reaches the top of the cleft he understands why.

Water gushing from the spout above his head falls in an arc that takes it directly down the narrow cleft, polishing rocks and tumbling any soil it can find. He reaches a hand to pull the Doktor the last few feet.

The Doktor cups his hands to drink. 'Where do we go from here?'

'We go to Aegila.'

'We left there just yesterday. Has the journey taken your senses?'

André studies the horizon for the tip of a mast he thought he had noticed, but it's no longer there.

'No, but there are things I need to do first. Help me with this stone.'

They slide a large, flat slab to bridge the point where the jet of water has eroded the ground. The water splashes against it, shattering into a thousand sparks and rainbows that ebb and flow in the breeze.

The Doktor walks around in them until they cloak his body with a fine mist. 'Very pretty. How does this help?'

'It might one day help two people find each other, but for now we need to wash ourselves thoroughly before we return.'

MESEMBRIA

André heads westward, scanning for the foot of the path that will lead him to the tower, before realising that he is over two thousand years too early.

The Doktor climbs behind him, their feet breaking fresh soil. Above them, the tower is outlined against the sky, its crenellations sharper and more complete than André had expected.

The Doktor pauses beside him. 'Why go to the tower when Aegila is in the other direction?'

'Because every animal seeks shelter from the mid-day sun.'

They cross the shattered doorway into the shade.

Perished, bleached timbers strut the inside of the tower at high level. Across them, blown brushwood has gathered under the stone eaves, affording respite from a sun directly overhead. There is a rustling noise against the far wall and they wait a moment until their eyes adjust.

'It's a goat.'

'No, Doktor. It's several goats.'

'Then stand in the doorway and let them all pass… save this one.'

The Doktor grabs the horns of a goat. It bucks and rears, trying to butt him with great violence until he subdues it by pushing its head to the ground. Its forelegs buckle under his strength until at last it falls quiet under his hands.

He releases the grip of one hand slowly, then stuns the goat with his sword pommel at the point where the spine meets the skull. The goat collapses into the dust. He ties the back legs together with the cord from his tunic and hauls it upside down into the air. He kicks his sword over to André.

'Quickly. Across the throat.'

'Wait!' André holds the sword in the air, pointing into the shadow behind the Doktor. 'Look…'

AKTÊ

The smoke from the searing goat meat percolates the brushwood ceiling and is lofted by a wind from the sea. The flame reflects in the cow's eye, illuminating the terror in its soul. The Doktor has built the fire close to the entrance of the tower so that it dare not pass and it huddles, limbs shaking, under the edge of the wall.

André examines its udder closely in the flickering light until he finds the marks he was hoping for. He leans his back against the wall and rubs his hands in the dust.

'Thank you, Alec.'

'What is an Alec?'

'That might take more time than we have to explain. How long do you think it will take to walk back to Aegila?'

The doctor points to a patch of sky around thirty degrees above the horizon. 'When the sun reaches there.'

'Dragging an unwilling cow?'

HESPERIS

Aegila is a collection of small flickers inside the city walls as flames are lit against the failing light.

André and the Doktor make their way around the wall until they find a barred gate.

There is a man at the gate. He holds the lock that fastens it against the night and the unwelcome.

'There is tax to pay.'

André steps up to the gate. 'Find me Strátos, the young man from the cloth market… or Decimus the chicken seller. They will vouch for us.'

'There will still be tax to pay.'

'To enter the City?'

'No. For the agelada.'

'I don't intend to sell it.'

The Guard shrugs. 'You say that now. But once you are inside?'

'It is for the good of the City.'

'So is the tax. Wait here.'

The light around them fails while they wait. The mood of the Doktor changes with it.

'*Kathigitis*? What do you know of my work?'

'You heal the sick.'

The Doktor shakes his head. 'If only that were true. I'm fated with those decisions the Gods are slow to make.'

André peers through the bars of the gate but all seems still on the path up to the wall.

'How good are your decisions?'

The Doktor laughs out loud. 'No-one complains, except my ghosts out there in the night. They hang upon Vela, the sail of my eternity, and moan in my ear like the keen of a tradewind.'

'And if you could change that?'

'Whose decision shall that be?'

'Yours.'

'Then bring that change before me so I can decide.'

'If it lives or dies?'

The Doktor shrugs. 'This is all I am used to.'

DYSIS

The man appears at the bars of the gate, half-dragging Decimus. He pushes the old man's face against the timbers.

'Do you know these people? They say you will vouchsafe them.'

Decimus struggles free from the man's grip. 'How can I vouchsafe those I cannot see?'

André pushes one hand through the bars and grips the old man's shoulder. 'Did Strátos' head fit in the oven?'

'Ah!' Decimus returns the grip. 'Man of Gaul. You're a fool to return here.'

'Fool or none, I'm glad to see that you are well.'

Decimus turns away from the gate, steadying himself with a hand to the stonework.

'Let them in. On one condition… that I can ride the agelada back down into the city.'

The gatekeeper pushes him aside.

'There is the tax to pay…'

In the darkness, André can feel the heat rising from the skin of the Doktor close beside him. He puts out a hand to stem the flow of his temper.

'Decimus, do you carry the pouch of coins you took from Strátos?'

'Yes, I do.'

'Then pay the man the tax he deserves.'

The cow is poorly fed and its haunches stand harsh as bony ridges under Decimus' loins.

'This isn't the most comfortable cow I have ever ridden.'

André laughs. 'You have my interest.'

'I have ridden many things in a long life. Ships, chariots, goats, cows, men and even women occasionally. I once rode a horse.'

'A horse? Where did you find that?'

'It found me. It was given to me by a Roman.'

'Those you have fled? Metellus?'

'The man of whom I speak would not be bounded by plain sight and his pursuit of that sight stretches into many of our futures.' He looks down curiously at André, studying the lines of his face, the shadow of his eyes in the darkness.

'Even into yours.'

'Sulla.'

'And his name not even a question on your lips, so far has his vision entered your fate.'

'And the horse?'

'Was fated to be eaten. But not until after I had served Sulla's purpose.'

'Which was?'

'His Immortality.'

'But Sulla is now dead.'

'And I am a man. And, as such, we are fallible.'

'Then you failed him.'

'Not at all. Sulla knew better than most that flesh is mortal and that only ideas can be thought of as eternal.'

André pauses a moment. 'Can you ride an idea?'

'For as long as you wish. It never tires nor stops to eat… yet still it grows.'

'Is your wisdom not wasted here?'

'Wisdom informs me that there are times when it is more profitable to ride a cow.'

MOUSIKÊ

In daylight, the cow becomes a curiosity. Undaunted and passive despite the awnings flapping about its head, it draws in people from the stalls around them. Some run their hands across its haunches. Some stare deep into the black of its eyes, looking for a lost soul in their midst.

Strátos keeps his sandalled feet safely away from its hooves. 'I have seen these before. There are a few down in the valleys where grass stays green in summer. But never here in the city. Which bit do we eat first?'

The man with the gyros stall stands by the cow's head, studying the width of its flank while counting coins blindly from one purse into another.

André waves him aside. 'Strátos? Where can I take this cow without disturbance?'

'Not here. They will never leave you alone.'

His grandmother tugs André's sleeve and points up the hill behind them.

'What does she mean?'

'She means the Governor's House. Outside the wall, up the hill. We will have to pass through the gate again. There will be tax to pay.'

'We have already paid the tax.'

'That was to come in.'

GYMNASTIKÊ

The bright pinks and whites of the house swagger colour against the monotony of the ochre landscape around it. A line of hives banks the wall of an enclosed garden and the sound of bees is a pervasive vibration.

Air flows in the opened house doors, then out again above, fluttering the window canopies. Beside its flat walls is a small outbuilding where goats crowd to find shade.

'It's a big house for one man. Even with servants.'

Strátos smiles broadly. 'He has a daughter.'

To André, the look on his face is an open book.

'And you like this daughter?'

'Everyone likes this daughter. You will like this daughter, but she is old for me.'

'How old is she?'

Strátos studies him, frowning in the sunlight at the lines on André's face. 'Old like you.'

'Ah, I see. Ancient, then.'

'Old like beautiful statue, but this daughter also has a daughter, and she is beautiful like me.'

Strátos runs nimbly across the gravelled frontage and into the gloom of a doorway. A woman appears from it and walks calmly towards him.

'*Kaliméra*, André.'

The light timbre of her voice rises inside him like the shock of a fresh spring.

'Minerva?'

She reaches out to embrace him. Equal to his height, her white-blonde hair wraps around his face and shoulders. He is shaking in her arms.

'Don't be afraid.'

'It would help if I knew what not to be afraid of.'

She pushes him away so he can see her face. 'Let's start with me.'

'That's the one thing I know I'm afraid of.'

'Have I hurt you so far?'

André feels this woman insinuating herself again into his affection, despite her earlier disregard of his feelings for Fabrienne.

She slides her hand along his arm until their fingers meet. 'Come and meet my father.'

André hesitates and she finds him immovable, even to the persuasion of her hand in his.

'I have a job to do.'

'Yes, you do. But honour us with your presence for a few moments.'

André glances back to where Strátos is holding the cow.

The Doktor is behind them, sword pommel guarded by his hand.

'They don't know what to do.'

'Tell them… then come up to the house alone.'

'First wash your hands properly.' The soap is crude but rich in tallow and slips in André's hands easily. 'When they are clean, use this soap and water on the blade of your sword. Don't wipe them on your tunic. Let them dry naturally in the sunlight.'

The Doktor glances up at him angrily.

'Where is the decision in this?'

'Do you want to make decisions worthy of your name?'

'More ghosts to hang from my sail?'

'Or ones that will sing your praises to the wind?'

A shade has been withdrawn in the stable, casting light on the place where the cow is tethered head-down to the ground.

'So I do not need to kill it first?'

'No, nor after if we have any compassion. Just scrape the *micro stoma* from the udder onto the blade of your sword, then put the scrapings into this bowl. But only when you are sure everything is clean.'

NYMPHÊ

'Father? This is André.'

The Governor is lying on a deeply cushioned bed, his legs are wide and bare under a short Romanesque toga.

Between his knees is a bowl of dark olives. He rips a handful from the bowl and plunges them into his mouth, dribbling oil down his chin. He separates the stones from the flesh in his teeth before spitting them back into the same bowl. He offers the bowl but André declines.

'And who is André?'

'André is the man we have waited for.'

'And what does he do now he is here?'

'He tries to save us, Father.'

'Excellent. Excellent. From what, may I ask?'

'From ourselves, Father.'

'From ourselves! I say. Good man. Do it more often. Tell me, have you been slacking? Is that why we have waited so… how long was it?'

'Nineteen years, Father.'

'That's a lot of slacking.'

'He's here now, Father. Don't you think he was worth the wait?'

'Then get him doing what he's supposed to. I can't abide procrastination. Move on, sir. Move on.'

'Are you afraid to move on?'

Minerva leads André up a narrow staircase and through a door built into the wall of the first floor. She leaves her sandals at the entrance and motions him to do the same.

The floor is heavily patterned and cool beneath his bare feet. In the centre is an inlaid relief that André recognises immediately. He moves around it slowly, marvelling at how well preserved the tiles still are in his own day. He moves over to the wall, where the shaded window calms the reflections of the market and harbour far below.

'I'm not sure I can do this.'

'You can, because I am the only road that leads you back.'

'Why me?'

'I have only known one other with your persistence of vision. My daughter was his gift to destiny.'

'Your marriage was arranged?'

'No. It was a desperate act of preservation.'

'By whom?'

'By the Mechanism.'

'And what of Fabrienne?'

'She is just an Echo.'

He pushes her away from him.

'How can you say that?'

'Because you are both Echoes. The Fabrienne of your time carries the echo of every woman destined to fall to your attraction across the centuries, as you carry the echo of her every man.'

'Don't echoes diminish over time?'

'On the contrary, there are moments when they combine to resonate such a powerful dream of opportunity that it can change the direction of Time. So enjoy the dream you are creating.'

'Are we no more than a dream?'

'No. You are not dreams. You are both Bells, first struck nineteen years ago by myself and Marcus Germanicus. Our echoes will reverberate throughout your time and, when you think you have heard the last of it, listen again. In your own language it bears *L'anneau de la vérité.*'

'And where is your daughter?'

'She he has hidden herself since you arrived. She does not tell me her reasons.'

'Then maybe I should ask her myself.'

'My daughter is far less important to you than I am. You should be trying to save my city.'

'But for how long? I couldn't find it in my time.'

'You will save it for now and, to Time, now is all that matters. Sit with me a moment.'

Minerva leads him to a low couch set where the breeze flows through the room. André shudders in a sudden swirl that sweeps dust from the entrance and back out over the city through the opened shutters.

'Are you still afraid?' She places a calming hand on his forearm. 'There is no need.'

'You have no idea of what I'm afraid.'

'Then tell me.'

He brushes his bare feet over the patterned floor while trying to coalesce a thought. 'It seems I now have a duty to Time itself.'

'Why be afraid of the inevitable?'

'That's exactly why. It is inevitable that I will fail.'

'Time will be the judge of that.'

'I am my own judge in all that matters.'

'And what is your judgement?'

He gently removes her hand from his arm.

'I failed in my career. I take intuition from others and distil it until it becomes mine. I failed to protect my wife. I have so far failed to find the remains of your city and I have failed in all my relationships.'

'Yet still you live. Is that not a sign of success itself in situations beyond your control?'

'Is that not also a failure, to live beyond the bounds of your ability to control?'

'No. That is bravery.'

'Then why do I continue to fail?'

'By its very nature, bravery does not always succeed.'

André stares at the patterns under his feet. A man in a blue toga wrestles violently with a green serpent much larger than himself and around them are silver stars, differing in brightness. The man's struggle is apparent in his expression of great determination.

Minerva reaches down to touch the tiles.

'This is Ophiuchus, the Eternal Serpent Bearer. His star is here, behind his heart. He is also my birth sign, the thirteenth of the known Zodiac. When we were summoned by the Mechanism my father brought these tiles from our home in Cimmeria and had them installed here.'

'And does the Serpent Bearer succeed?'

'He is the embodiment of determination. The Serpent is his enemy and, although he can never defeat it himself, he holds it in eternal stasis while he waits for a Hero.'

'How does he stay so strong?'

'He has Faith.'

André turns quickly to capture a look in her eyes.

'I would hope for one such success before I die.'

'It is you he waits for, and you have only one Serpent left to defeat.'

'Myself?'

'No… fear of yourself.'

SPONDE

Inside the shelter the Doktor and Strátos have scraped the udder clean but only a small amount has been scraped onto the edge of the bowl.

The Doktor holds it up for André to examine.

'This is all.'

'Then that will have to be enough. Once we start the infection off, you'll have many donors. Strátos? Who spins cloth for your grandmother's robes?'

'Aglaïa. She lives down by the harbour where the sea air stops the yarn breaking.'

'Go down there now. Bring her back with you and ask her to bring her sharpest comb.'

'This may take some time. Her legs… she sits all day…'

They are back within half an hour, Aglaïa cradled in the arms of the Doktor.

In the old woman's hands are several combs. André takes them gently from her and holds them up to the light. He selects the best one and hands it to the Doktor.

'Break the tines from this until there are two left, side by side, then sharpen them as much as you can.'

The old woman looks on horrified.

Minerva takes her hand and reassures her that the Governor himself will find her a new comb.

'Minerva. Lift her sleeve.' André dips the sharpened tines into the scrapings in the bowl, then draws them across the old woman's upper arm until blood appears in the grooves. The old woman starts in pain as André rubs the scrapings into the cuts with his thumb.

'This will make her feel ill for a few days. She will have sores but she will not die.' He looks quickly at the others around him. 'I need a list. Someone keep a list of those we treat.'

Decimus heaves himself from the stool by the window.

'Give me parchment. This much I can see to do.'

André cleans the tines then repeats the treatment on Strátos. He takes Minerva's hand to lift her sleeve but she shies away.

'There are others more important.'

'Alright, you can wait. Take me to your father.'

She holds up her hand in refusal. 'There was a time when my father spoke that even birds stopped to listen. Do not prolong his confusion.'

'And if he should die?'

'Then his past lives on, untainted by the erosion of age.'

AKTÊ

'Strátos, gather as many people as you can in the market place.'

'What do I tell them? That there are free chickens?'

'Tell them that with every chicken they buy they get a free chance to live.'

The Doktor grips André's wrist before he can turn away.

He holds the bowl angrily between them, gesturing at the futility he finds in it. 'What is this? There is no offering to a God here. What are we doing to these people?'

André wraps his hand over that of the Doktor. 'We are making them ill.'

'I ask again, by what magic?' The Doktor shakes the bowl violently. 'I see nothing in this.'

André takes the bowl from him. 'You have never seen the wind, yet you believe in it.'

The Doktor holds the comb in the air. 'This is true, but I have seen it shake a sail. Now show me the wind that blows through this.'

'I can't, but I ask you to believe in it the same way.'

'So what do I have to decide?'

'To help me.'

'Then teach me… *Kathigitis*.'

HESPERIS

The market stalls are strapped down against the evening

wind and wandering fingers, but people are still milling around in the area by the gyros. The Moroccan is carving meat into a platter and it is disappearing as fast as he can scoop the coins from waiting hands. Strátos is driving more people before him, ragged as geese.

André does a rough head count. 'I'm not sure we have enough to treat them all.'

'But you said that once they were ill, we could scrape the micro stoma from them and use it.'

'I did, Doktor, and although the incubation period for cowpox is shorter, the disease has three days march on us. It will be a race to an uncertain conclusion.'

'How many will die?'

'Some, but we can give them any chance they might have by persuading them that this is necessary.'

'How will you do that?'

'Do you remember that I asked you to make one last decision?'

'I do.'

'Then climb up on this stall.'

André climbs up beside him. The crowd grows steadily more quiet, watching the two of them, waiting for whatever Strátos has promised them.

The Doktor opens his arms wide to the crowd and calls out to them, sword in hand. 'You who know me. You know what I am.'

There is a stunned silence and the shuffling of feet.

Strátos cups his hands to his mouth. 'Doktor…'

The crowd pick up the shout. 'Doktor… Doktor…'

The Doktor waves the sword above his head. 'And you recognise my device, The Releaser of Souls. The Bringer of Peace and an End of Suffering?'

He slides the sword back into his belt. 'And if I tell you now that there are other ways to cure this sickness? That with this…' he holds the twin-tined comb above the crowd. '…the disease brought here by the ship can be swept aside from this city.'

The crowd reply with shouts.

'I am not ill. I have no disease…' 'I was not here when the ship came…' 'Where is my free chicken…' 'Why should we believe you?' 'Strátos lied about the chickens. Where is he?'

The Doktor glances at André in despair. 'I am losing them.'

'Not yet.' André addresses the crowd. 'In five days time some of you will develop the disease brought here on the ship. In nine days time you will begin to die. The first will be your elderly. Your mothers and fathers, aunts and uncles… then your children will fall like olives from your trees… and you will share in each other's misery until at last, in fifteen days, most of you will die. You will carpet this hill with rotting flesh and your souls will moan along the wind.'

The crowd distance themselves from each other until only families are touching. 'What shall we do?'

'This…'

André lifts the sleeve of his tunic. The Doktor dips the comb into the edge of the bowl and pulls it quickly across André's upper arm, drawing blood behind it. He rubs at the scratches with his thumb until the blood blends into his skin.

The crowd gasp as André does the same to the Doktor.

He grasps the Doktor's hand. 'We are now brothers in blood.'

The crowd has fallen quiet below them.

The Doktor returns his grip. 'They are waiting now.'

'For what?'

'For us to die, of course. Or for me to kill you. Either way, *Kathigitis*… they are in for a disappointment.'

'That must be half the population inoculated… and that is all we can do for now.'

The Doktor examines the empty bowl. To him it has been empty from the beginning.

'How big are these inoculas? I see nothing more nor less than when we began. How can so little be given to so many?'

André sets the bowl aside and waves away the rest of the people around them.

They are mikro, mikro, mikro. Impossible to see without the proper device.'

'Then how do I know they are there?'

'They are in everything we touch, but our bodies have adapted to live with most of them.'

The Doktor shakes his head in disbelief. 'Then there is no escape from disease?'

'You have carried it on your sword from corpse to corpse and from there onto living men.'

'Then what have I been doing with my life? Am I nothing but a harbinger of death?'

'That has changed today. You have brought a new disease to them, one that will make them ill for a little while and then will protect them against a greater peril. This is a work worthy of your name.'

'My name is Nikolaus, *Kathigitis*. And I bow to your wisdom.'

'And I bow to your ability to take decisions and dispatch them without regret.'

MOUSIKÊ

André follows the dark-haired girl from Minerva's house to a small cove hidden by the Point of Glyphadia. For some distance the white of a dress amongst the rocks has been his only point of focus. As he approaches, that shifts to the white-blonde of her hair. She doesn't turn, even though their footsteps must have been evident for some time.

'Mistress Artemisia?'

Artemisia doesn't acknowledge the servant's voice. Her gaze remains out towards the waters of the cove but André notices a subtle settling of resentment across her shoulders.

'Has my mother sent you?'

'No, Mistress. This man wishes to address you.'

'A man?'

Artemisia turns to see who has come. 'I thought you were alone. You always make enough noise for two… and what is the matter with his face?'

André recovers himself with a growing smile. 'I am admiring your hair.'

She strands it through her fingers into a breast-length fan. 'Why? Should it be different to this?'

'I can even tell you how it will smell.'

She holds a strand under her nose. 'And of what does it smell?'

'It will smell of… Fabrienne.'

'Fabrienne? I like that name. Does it have meaning?'

'In my language, it means one who is still learning.'

'And you have come to teach me?'

'There is nothing I can teach you.'

'Then you are a wise man.'

'Wisdom comes from knowing your limitations. You

have already exceeded mine.'

'Are you going to like me?'

'No, but one day I am going to love you.'

She studies the lines that life has burned deep around his eyes.

'Like a father?'

'No.'

'Good.'

MESEMBRIA

'Come quickly, *Kathigitis*. Decimus is ill.'

André resists Strátos' pull. 'So is half the city.'

'This is not same. Decimus does not have these.' He runs his finger across the parallel lines of his own inoculation.

André allows himself to be pulled along until they reach the old man's market stall. Unusually, there are no chicken carcasses and the oven is cold. Decimus is slumped in his seat by the counter. His frailty is apparent at a glance.

'What's the matter, old man?'

Decimus glances up, his eyes wet and rheumy. 'I have an *adiathesía*.'

'And how does this sickness make you feel? Do you have the mikro stoma?'

'No… no. I fear it is here…' He places a hand across his chest. 'Somehow I feel the need to run, but I no longer can. What shall I do, man of Gaul? Run, fight or die?'

André places a hand on Decimus' forehead. It burns with fever. 'Which do you feel most able to do?'

'Die.'

'What makes you think that you must choose?'

Decimus lifts an edge of cloth. Underneath the counter is a dark box made of olive wood. 'This.'

André slides the box out from under the bench and turns it in his hands. 'I thought this was beneath the waves.'

'This was made in the shadow of the first. Its predictions may fairly be said to describe the darker side of fortune.'

'And what would it say of me?'

'I do not need the mechanism to foretell that. Death haunts your footsteps. In three days you will feel his breath against your ear.'

'What can I do to stop him?'

'You cannot. But you can prevent the escape of a knowledge that would ruin mankind.'

'How so?'

'If you woke each morning with full knowledge of what would happen, would you still rise from your bed?'

'So, once a prediction is made, there can be no such thing as free will?'

'Free will was only ever an illusion. Where would a man turn if he knew all his directions were the same?'

'So the paradox remains. And if this is destroyed, what then?'

'The illusion continues.'

'Is that all we have? An illusion of life?'

'Would you sooner it be an illusion of death?'

'I would sooner understand its secrets.'

Decimus takes the box from André and pushes it back under the bench. 'Then make your choice, you have only three days in which to learn.'

ELETE

'*Kathigitis*!' From the garden of the Governor's House, Strátos points to the horizon. 'Sails.'

André shades his eyes to discern the vague shapes far out at sea. 'Levies?'

The Doktor turns away in disgust. 'Romans.'

He lifts his hand into the breeze. 'The wind is keeping them away from us. If we are what they are seeking, soon they will have to lower their oars.'

'And then?'

'One day… maybe two if this wind holds.'

'Then we have little time to prepare the city.'

'Three quarters of the city are sick. How much can they do?'

André pauses in thought for a moment. 'We can make them more sick.'

'They cannot fight even now.'

'They may not have to. They have seen the sails. Gather as many as you can into the market this evening. Strátos… do you know where Decimus keeps his chickens?'

'Yes, *Kathigitis*.'

'Then find as many as you can and take them to his stall.'

'What if he refuses me?'

'Tell him I have made my choice.'

HESPERIS

'Man of Gaul, I will not let you kill my chickens.'

'Then what will you do, Decimus? Barter for your life with them?'

'Perhaps.'

'Then the Romans will hear the crunch of your bones under their feet.'

'Man of Gaul, you say you want to save this city, but you have rendered sick any man capable of fighting for it and the rest have fled.'

'If they had escaped the disease they would have died at the hands of the Romans.'

'And instead they have you. I know what it is the Romans seek. Take this box and place it alongside its sister device so they may be destroyed together.'

'It is too deep. I have no equipment that will allow me to go so deep.'

'Have you sounded the depth of your soul?'

'Many times.'

'Then you will know there are no depths to which a man can not go.'

NYMPHÊ

'This is just an old man's attempt to infuse you with his own guilt.'

'However well-intentioned, I have left your city exposed to the Romans.'

'André, we have always been exposed to the Romans. This is merely another time.'

'They did not get you the first time.'

'And they will not get me this time.'

'How can you be so sure?'

'They will not. But you must preserve the mechanism.'

'Decimus wishes it destroyed.'

'And so do I. But this is not the time. There is one who will need full knowledge of it in order to take their rightful place.'

'Decimus says this machine displays the darker side.'

'And after two thousand years dropped into the sea it would display nothing at all. Keep it safe and she will know what to do.'

'She?'

'André, it is time to understand that all your masters are mistresses.'

Minerva presses a fingernail against a small indentation and the door of the box springs open. Inside are a series of etched and gleaming dials. She slides the mechanism out of the box and turns it in the sunlight from the window until she finds the hole between the cogs.

The key she takes from the cord around her neck is cylindrical in design, with curves and flutes along its length.

Slipping it through the mechanism, she applies pressure and the whole engine rotates, shifting into a half-seen blur where suns and moons pass through one another without colliding.

She stops it with a finger. 'Enough. It makes no sense to me now and it becomes impatient. Here…'

She places the device back inside the box and passes it to André. 'Take the device and keep it silent. When you are finished learning, bring the key back to me. But do not let either out of your sight.'

ELETE

Decimus looks around him.

The market is unusually quiet. Stalls are empty where people have fled, either from fear of disease or fear of the Roman fleet. He shows André the hidden catch to the box.

André springs it wide and Decimus holds out a hand for the key.

'She gave it to you. Don't be afraid. We have so little time.'

'I thought…'

'And what did you think, Man of Gaul?'

'I thought of the danger of this combination.'

'The question *and* the answer?'

'I have no desire to be pinned to the board of Time like a butterfly.'

'I can only teach you to read this device as a man. As I said before, there are no depths to which a man will not travel, but this device holds a depth that no man *can* travel. You can never be the answer. A man can only ever be the question.'

'Then let me ask it.'

'Then give me the key.'

'And if I say I no longer have it?'

'I know you do. The device and the key seek each other and in your hands it already feels complete.'

Decimus shows André the silver coin with Metellus' face.

'This is the real key. It was struck in the Roman year of 668 *Ab urbe Condita*, also unfortunately known as The Year of Cinna. Without knowledge of that year, the device will never be of use to anyone.'

André slips it into the shirt pocket under his robe and

hands the key and device back to Decimus.

Decimus inserts the key into the device, setting the dials in rotation.

'With this key we unlock Time itself. With the knowledge from the coin we pin Time's Butterfly to our advantage. Now watch and learn.'

MOUSIKÊ

The air is heavy with steam and the scent of melted pitch. Strátos has stolen the best amphora he can find while the stall-holder is ill. It is glazed with bright stars and swirls of imagined galaxies and it sits in a bath of boiling water while Strátos stirs the slowly melting pitch.

The amphora is part-filled by the time André returns to the shelter.

Nikolaus shrugs at his unspoken question.

'This way it does not crack when we pour in the pitch.'

André wraps the box in waxed cloth and lowers it gently into the hot pitch. He thinks to drop the key in, then returns it to his pocket. He slips Metellus' coin and the broken comb in instead. Nikolaus fills the rest of the amphora and seals the lid both inside and out.

André dips more of the cloth into the pitch and binds it around and around the top, spreading more as he goes.

'Nothing will penetrate that. Except Time.'

NYMPHÊ

The line with the sealed wineskins attached holds vertical throughout the the deep water. The amphora has been lowered alongside it until it has reached the bottom. André sits on the gunwale of a small fishing vessel, hand through a loop in a cord attached to a large stone.

Nikolaus places a cautionary hand on his shoulder. 'Be careful.'

'Of what?'

'That you don't add to my ghosts.'

Artemisia pulls him away. 'My father wishes to speak with him. Let him go.'

The water is colder than André has anticipated and the downward rush behind the stone is heady and fearful. The sunlight is left quickly behind but the water is so clear that the depths become apparent as he accustoms.

The pressure is crushing his chest and the wax pushed into his ears but the lines descending beside him are a reminder that he must remain mentally attached to the surface, no matter what else the depth tries to persuade him.

The mast of a ship looms from the darkness. He tries to catch it to slow his descent but his hand is ripped away by the mass of the falling stone. Blood flows around him as barnacles peel skin from his hand.

The stone finds bottom and the ten yard line to which he is attached gives the water time to cushion his descent. He slips his hand from the loop and allows the smaller stones girdled around his waist to give him the negative buoyancy he needs. He unties the rope from the amphora and drags it around into the lee of the ship's hull where it will be out of immediate sight. He uses the shaped stone that has dragged him downwards to disguise it.

He turns aside and swims into the shade of the wreck, following an instruction given by Minerva. Beneath the shattered deck is the black void of a small cabin. He swims into it, feeling his way in the darkness until he finds the sharp edges of a chest. The lid will not lift.

His eyes become better adjusted and he can see bones strewn across it beneath a large marble statue. The bones are a rib cage, slid along the statue's arm like a bracelet. The marble leans heavily upon the chest, too much so for him to move. His heart is pounding in his ears and his peripheral vision swims with sharp, jagged, rainbow-colours.

He spins upright to leave but something catches his foot.

In the darkness, he has become entangled in the crock of bones.

He tugs his foot but they fall closer, holding him there.

A voice sounds inside of him as though it comes from the very water itself, a voice he feels but not hears.

'A man is never more than the messenger.'

André pivots around to see where the sound has arisen, but the cabin is so dark it is impossible to tell.

He tugs harder at his foot but the grip grows tighter.

'You are not the message.'

The grip lessens on his foot. He unfastens the cord of the weighted belt and begins his drift upwards.

He reaches the first air sac, thirty feet above the deck, and breathes it in greedily.

TO LIMANI TOU POTAMOS
AEGILA

GYMNASTIKÊ

Despite an offshore wind, the now empty masts on the horizon grow larger by the hour. The water beside them is flecked white by the force of double-banked oars.

'How long before they reach the harbour?'

Nikolaus shades the sun from his eyes. 'Less than one half of the day. How shall we meet them?'

'We'll let them meet us. Do you have the chickens?'

'They are cut and bled as you asked. Someone will eat well tonight.'

André laughs, a desperate sound from a place behind his forlorn thoughts. 'Then hope it is not the Romans. Let's go and create the dead.'

MESEMBRIA

A Roman ship draws alongside the harbour, oars shipped across its lower deck.

The Master stands it off the harbour wall, just close enough to survey the scene that confronts him. Everywhere he looks there are bodies, some bloodied and shapeless as if bearing sword thrusts, some still twitching. Wherever visible they are covered in mikro stoma. Behind them is a huge pile of tinder and kindling made ready for a pyre.

'Take us in.'

The Master hesitates to issue the command. 'We must not. For our own sakes.'

Metellus speaks softly to reassure him. 'What I seek is here. I know this.'

'But the plague?'

Metellus laughs sharply. 'There are more plagues than this, and one all the more fierce when hiding something that he thought only he was aware of.'

'Sulla?'

'My erstwhile friend. Now my Nemesis.'

'I thought him dead?'

'Sulla's memory lives everywhere. Like this damned plague.'

Metellus brushes the scars on his forearms. 'Now take us in. Like both plagues, this one has burned me and left its mark. I will take six men.'

The Master surveys the human wreckage strewn across the harbour roadway.

'The men must not be allowed back on board.'

'I know this. Now take us in.'

Metellus strides along the harbour road, kicking the occasional body and eliciting groans from the sick lying in their own fluids. The house on the hill appears to watch them with lidded eyes that flutter, tokening the breeze that flows along the ridge.

Down by the harbour, all is now still.

Beyond the apparent dead and dying the rest have fled. Whether they have fled him or the plague is open to conjecture but their end will be the same. The men behind him wait for orders, watching the bodies for movement.

'Touch no-one, unless it is with the point of your sword. There is death in this place. Let it not be yours.'

They thread their way up the hill through a market place where no more than crumbs remain of what had once been bread, cheeses and cured meat until they come to a locked gate in the wall.

'Break it.'

The gate is heaved aside to allow Metellus through.

SPONDE

At the angle from which Metellus is now studying it, the house casts a sidelong glance at their approach.

In that glance he perceives a certain arrogance that he recognises. There is a power here, but he has no fear of raw power. It is just another form of sword. But the power of foreknowledge? To know the purpose and time of his own death? That remains his greatest fear… yet here he stands in fell pursuit of it.

The doorway is dark, and before he enters he sends his sharpened sense of survival into that space.

He hears breath drawn at the sight of his silhouette.

There is a sigh of cloth moving over skin.

These things build an image he has studied many times.

The house is far from empty.

He hefts the sword in his hand as a voice comes from the corner of the room. The voice is soft with resignation. It is also female.

'You will not need that in here.'

'Show yourself… and your companions.'

He waits, framed in the doorway, as shades are lifted and the light of day strikes the tiled floor at his feet.

The Doktor and André move into the light, keeping Strátos behind them. Decimus slumps helplessly in a seat beside the Governor.

Minerva glides into the centre of the room.

Metellus takes one step inside. 'Who are these people?'

Minerva points out the Doktor. 'This is Nikolaus, the Doktor for our city.'

Metellus grunts. 'I have seen his worth at the harbour. I had to climb over his 'cures' to leave my ship.' He points to

André with his sword. 'Who is this blonde one?'

André opens both empty palms towards Metellus. 'I am André.'

'And what is André?'

Nikolaus sheathes his sword. 'He is a Man of Gaul. He is *Kathigitis*.'

'Then for once there may be a chance of intelligent conversation. There is a distinct lack of it out on the water.'

Minerva moves within range of Metellus' arm. 'Can we send the boy home?'

'No. Outside are six of my men with one instruction. To kill whoever leaves without me.'

Minerva reaches out to touch Metellus' forearm.

His heart races in his chest and the floor swims beneath his feet as her fingers wrap over his wrist.

'Put away your sword, General. You will find little use for it here.'

Metellus unexpectedly sheathes his sword. 'I came to learn, not to kill.'

'And what would you learn?'

'I would learn the secret that Sulla dared not share, and that would have been the source of his power once in Rome.'

'And what would you do with that secret?'

'I would rid Rome of Cinna's assassins. His Socialism embraces monsters in its midst whose idealism is enforced by the sword. All who followed Sulla's Republic have either fled or been put to death. I have one such aboard a funeral vessel outside the harbour.'

'Which one?'

'Lucius Cornelius Sisenna. Sulla's personal historian no less, and the one to whom he owes most of his fame. We are taking him to Rome for burial in all his leaden, Funereal Glory.'

Metellus takes a deep breath but his hand stays away from his weapon.

Minerva releases her touch and watches the tension leave his shoulders. 'Was he…?'

'He fell to the sword on Crete, but to whose side in the battle remains an open question.'

'Then what is it you seek to learn?'

'The knowledge to kill Cinna's legacy… and those who would derive their power from it. Sulla failed… but in his attempt he vowed to release a philosophy abroad that would bring Gods too close to men and men too close to Gods. I would see an end to it all.'

'It will end. If only you wait.'

'I am told that Sulla's secret exists in two parts, and that he rendered one part no longer accessible. If I rid the world of the other, perhaps Cinna's legacy will fail.'

'You would pursue a dead man?'

'I would free Rome from the grip of his decaying corpse and be remembered for that.'

André pushes Strátos into the safe hands of the Doktor.

'Unfortunately, General, your history falls under the shadow of one who will soon replace you. Gaius Julius Caesar.'

'A mere upstart of thirty years? How can this be? I pacified your land for you, Man of Gaul. Will that not be enough for the world's memory?'

'Many have tried, General, but Gaul has a mind that twists its own image in the mirror and Time will not change that, nor render it ever at peace with itself.'

'Then sit, *Kathigitis*, and tell me how you can know this.'

'First allow your men to set Strátos free, General. There are people who depend on him and this is a long story.'

ELETE

Strátos makes his way along the outer edge of the city wall until he is out of sight of the patrol. Climbing the wall he makes his way down through the market, keeping his feet on a known path and his head below the bench tops until he reaches the harbour.

The wind has turned around and the ship that landed Metellus has been warped out into the bay away from the corpses and the sick. An anchor rope drops from the prow into the still water and the deck is empty except for the heads of oarsmen, resting across their benches.

Keeping the brushwood pyre between himself and the ship, he makes his way to its lee. In his pocket is the magnifying glass that *Kathigitis* has given him.

He has learned its power when held into the sun and the burns on his hand carry the scars of his first efforts. He focuses the sun onto the kindling.

Slowly, smoke begins to rise.

ELETE

Metellus rises from his seat in frustration. 'So you are telling me that it is impossible for me to capture Sulla's device? Even though its Adept is here under my control?'

'I am not under your control.'

Minerva holds herself in check, sensing that his anger has no ceiling but, surprisingly, Metellus bursts into laughter. He points to where Decimus is slumped in a chair.

'You think I do not recognise this man? This 'Decimus' who has weighed pure gold for Kings? Enabled a single man by use of his machines to lift unimaginable weight and draw water from the deepest of wells? By the word of my own eyes I have the creator of the device within my grasp again.'

'But not the device itself.'

'But I hold the Priestess of the Key.'

'Then you hold nothing.'

'I refuse to believe that.'

'General, take a look in this man's eyes. How can he create anything now he can no longer see.'

'He can advise if he cannot see. Therefore I have the two parts I need to succeed where Sulla failed. It will just take more time.'

André is staring out of the window at the smoke rising from the harbour.

'Time is something you may not have.'

AKTE

On the harbour side, the wind is tumbling flames from the brushwood pyre onto the ships already moored there. Furled sails are catching and spreading their sparks as ropes are consumed and the canvas is set free.

The anchor stone is rapidly lifted on Metellus' ship and the oars power it away from the heat into the middle of the bay.

Hidden from sight behind the pyre, Strátos is caught by the flame he has set. He drops the magnifying glass to beat at his tunic. He reaches into the fire to retrieve the glass. The heat from the scorched handle sears into his palm but he will not let it go, even as the wind lifts and scatters sparks across himself and the market.

HESPERIS

Metellus stares out of the window at the burning stalls.

'It seems you care little for this city, Man of Gaul.'

'On the contrary, I care more than you could know.'

'So you burn the city to raise the Phoenix?'

Minerva joins them at the window. 'As Chiron told Achilles, the Phoenix outlives nine ravens. It will rise again.'

Smoke obscures the harbour activity but she points to a mast moving in clear air above it. 'Your ship deserts you.'

'It dare not while you or I live'

'Chiron also said that we, the rich-haired Nymphs and daughters of Zeus, outlive ten Phoenixes.'

'And if I kill you now?'

'You will fulfil the prophecy.'

'And if I piss on your ashes?'

'I will be damned to hunt you for eternity and your soul will never know peace.'

'I have never known peace.'

Minerva reaches out to him. 'Peace never exists in the point of a sword. It exists in the hand that sheathes it.'

Minerva wraps her fingers around his where they rest on the sword pommel. 'I will show you that peace.'

Metellus' legs begin to shake. His stance loosens as if he is about to fall. His arms lose control and only her grip maintains his hold on the sword. His eyes flash wide and unfocused. His mouth is slack and words tumble unwilled from his lips. 'I have seen…'

Minerva maintains her grip as she unsheathes his sword.

'Tell me what you have seen.'

Metellus continues to shake, barely staying upright.

'I have seen Death.'

'Whose death have you seen?'

'My own… and so quick to come.'

'And…?'

'And yours.'

Minerva pulls Metellus' sword close before André or the Doktor can move. The tip enters below her ribs and slices straight up into her heart.

She drops to the floor as André rushes to hold her.

He lifts her in his arms. Her lips are losing colour.

'Minerva? Why now… why here?'

'Antikythera is… forever… between… two worlds…'

Her eyes open wide. She stares beyond him, intensely, as if she is witnessing a distant event.

'… don't break the circle.'

Her eyes remain fixed. The Doktor taps André on the shoulder.

'Come away my friend. She has gone.'

Metellus is shaking from Minerva's revelations, oblivious to anything except the vision of his own death.

Out of his sight, André takes the key from his pocket and hangs the fine cord around Minerva's neck. 'I can no longer stay here. Will you look after her, Doktor?'

'This woman had one foot on Earth with the other amongst the Gods. She shall have no less than she deserves in the customs of her kind. I will do all that is necessary.'

'Is there anything you will need?'

'The house itself will provide much. I await the will of the Gods for all else.'

'I hope they don't fail her.'

'The Gods never fail one of their own.' He sees the look of consternation on André's face. 'What ill befalls you?'

André stares hard at the walls surrounding him while still hearing the crack and rush of flames consuming the market on the lower slopes.

'I didn't expect to still be here after…'

'Where did you expect to be, *Kathigitis*?'

'Not so much where, as when.'

'How did you first enter this city?'

'Through a small gate in the outer wall, but I have lost track of it.'

'Perhaps she has withheld it from your sight. What was the first thing you saw on entering?'

'Strátos.'

DYSIS

Metellus staggers to his feet in the doorway and falls outside into the arms of his men. They support his weight as he stumbles along the side of the wall, avoiding smoke and heat until they reach the city gate. Beyond it, a roar of flame guards the approach to the harbour.

Metellus shrugs himself upright. Sensation is returning to his body, the heat of the fire keen on his exposed skin.

'Take me down there.'

'We may die in the fire, General.'

'I know this, but today or in three years time is of little consequence to me now. It appears I shall remain unfulfilled whenever, damn that Witch.'

The soldier slowly removes his hand of support. 'If your enemies should share this knowledge, General…'

'They will never know.'

'But should they find out?'

A genial expression flits across Metellus' face. 'I know *I* will never tell them.'

'We swear as one, General. Neither shall we.'

HESPERIS

Metellus' bireme has been moved out into the bay away from the heat to where a small reed boat can be lowered safely from its deck. It sculls slowly towards the end of the harbour furthest from the city where Metellus is helped into it by the soldiers.

'I shall send a boat out into the harbour. If you can reach it you may take it and follow.'

The bireme carrying Metellus makes its way out of the bay.

André and the Doktor wait along the harbour path until they catch sight of two boats entering.

The first is a small landing vessel, towing behind it Sisenna's un-crewed funeral ship. Cast adrift into the wind that now blows from the sea, the funeral ship is taken towards the remains of the fire but it holds off at a distance, entangled in the debris of the bay.

The soldiers shed their leather and weapons onto the harbour path and prepare to swim out.

Archers in the landing vessel stand upright and stud them with arrows.

DYSIS

The cow is in the small outbuilding. There is smoke in its nostrils and fear in its eyes and Strátos is holding it tight to stop it bucking. André approaches them warily. The cow is tethered to the wall behind but anything within reach has been trampled in its anxiety.

'Let the cow go, Strátos, and bar the door.'

'This is now all I have.'

'Then rope it and bring it with you. I need your help. Do you remember the day I first came here?'

Strátos holds up the magnifying glass. '*Ne, Kathigitis.* I remember it clearly.'

'Then show me where you first saw me.'

'It was over that way.' Strátos points to a place beyond the market. 'By the beehives against the outer wall.'

André catches hold of the rope with the cow attached.

'Take us there.'

ARKTOS

In the afterglow of sunset the gate carries a worn and deserted air. The hinges have dropped and it ill-fits against the stone supports.

'How have I missed this, Strátos?'

'It has always been here, *Kathigitis*. But never have I seen it look so old.'

'Perhaps it has been waiting a long time for me.'

'Shall I go first?'

'No, Strátos. This leads to a place where you cannot be.'

André slips out of his blue robe and hands it to him.

'You have a job to do here.'

'My work, *Kathigitis*?'

'Find Minerva's daughter and keep her safe. I need you to grow into this robe and become the man I know you are, then make sure Minerva remains undisturbed until people have forgotten she ever existed.'

'Then I will return this.'

Strátos hands André the magnifying glass. The ivory handle is recently heat-scorched and he points it out.

'*Signómi gi aftó*. I know it belongs to your *patera*. If you were *patera mou*, I would want you to keep it while you live.'

André smiles and tucks it into his shirt pocket as he opens the gate. '*Antio sas*, Strátos.'

'*Antio sas, patera mou*.'

'Wait…' André turns Strátos around and lifts the hair at the nape of his neck. What he finds there brings a wry smile to his face.

He takes the magnifying glass from his pocket and presses it into Strátos' hand.

'*Oche*, Strátos… *Antio sas… patera mou…*'

CHRONICLE

XV

REVERBERATIONS

2006

**JUNE 24th.
SATURDAY**

11:42 A.M.

'Why does this camp suddenly reek of goats?'

Alec lifts his arm. 'Sorry, Manon. That might be me.'

André is silent by the dead embers in the hearth. In his hand is his father's magnifying glass that he has carried in one pocket or another since he was thirteen.

The ivory handle is charred along one side. He rubs the old stain absently. For the first time, black carbon transfers to the pad of his thumb.

'André? Are you okay?'

He shakes his head. 'Sorry, Manon. I will be. There are plenty of other tragedies you can sympathise with around here.'

Fabrienne gets to her feet and strides off along the road towards Potamos. André climbs slowly to his feet to follow.

She spins around to confront him. 'Of which tragedy are you most afraid?'

He drops his hand away. 'Should I be afraid?'

She turns away. 'Yes. You should.'

'Of what?'

'Have you not listened? Are you not aware of the responsibility that I contain?'

'It will also be *my* child. I have no greater responsibility.'

'She is not just a child.'

'*She..?*'

CENTRE HOSPITALIER DE MONTFAVET
2 AVENUE DE LA PINÈDE
84140
AVIGNON

2006

JUNE 19TH.
MONDAY

4:10 P.M.

'Mme Merle? Mme Merle, wake up. You have a visitor.'

Mignon stirs fitfully but finds it difficult to lift her head from the pillow.

The sedation keeping her functions stable is giving her liver the time it needs to complete the healing process.

Her lips feel like two feather pillows. She struggles the words past them. 'Is it… Fabrienne?'

'No, Mme Merle. Like I said, you have a visitor.'

The nurse helps Mignon into a more vertical position.

'Why isn't it Fabrienne?'

The nurse leans over and tucks in the sheet.

'I haven't seen your daughter since we told her you were expected to make a full recovery. If she was my daughter I'd give her a slap.'

'Is it Oriel? … I mean… Mme Beaufort?'

'No… it's a nun. And I had to make her wash her feet before I would allow her anywhere near you. Filthy, she was.'

'I don't…'

'And neither do I. Silly things… wasting their lives… and this one was filthy… like I said.'

Mignon collapses back against the pillows. 'I only ever knew one nun.'

'I'll show her in… but only for a minute, mind.' She tugs a crease from the folded corner of the sheet. 'Not that *they* ever listen.'

Somewhere outside the open window is a movement of vehicles, a ghost-like whisper of spent diesel oil filtering the curtains. From down the corridor comes a recurring bleep. It becomes a single line of sound before becoming a screech in Mignon's head.

A cool hand is placed gently on her forehead and the growing anxiety ebbs away.

'Mme Merle? May I?'

The nun indicates a wish to sit beside her on the bed.

Mignon nods willingly. 'But the nurse will say no.'

'I think the nurse has other things on her mind at the moment.'

Mignon studies the face within the coif for some small recognition or a shard of memory… but there is nothing… except…

'I saw from your look that you were wondering… but you do not know me. I am Sister Acéline…' She waves away the question in Mignon's eyes. '…but that is not important. What is… is this.'

She takes a letter from a fold in her dark brown habit and offers it to Mignon. Mignon instinctively shies away.

Acéline holds it out between fingers that are slender but calloused from working the soil in the Abbazia garden.

She had no idea why she'd been given the task. Until the moment she had walked into this room.

'It is only a letter.'

Mignon settles back into the pillow and turns aside.

'You have no idea how much heartache can be written on one small piece of paper.'

'Mme Merle,' Acéline lowers the letter to the sheet and allows it to lay there. 'I have not read this letter… although I know from where it comes and by whose hand… and so I cannot imagine that it contains anything other than love and salvation.'

She sits further onto the bed, bare feet swinging clear of the hospital floor.

Mignon notices she has good ankles… consistent and parallel. She watches the hand that approaches her forehead. It is worn… but perfect. The fingers caress her brow. A cool certainty washes away the anxiety rising in her skin.

She allows her own fingertips to rest lightly on the letter. For a moment they are content to lie there.

'Mme Merle?'

Mignon pushes her fingers onto the paper, obscuring her name marked there by an ancient hand.

'Mme Merle, can I help?'

Sister Acéline reaches for the letter but Mignon covers it with the flat of her palm.

'No.' Her fingers turn it over. She holds it close to her eyes to examine the seal. 'I don't know anyone in Italy. I no longer know anyone… anywhere.'

She allows the letter to fall from the bed.

Acéline pushes it back under her hand.

'Maybe not, but people know you… and I know that you are loved. I think there is nothing you need fear from this letter.'

She leans across the bed to kiss Mignon's forehead. Her breath flows cool and clover-scented… the skin of her cheek is the palest honey.

Reassured, Mignon slides her finger under the seal.

It parts so easily.

She unfolds the paper…

Abbazia di Novalesa
Alta Val Susa
Piedmont
Italia
June 16th. 2006

My Dearest Mignon

I call you 'Dearest Mignon' because you are the dearest thing on Earth to me. You are the only child I ever held in my arms. Since that day, my shadow has never left your own.

As you read, I will try to answer the question that poses.

Firstly, I would ask you to be gentle with the Sister who has brought this letter to you. She does not know why she was sent, so I will say this only to you. She is a hard worker but in the past has lacked humility, thinking herself above all things, but within that pride I found a certain ability of persistence that reminds me so much of your mother I was left with no better choice. If you are reading this letter, I know you will have experienced that ability.

Your mother was brought to stay with us by Doctor Beaufort at the tender age of fourteen. I have tried to be annoyed with her and have consistently failed. One memory of Oriel's sweet face and I am consumed. As was Artus, your father. From the moment they met, under circumstances which I shall explain when you arrive, their destinies were inevitable and if they were guilty of anything it was an inability to wait. Such is Love.

We made every effort to encourage your mother to commit to the sisterhood but the sheer gravity of Artus' star was more than the combined endeavour of the entire Abbazia. It broke Madre Honoire's heart when Oriel returned to La Roque, despite her vow never to marry Artus while Honoire was alive.

My only wish is that the letter I sent to her in that respect had been in time to bring her the happiness she had grown to deserve.

327

I have known every move you have made since the day I oversaw your adoption. Madre Honoire appointed to me that task in the full knowledge that it would disabuse me of any prideful thoughts I may have possessed. In that, she was right. The hardest thing I ever did was letting go of your perfect little hand.

There is a thing I may tell you that I thought Madre Honoire never suspected. In my pocket I have a corner that I secretly snipped from your blanket. While I was clearing away after Madre Honoire's death, I found one in hers, too.

I have been responsible for each move you have made... every fresh foster home when they became too uncomfortable... and if you wish to blame me for that then I shall be pleased to hear it from your own lips... if you also recognise that they improved over time, then I shall be happy with that... but when you met and married Chrétien Merle, all I could do was stand and watch in silent anguish.

My position would not allow me to interfere in the sanctity of marriage vows made before God. All that was left to me was to besiege Santa Teresa with earnest prayer until at last She sent you her Angel.

I am told that you are expected to make a full recovery. Sister Acéline has been instructed to await your release from Hospital and to accompany you to the Abbazia.

Once here, you may stay for however long you need to effect your convalescence, or until you tire of being regaled with my stories of your wonderful, beautiful, Grand Mère... whose life I miss more than my own life itself... my dear Sister Minette.

The saviour of our order, Santa Teresa De Ávila, once said that she had 'little more to work with than two ducats and God'. I now have only one... until I hold you again in my arms,

Madre Mirais

Mignon folds the papers together to slip them back into the envelope. The seal now feels clumsily hard between her fingers. Sister Acéline is watching her face for an answer.

'You know I cannot go.'

Sister Acéline takes the letter from Mignon's hand and places it on the bedside table.

'I only know that unless I can convince you to return with me, I shall spend my life in eternal penance… and *Ave Maria* shall become the only words to pass my lips for time without end.'

'I have to wait for Fabrienne. She must know where to find me… she is all I have left.'

Acéline places her fingers either side of Mignon's brow, watching the eyes clear as her anxiety drains away.

Mignon drifts into complete relaxation.

Acéline smiles in recognition of the grey-blue iris with the small green fleck that she sees reflected in the still water of her own basin each morning.

'Fabrienne will always know where to find you… and she is safe. One of our Sisters is keeping her *very* close.'

2006

JUNE 26th.
MONDAY

10:35 A.M.

'I can not do. You too old.'

'You took my money, Fuentes. Was that too old?'

'*Mira!* I make a promise I do not see. For now I see no money.'

Frank spins gracefully on one heel as if to walk away. His hand drops fleetingly into his pocket then out again.

He holds out an empty palm. 'How did you get the rig… and the boat?'

'They here… and Jorgé… he see to…'

'And the plane fare?'

'I no care. I no live on plane fare. You be quick. Ferry boat is still here.'

Frank slides his hand into his coat pocket. When it reappears it holds a clip of Euro notes. He counts them slowly into Fernando's hand until a smile appears on his face.

Fernando hesitates, staring at the pile of notes, then folds them across his palm and stuffs them back into Frank's hand. 'If I do this thing I kill you.'

'Eight years ago, my friend, an old acquaintance of mine spent nine days circling the earth in a space shuttle. Now I can't claim him as a playground buddy, he's a while older than me, but for a time back there we shared a different kind of playground. Know what I mean?'

'So where is your medals?'

Frank's hand slides back into the pocket.

'I'm waiting to pin them to your chest.' The hand lifts something small and black almost into the light. 'Would you like to see the pin?'

Fernando takes a step back. Frank holds out his other hand, palm up. 'Whoa, boy. Don't you shy on me. I'll have you broke and saddled before you take another step.'

Fernando stops, relaxing a little as he notices the truck rolling quietly across the harbour apron towards them.

Frank turns as André climbs out of the passenger side. Another glance finds Jorgé behind the wheel, gripping it tightly.

'Looks like we got company, Fuentes. That's good. I'm always a gentleman in company. You'd best to remember that. So introduce me.'

'Hi, Fernando. Found yourself another fight?'

'Hell no, Mister..?'

'Professeur…'

'Ok… *Prof.* We were just re-affirming the terms of our charter, here.'

'You chartered Fuentes? You must have a sense of humour.'

Frank looks away to stare Fernando in the eye. 'Do I need one, Fuentes?'

Fernando shakes his head and begins to throw the refilled bottles into the bottom of the rib. Jorgé puts the brake on the truck and climbs down into the boat. The next air bottle knocks him flat on his back.

Frank extends the handle on his case and catches André by the elbow.

'Let's leave these girls to get settled. Where can I buy you a drink around here?'

André removes the fingers from his arm. 'You can't.'

GALANIÁNA CAMP

11:16 A.M.

'How come you got to bring the truck back, Boss?'

'It's only until the next boat, Alec. I said you'd go around and pick up all the rubbish.'

'Another bad smell is all I need. Thanks, Boss.'

André strides off towards his tent.

Veronique appears from between the guy ropes with a bucket of honey crystals from the sarcophagus.

'What's eating him?'

'Hadn't noticed anything was.'

'The moment he saw me…'

Alec snatches the bucket from her hand.

'Then shut your mouth and learn the lesson.'

12:40 P.M.

A battered old pickup slows to a halt some distance from the camp. An easterly wind sends the dust skittering towards the dig site. Frank waits until it passes before alighting from the cab. The driver immediately reverses back along the road. Frank turns and holds up his hand but the driver ignores him. The truck spins in the end of a simple pathway and speeds off.

With a glance at the high sun, Frank takes off the coat and slings it over his arm.

'Were you expecting anyone, Boss?'

André rises to his feet. 'No, Alec. Least of all him.'

Frank crosses the last hundred yards with ease.

Alec gets to his feet beside André and waits, his features unusually passive.

'Hi. I'm Frank.' Frank holds out his hand but no-one offers to take it. 'I want to ask you about Fuentes.'

André dismisses him with a gesture. 'Whatever you have going with Fuentes you can leave me out of.'

'Now I heard you might have a certain… sphere of influence… with our mutual friend.'

'Then you heard wrong.'

Frank hitches his coat over so that the side pocket is in easy reach. 'Well… I guess that's where you and I agree to differ. See, I think you have some kind of a relationship thing going there…'

'It died with my wife.'

Frank shrugs. 'You want I should empathise here?'

'I want you to leave. We have nothing for you.'

'*Au contraire*, my friend, *Au contraire*. There is more here for me than you can imagine. Sit down.' His hand slides into the coat pocket.

André takes a step forward.

Alec catches his arm to hold him firmly in check.

'Let's just sit a while and hear what he has to say.'

He drags André down to the camp-chairs behind them and kicks over a stool from outside Manon's tent.

Frank rights it with one hand and sits down. 'Let's talk about Fuentes…'

'That's not why you're here…'

'Alec… let's hear him out, you said, and then he can leave.'

'He won't leave, Boss. Not until he finds what he thinks we have.'

'Boy's got a point… *Boss*. Fuentes is only one means to an end. In my book, there are several. I don't care which one I follow first. Right now I'll settle for talking to a little bird.'

Alec glances at André's watch and pushes around the kindling in the hearth.

'And what will the little bird tell you?'

'Whatever she knows. She may hesitate… but she will.'

'And you've no objection to us eating while we wait?'

'Go right ahead. Might even have some myself…'

Alec turns away to reach into his tent, pulling out a few selected tins. 'You need both hands to do that.'

With Frank watching him carefully, André tries to calculate the situation in degrees of survival… whatever happens, he will not allow this man to bring harm to Fabrienne… he catches his thought… or anyone else here for that matter.

Frank stirs on the campstool, stretching out one leg in front of him, massaging a knee with one hand.

'When it's real quiet like this…' He smiles across the hearth at André. 'I can even hear your thoughts creaking. If you think you're fast… go for it… but in terms of speed I can tell you… *Boss*… that you ain't seen nothin' yet.'

Alec fumbles through his pockets before putting a light to the kindling. Smoke swirls the air between them. André's eyes are shifting… constantly reassessing.

'He's right, Boss.' Alec throws a spoon to André. Frank snatches it from the air between them without looking. 'Sit back and chill.'

André stares at him through the smoke.

Alec throws him another spoon. 'The others will be back in a few minutes. Manon won't be able to resist the sight of the smoke, no matter what she says about my cooking.'

André eases his chair back from the fire. 'No chance of stopping them?'

'I'm a lot of things, but not Canute.'

Frank drapes the coat across his knee and takes a handkerchief from the pocket. 'I see you girls have a thing here.'

Alec empties three cans into a large pan. 'It's what keeps us going. Digging all day gets boring.'

'As long as you don't dig too deep.' Frank wipes his

forehead with the handkerchief. 'That's when it gets exciting.'

'And you'd know all about that…'

An expression flickers between them. 'And how would someone like you know?'

Alec stares him in the eye for the briefest of moments.

'I recognise the sign.'

12:57 P.M.

Manon arrives with Veronique, sharing the bucket handle. Fabrienne is half the slope behind them, having stopped to rinse the dust from her hair.

'We have company?'

'Manon, sit down.' One glance at Alec's face and she does as she is told. Veronique puts the bucket beside the fire and makes to head for the latrine.

'Hold on there, Missy.' Frank raises a hand to stop her as she brushes past him. 'Go and sit with your friend over there.' He indicates where André sits perched on the edge of the chair. 'We don't have a full complement yet.'

'But I need…' One look from André quietens her. She crosses the hearth to sit on the floor beside him.

She insinuates an arm around his leg. He brushes it aside, but she replaces it just as quickly when Fabrienne appears between the tent lines.

'Now we have the little bird. When I've heard her sing you guys can get back to your lunch… or whatever that is.'

Alec relinquishes his seat and insists Fabrienne into it. He takes another one, close beside Frank.

She grips the chair arms until her knuckles bleach white as bone. 'Why are you here?'

Frank slides a hand into the coat pocket. 'You know why I'm here.' He flicks a piece of paper onto the earth between them.

Alec picks it up and unfolds it. On the paper are two

perfect arcs. Between the top is the word. '*Oriel*' between the bottom is the word '*Artus*' and in the centre…

'My mother.'

'You drew this?'

'Yes. Many years ago…' She glances quickly at André.

'…before my life began.'

Frank draws in his knees so that in one fluid motion he can move. 'Then it seems I have the right little bird. All that remains is to hear you sing.'

'What song would you like?'

'Hold on a minute…' André slides to the edge of his seat. '…you know this man?'

Fabrienne sits back into her chair. 'I'd like you all to meet The Tooth Fairy.'

Manon pokes around in her back teeth with a finger.

'Then I reckon he owes me twenty centimes.'

'This fairy doesn't give you money, Manon. You'll find death, pain and destruction under your pillow when this one leaves. Ask my brother, Raoul…'

'Now there was a good old boy. Had something… but he just wouldn't…'

'And my *Grande Maman*?'

Frank shrugs. 'The strong do what they must.'

'Even to old ladies?'

'Even to young ones. That Marilyn turned out to be a false start. She had all the attributes but none of the sense. It was driving her insane. I was a blessing in the end.'

He turns away from Fabrienne's incessant stare.

'Sometimes I wonder if you people know what keeps you safe in your little boxes at night. If you did, you'd never sleep again. An old friend of mine, God rest him, used to say that we were like 'royalty travelling incognito through a semi-conscious mist'. Never was sure about the last bit but there you go… that was Howie getting all poetic on me.'

Alec reaches over to stir the food that is sticking in the pan. "Evil sometimes seems good to a man whose mind a god leads to destruction.' "Antigone."

'Thanks for the history, young man, but *here endeth the lesson.*'

André shifts his feet onto the front rail of the chair where it presses into the earth. A slip of even one foot could be fatal.

'What do you want from Fabrienne?'

Frank glances around the group, flicking from one individual to another. 'You guys don't even know what you have here.'

'We have a friend…'

'To die for? Who's the volunteer? Anyway, it's not her I want. She has a parcel for me. I'll take it and go.'

'I think you can just go.'

'Sorry, Prof. Not without what I came for. Oh…' he stares directly across at Fabrienne. '…and the key you made.'

'I made no key.'

'Now, like I said about Raoul… and you got no idea how extreme the provocation that boy could take… but in the end you'll only have yourself to blame. Should've known better than to confide your little secrets to *Professeur* Henri. What was that about? Pillow talk?'

André's anger deepens at the thought behind that last comment. He fights hard to keep it from showing but Frank reads him in an instant.

'Oh… I see now. Didn't see that one coming. Our little bird here sure pulls people in. You're in love with her, too. That Henri told me he got nowhere so put your mind at rest on that one. I'm just pushing. So just you sit still and be pushed. Take that disappointment out of your face. We'll all soon be done here.'

Deep within the timbers of the hearth, the rifle bullet

Alec has slipped into the flames is growing in impatience.

Within the first few seconds the fine coating of grease that had kept it safe in Auguste's workshop for the last sixty two years has bubbled into the embers, adding fuel to the heat growing around it.

André begins his leap from the chair. Frank's hand strikes into his pocket, emerging with a gun.

1:01.0.1 P.M.

The embers settle, bringing the base of the casing hard against the dug-in upright of the iron tripod. Within the centre of the rim, the primer becomes unstable. The bright brass casing that the grease has uncovered glows dully when compared with the breeze-fanned charcoals surrounding it because, pressed inside it, is a one-hundred-and-twenty-four grain, seven-point-nine millimetre Spritzer projectile in a copper jacket with a soft lead nose.

1.01.0.05 P.M.

The chemicals in the centre of the primer oxydate violently under the heat, catalysing the powder beneath the bullet. The tripod leg shoulders the reaction. The bullet, freed at last from the gravity-well of the war for which it was first pressed, leaps through the space beyond the flames.

1.01.0.06 P.M.

With a pre-ordination it could never understand, stripped of any spin that rifling would have given it, its trajectory becomes a straight line towards Fabrienne. She blinks, as if the dropping of an eyelid will deflect this object crossing the slow space towards her. She reaches out but the copper is slick and sheer as if it belongs in another dimension, only the image existing here and now. Her fingers twist and turn around the metal while it continues to flow over her skin. The bullet is dragging behind it a cone of silent darkness that will engulf her forever. She makes one last effort but the bullet is inescapable.

1.01.0.07 P.M.

Another hand reaches out, brushing hers aside. Tiny fingers tease the metal, reshaping the shockwave to re-pattern its future in a way that it is obliged to answer.

The bullet begins to drift.

1:01.0.08 P.M.

The tripod tips, scattering hot food in the direction of Manon. She begins a scream as it splashes across her naked legs. André leaps from the chair. Anchored by Veronique, his leap falls short. Frank continues his aim, pursuing a moment of pure instinct. Fabrienne throws herself across the fire to land on top of André, her bare feet scattering the coals as she waits for the dull impact that will separate her from life.

1.01.5.40 P.M.

Silence falls around them.

Fabrienne opens her eyes.

Frank is on the stool, smiling down at her, gun hand resting on his knee.

Veronique is scrabbling in the dirt at André's feet, her mouth hanging open. Mewling noises are escaping from her, whipped away with the smoking debris from the fire.

Manon is shocked into silence, staring blankly at the heated food covering her legs.

Fabrienne pulls her own feet away from the flames. They

emerge unscathed.

Alec is in the chair where it seems he has been all along. A broad grin flickers in and out of existence as he watches her.

Frank is still smiling as Fabrienne looks up at him. The hand with the gun is implacable in its steadiness of aim. She searches his face for the flicker of expression that will signal the subtle flex of a finger.

Frank continues to smile. His right eye has a slight squint, the way you would centre a distance shot, but the iris of the left has disappeared. From the black hole remaining, a tear of blood emerges onto his cheek.

Fabrienne searches beneath her into André's shirt to find his life still pulsing under her fingers.

1:04 P.M.

Manon is brought abruptly aware as Alec sluices the food from her legs with the water bucket. 'It seems I have a new signature dish. 'Death by Lasagne'.'

Fabrienne bends to examine Manon's skin. 'You've tried with everything else…'

André is walking away from the hearth, fingers pushing vehemently through his hair. He has done this several times now, taking around ten steps before spinning on a heel to come back and squat down, staring up into Frank's smiling face. 'I don't understand…'

'It's called 'Providence', Boss. It can't have you expiring before your star arrives.'

Across the hearth, Fabrienne is gently stroking Manon's shin, looking for blisters, the heated skin cooling under her touch. André pauses to study her.

'I think it may have its work cut out.'

Manon's hand stops Fabrienne's. 'I hoped for a minute.'

'What did you hope?'

'That it had made me perfect… like you.'

Alec's shadow falls across her as her eyes close.

'One perfectionist is enough, thank you. The food wasn't even hot.'

Manon's eyes snap open. 'Then perhaps we've been missing a trick here. Instead of eating it we should have just thrown ourselves under it…'

'Anything that makes you feel at home…'

'Leave it, you two. What do we do about him?'

André nudges Frank, who slides gracelessly from the stool into the dust. 'Am I the only one here who cares about the consequences?'

'What consequences, Boss? Guy comes along here… obviously in distress… everybody knows he was arguing with Fernando… and decides to shoot himself in the eye. What are we supposed to do about it?'

'How very convenient, Alec. But he never fired a shot.'

Alec wraps his hand around Frank's and fires a bullet into the hearth, spraying the air with hot ash.

1:58 P.M.

'… and I never get chance to give back his money.'

'Shame on you, Fernando. What about his wife and kids?'

'*Es verdad*, Alec. Perhaps they pay me extra *para el favor?*'

'Only if you own up to killing him. Might save the rest of us a lot of trouble…'

Frank's body lies sprawled across the bed of the waste truck, the small pistol tucked neatly into his hand.

Alec had searched amongst the remaining coals for the old rifle shell case, dipping it in the bucket before throwing it to Fabrienne.

'For luck…'

She had slipped it back into her rucksack.

'By the way, I also borrowed this.' Alec hands over a large wrought iron key, blackened by fire. 'I've been trying to work out how to give it back without seeming dishonest.'

'That depends on what you were going to do with it.'

'I was intrigued by it, that's all. The weight of it alone says it's important… and the workmanship. What on earth does it fit?'

Fabrienne takes it from him. Her hand wraps around it, taking some of the char into the whorls and grains of her fingertips.

'Something you've been trying to unlock ever since I came here.'

'What's that?'

'My History.'

2:12 P.M.

'I never see this man before the other day.' Jorgé looks

up from his study of the body in the truck. André riffles through the papers in the coat pocket. 'No real ID, apart from the passport.'

'What is his name?'

'Why would you want to know that, Jorgé? You'd do well to keep your nose out of this. I can handle the trouble. I have witnesses…'

'Fernando says I take this man's money for charter. I want to know if this is him. He contacted me by email to come here to learn to wreck-dive. He said nothing about shooting himself.'

André flicks open the passport. 'His name is Frank. Does that ring any bells?'

'No… no. This guy… his name was… *Henri*. Wait. I have the name on my boat.' Jorgé rushes off to return with a printed webpage. He pushes it into André's hand. 'Do I got that right?'

'Yes, Jorgé. You certainly do…'

A small boy tugs at André's pocket. He stares down into a gap-toothed grin, reaching into his pocket for a coin.

The boy ignores the half-Euro and continues to tug.

'*Kathigitis..? Kathigitis..?*'

'*Ne…* I am *Kathigitis. Parakalo, ti theleis?*'

The boy points towards the bar. '*i giagia mou!*'

André spins around to see the old woman from the bar walking with precision across the harbour towards them.

In the sunlight, the frailty of her bones beneath the black shroud shows white at her ankles and wrists. Her face is a collapse of fine shadows beneath a hood of shawl. Her right fist is clenched tightly before her as she approaches.

She pushes André and Jorgé aside with withering glances. Alec waits at the foot of the truck. The old woman stares at him until he too is forced to turn away. She reaches over the side to study Frank's face. She turns it towards her, studying the grimace of his death smile. She opens her fist. Inside it is a small, pitted black olive. She pushes it into Frank's left eye where it neatly replaces the missing iris.

With the brine coating her palm she brushes away the tear of blood. Her fingers reach up and hold both lids until they stay closed.

She speaks slowly to the boy before setting off back to the bar.

'*i giagia* say…' The boy rubs his eyes with the heels of both hands, as if to shake loose the smattering of language behind their lids. '…say come.'

He points to the body in the truck. 'Say he come too.'

2:18 P.M.

The bar is darkly shuttered against the sun.

The old woman has cleared away a table from the corner and has pushed aside the wooden stools that normally clutter the floor. She motions them with a formidable grace to sit Frank's body by the corner on a seat built into the thick walls. Nudging them aside, she replaces the table in front of him and bangs shot glasses down onto the hard wood. She splashes them liberally with ouzo.

The boy tugs again at André's pocket. '*Trink… Giagia sas thelo trink…*'

Alec pulls up a stool and lifts a glass to Frank's body. 'Bet he never expected a wake.'

André hears the ship's klaxon sounding across the bay.

'With all the excitement I'd forgotten what day it was.'

'That's what's called a 'senior moment', Boss.'

'And I'd like the chance to have many more, Alec, so how do we get around this?'

'Leave it to Providence.'

The old woman taps the table by Fernando and Jorgé. '*Adeia!*'

The boy takes their glasses away. *'Giagia sas thelo* leave.'

She follows them out across the jetty, her footsteps as precise as before, her hands sweeping them away from the approaching ship and towards their rib.

Fernando hesitates for a moment beside the truck, then holds out his hand for Jorgé's boat keys.

The rib's engine fires unevenly while Jorgé casts off. An inch of throttle blends it to a soft burr across the bay.

3:02 P.M.

The boy stands beside his grandmother, holding tightly to her hand as the ramp grinds up the concrete towards them. André watches them from the doorway as they stand, patiently fragile against the bulk of the oncoming ferry.

A reflective green uniform appears amongst the crew gathered at the edge of the steel tongue. The boy releases her hand and runs into the ship where he is caught and lifted.

The Paramedic carries him shoulder-high from the boat to set him down on the concrete. He hugs his mother briefly.

André sees her point back towards the bar. He is caught for a moment in indecision… should he be seen watching?

The paramedic runs back into the ship and returns carrying a case. His mother shakes her head, trying to push the case to the floor but he gently shrugs her away.

André watches him match her steps, small, precise and inevitable, towards the bar.

3:08 P.M.

'I first think archaeologists boring… but you are reason of much excitement here.'

'I hope not.'

The paramedic takes the time to steal a glance at André.

'My mother… I hope she is right about you. Where is the dead one?'

'He is here. In the corner by the window.'

'Ah… such a smile.' He lifts the lid of Frank's right eye, flashes a penlight in it then away again… touches the side of his neck. 'When this happen?'

André finds himself pushed brusquely away. The old woman stands squarely in front of her son, both hands clasped and knotted above her heart.

She speaks rapidly in Greek and then with a large groan, collapses suddenly.

André grabs her from behind to stop her slipping to the floor. The Paramedic peels away his fingers and she stands upright on her own.

He smiles over her shoulder at André.

'Do not worry. I call her 'Greek Tragedy'. It worked when I was ten years. No longer.'

He lifts her face to speak to her. She replies, nodding at Frank's body in the corner, turning and smiling harshly at André.

The Paramedic pushes his bag under the table and sits down. 'She worries about her city. She says if you do not find it… no-one does.'

'We can explain…'

'No, no. Say no more. You know how many times heart attack I see in one year? The Greek diet… she is terrible if you do not grow up with her.'

He pats his own waistline. 'And when you do.'

André picks up a glass of ouzo from the table, swills it around before setting it down again.

'When you have finished here… I have something else you ought to see.'

4:02 P.M.

'She was… is… beautiful.'

André leans over the box beside the Paramedic, looking for something he might have missed… and finds it. The honey in which she has been embalmed has achieved total fluidity since her exposure. The lines in her face are flowing outwards, leaving behind the planes of her skin as soft… the arc of her cheekbones as delicately pronounced… as he recalls.

He looks around for Fabrienne, but unusually she has chosen to remain in the camp with Manon and Veronique.

'How old you say she is?'

'Fabrienne says two thousand and ninety two… give or take the occasional change of Calendar.'

'How does she know this?'

'I'm not sure I'm ready to find out…'

4:09 P.M.

'Come here…'

Fabrienne beckons Manon over to stand beside where she sits. Manon hesitates, but Fabrienne reaches out to the faded denim of the jeans she has worn every moment since the incident by the fire.

'Take them off.'

Manon's fingers push through Fabrienne's hair, drawing her closer. 'I can't.'

She looks up to find Veronique studying them.

'I keep seeing…'

Fabrienne's fingers find the buckle. Manon's hands shake as her jeans are slid past her hips.

She catches Manon's chin in one hand, tipping her face downwards, forcing against rigid resistance. 'Look down.'

'I can't.'

'You can. Open your eyes.'

Sensing Manon's soul is becoming unstable, Fabrienne places a finger in the centre of her trembling forehead.

'Tell me what you expect to see.'

'I expect to see… you.'

'You will have to look inside yourself to find me.'

Fabrienne presses harder with the finger, closing her own eyes. 'Look *now*…'

Manon's breath tears into her throat. She chokes on the inexplicable volume of it, holding it in, allowing it to diffuse amongst the rush of her cells.

Her eyes flash open. Taking her fingers from Fabrienne's hair she runs them along the unsophisticated length of her own shin, experiencing soft, dark hairs.

Within Manon, all sense of self-rejection has flown.

In its place there is a stronger presence. And a decision

still waiting to be taken.

'I am still… me.'

She steps from the jeans and kicks them into a heap by the hearth.

Fabrienne stands and embraces her.

'You always were.'

4:14 P.M.

The sound of feet sliding through the scree comes to them on the breeze.

'André. Come with me… now.'

Veronique's hair is sticking to perspiration on her face.

André has rarely seen such alacrity from her in all the time she has been here. 'I hope this is important.'

She drags him away from the Paramedic to whisper to him.

André pushes her away sharply.

'I said I hoped it was important.'

She takes hold of his hand in hers, brushing their combined fingers through his hair. 'I… I thought it was… I thought that she… they…'

André shakes himself free of her touch.

'It's not important to me what you think, Veronique.'

The Paramedic steps away from the sarcophagus. 'If you need to leave, I also have to get back to the bar. Please let me know when you intend to release her from this box.' He chuckles lightly in an attempt to break the atmosphere he can sense descending around them. 'And also how…'

André takes his hand. 'Thank you. At least now you have seen her I know we're not suffering from some kind of mass hysteria.'

The Paramedic returns the firmness of André's grip. He glances quickly at Veronique in full retreat up the hill.

'No… only one of you.'

4:26 P.M.

Veronique kicks hard at spent embers in the dust around the fire, sending them flying in the air.

'I am going down to the Port with the Paramedic and nothing you can say will stop me now. I cannot stay here.'

They all watch Veronique in silence for a moment.

Alec opens his mouth but, before he can speak…

'No… There is nothing left to say.'

'I was only…'

'Be quiet, Alec.' She shoots a glance at André, whose face remains an example of impassivity. 'I will not stay with someone who accuses *me* of sexual harassment.'

André's face loses some of that impassivity. 'I never said that, but now that you mention it…'

'Be quiet! You *kāfirūn* think you know the way women should be treated, but you know nothing. My father was a *kāfir*. He joked about it after he raped my mother in the camp at Shakila. Said his name meant '*Christian*'. And he was supposed to be protecting her? How Christian is that? And he was French, too. So forgive me if I try to leave here with *some* dignity…'

André offers his hand. 'If there is nothing else we can say… then can we all say goodbye as friends?'

In reply, Veronique throws her rucksack into the footwell of the Paramedic's truck.

The cab door slams shut.

They stand and watch as it gathers speed along the road.

André turns away from the cloud of dust it leaves.

'If you'll all take a deep breath, then come with me, I have something to show you.'

4:47 P.M.

Alec rolls up the canvas cover. The underside is heavy with dew from the now fully liquid honey in the box. He places it on the metal lid they had earlier set aside.

André stands back out of the sunlight to allow them to look more closely in.

'I didn't expect this…'

'I don't think anyone could have, Alec. That's why I brought the Paramedic up here. I was afraid to believe it myself.'

Hesitant at first to touch, then bursting through her fear with unprecedented confidence, Manon reaches into the box to stroke the proud line of nose rising out of the honey.

'She is just like you, Fabrienne.'

Fabrienne slides an arm around her shoulder.

'And she loves you too.'

'I'm not even going to ask…'

'Just believe it.'

GALANIÁNA CAMP

There is a darkness outside, total from the lack of a moon. Invisible cloud coats the more willing stars with a dull rime but inside the tent it is sheerest black.

Fabrienne is enveloped by the cling of fabric… the sleeping bag, unzipped and spread… the harsh mesh net across the opened flap… the fine muslin of the canopy liner, but she can not find her path to sleep amongst the touch of these things.

Her thoughts attempt to make sense of her memories, placing them around her in time as if it were a scent she could follow, like Manon's breath against her neck… the hard skin of André's fingers when he'd touched her cheek… the clarity of the air above the island… a salt wind brushing the feathers of a cormorant… and the quick-flash-silver of a lost fish.

She lowers her hands, leaving behind the suspended muslin only her fingers could have seen… and it feels as though they are still there… the slubs and false-weave beneath her fingertips mingling with memories being drawn up like a fine veil, drawn without conscious wish… or her ability to suppress them.

She reaches up to find these other hands.

They are acquiescent under hers, though now less certain of their direction.

Slowly, she crosses them above her stomach.

The pressure of searching ceases.

The hands within hers are tiny, but warm and still.

They drift Fabrienne's senses onto the path of sleep.

TO SKÁPSIMO
GALANIÁNA

JUNE 27th.
TUESDAY

11:54 A.M.

'Manon, can I have a hand here?'
'It is not usually my hand, Alec…'
'For once… can we have a little less attitude?'
'What do you want me to do?'
'Help me pour the buckets of honey back into the box.'
'We only just took them out.'
'I know, but we are putting her back as we found her.'
'What does the Boss think about that?'
'He agrees with her that it's for the best.'
'With *her*..?'
'Manon… just lift the bucket.'

2:21 P.M.

Fabrienne clears the stone chips from around the edge of the sarcophagus with the tip of her trowel.

'How do you propose we seal it, Alec. There is no cement on the island.'

'We could wait for the boat and order some… but I have a more immediate idea. Jorgé, can I borrow your truck?'

'It is not my truck. I only borrowed it myself.'

'Then you had better drive it for me. I have something precious to carry.'

3:02 P.M.

The bar door is latched and bolted by the time they arrive. Jorgé checks his watch.

'Sieste.'

'We don't have time for sieste, Jorgé. Pass the bucket out of the cab… and throw in some of that rag off the floor.'

Alec strides around the corner of the bar. At the back, a low wire fence encloses an area where chickens scratch and bicker. They shy away as he steps over, brooding into a huddle.

'Good girls… now just keep quiet long enough for me to…'

He fills his hands with still-warm eggs from the roost, placing them carefully amongst the rags. Finding only ten, he steps back over the wire.

'Will that be enough?'

'It's all there is, Jorgé. I can't make them lay.'

'Are you sure? Do you not see the way they are looking at your hair?'

3:42 P.M.

'Careful… keep the yolks separated out. Manon, scrape the other buckets clean. Enough honey is clinging to the sides for what we need. Fabrienne? Have you pounded that rock to dust yet with your little hammer?'

Alec sits on the edge of the stone box, beating air into the egg-whites with a forked twig. The foam stands in peaks as he lifts it out. 'I think that will be enough. Fabrienne… Two handfuls of the rock powder. Manon? Any honey you can give me.'

Reversing the stick he folds and blends until the bucket holds a homogeneous beige substance that supports its own weight.

André's fingers reach in through the sea of honey.

Fabrienne grabs his arm but he shakes her free. Ripples form sluggishly around his wrist as he plunges his arm down into the box. Through the dark veil of the honey, he finds an edge of Minerva's robe. He lifts it, rolling it slowly aside to expose the skin below the ribs on her right. His fingertips trace a small, bloodless slit before moving up to catch the cord around her neck.

He looks up to find Alec watching him. He palms the key and presses the robe back into place, adjusting the edge as carefully as he can.

'I thought… at least we should make sure she looks… properly dressed.' He sweeps the honey from his arm with encircling fingers.

Alec passes him the bucket. 'Trowel this around the edge. It will blend with any moisture condensing under the lid and form an effective plastic seal. If we give it a couple of hours in this heat, we should be able to start refilling the box with loose earth.'

'Will it work?'

Alec wipes his hands on his jeans. 'She will never forgive you if it doesn't.'

'What about the tiles?'

'You ought to have something to show for all your hard work, Boss. I think they have your name on them.'

11:48 A.M.

Fabrienne has refused an invitation to walk down to Potamos Bay to meet the boat. Alone at last, she unwraps the loose bedding surrounding the wooden box. Sunlight beats a slow path through the dark material of the tent, diffused lightly by the muslin liner, but there is enough for her to admire Raoul's handcrafted dials and gearing.

There are no jewels encrusting these carefully marked plains of flat bronze. Graduations and symbols alone adorn the dulled surfaces.

Raoul had told her, 'all that glisters is not gold', and she had thought that was his excuse for a lack of skill.

She inserts the key into the aperture, following the half-twists and turns that take it deeper and deeper into the turning metal. The device resets itself as the key becomes fully inserted. She turns it, faster and faster, feeling nothing.

All sensation this device had instilled in her before is now effectively lost. This may as well be the shapeless lump of metal brought to the surface by Elias Stadiatos at the pivot of the twentieth century.

She is startled by the sudden unfolding of her tent flap and shields the device with her body, wrapping it hurriedly into a parcel of her working clothes.

André reaches around and takes it from her hands.

He unwraps the device, cradling it in his lap. 'So this is what the attraction has all been about. For a moment there, I thought it might have been about me.'

'Why should you think that?'

She takes his breath away with that one simple statement.

He turns the device in his hands, studying the grain of the wood closely. With a fingernail he pops open the hidden catch and peers inside.

'This is almost perfect…'

'How could you know that?'

'Because…' André hesitates, choosing his next words with care. 'Because it reminds me of you.'

'How?'

'Well, it's precise, for a start.' He sits back against the tent wall. 'And it's also perfectly interlocked and, like yourself, perfectly useless without the proper key.'

She lifts the device from his lap. 'Oh. I see…'

He pushes his hand up to his hair. 'And now… so do I.'

Fabrienne reaches out to stop him. 'You do not need to do that anymore.'

He brushes her hand aside. 'I am just checking to see which hat I am wearing. Perhaps it's the *friend* one…'

'No, no… it isn't that…'

'Oh, yes… I remember now…' His fingers track through his hair in defence of the broken habit. 'I left the *lover* one up at the rock some time ago.'

She reaches out to him with the device but he flinches away. 'Don't you want to meet your rival?'

'There never was one. Only one person basks in your affection.'

'The device isn't a person. It is the whole of humanity.'

'Competition I can handle. You, Fabrienne…?'

'Do you not wish to know how special you are? Why *Grande-maman* chose to speak to you?'

'I only wish to be special to you.'

'You are more special than you could ever imagine. There is a chain between us that we cannot deny.'

'But you would wish to…'

'There would be little point trying. We *are*.'

'And is it that simple?'

'Yes.'

'And you feel nothing for this? No love for me? No...' He shakes his head, brushing the muslin with his hair. 'Then where is the point of all these hats I am forced to wear?'

Fabrienne holds up the device between them. 'I have always known which hat you would wear... and when... and now, thanks to you...'

'There is no need for explanation. To you this is the unfolding of a play where you hold the script. Tell me, do I exit stage left... or right?'

'I am sorry to tell you... you have no exit.'

'Then I am trapped on stage.'

'With me.'

The light inside the tent is subtle and André studies her face, attempting to fill the blank spaces of her expression that even sunlight fails to search out.

'I think I need to consider this.'

'What I am telling you is not an option.'

'Then you are as trapped as I.'

'No... I am free. It is my choice to remain with you.'

'Why do *you* have a choice... and I do not.'

'Because you were the key that set me free.'

'And who will do the same for me?'

'No-one who yet lives.'

Fabrienne removes the device from the box and sets it aside. Her fingers lift the key from around her neck and insert it into the side of the mechanism. The dials and cogs spin, seemingly at random.

'There was a time when I could have asked the device for the answer to that question, but since you have set me free there are no answers. If Time is telling me anything... it is telling me to wait. There will be another moment. There always is.'

She spins the key again, ages flashing by described in blinding arcs of moon phases, declinations and shifting orbits. Before the device slows to a stop, the hands she had experienced in the darkness reach out invisibly. She feels them shy away as they touch the device. A chill settles… inches below her stomach… an icicle thrust. She stops the device with a finger and puts it back into the box.

A decision she has been trying to convince herself to make ever since she set foot on Antikythera has just been made for her.

André takes the box and sets it between them. 'Why have I been drawn into the orbit of this?'

'What do you know of gravity?'

'Only that where it applies to two large egos it becomes a fatal attraction. And I do have my own perturbed star…'

'There are many kinds of gravity. Emotional, physical, but these are just subtleties. The main two are Ordinate and Pre-ordinate. The inevitable and the perceived.'

'Then I do not envy your perception.'

'Do you not wish to know who will finally set you free?'

'I had hoped that you…'

'I am no more than a subtlety…'

The heat is building inside the tent as the sun strikes it vertically. The air is thickening with their breath.

André inhales the combination as if it were lifeblood.

This close, Fabrienne exudes an invisible aura… intangible yet infused with great substance… enough to fill any empty space left within him.

He sits up slowly, thoughts rising like the early sun through his canvas, following the line of a question that had formed the day before but that he hadn't found appropriate to ask. Now that Fabrienne was so firmly under his skin, he hoped the attachment would allow him some license.

'Why did you discuss this with Henri Lefevre?'

'It was not 'pillow talk' as you may be imagining. He would have liked it to be, but no. Do you think me so shallow? I only asked that he translate the date for me. The one that Auguste had written on the corner of the paper, 668 *Ab urbe Condita*. Henri said that would be 86BC. He asked why I wanted to know. I told him it would help me decode something of archeological significance.'

'How could you not be aware that the discovery of the Antikythera device was one of his pet obsessions, and that he would immediately recognise the importance of that date?'

'I did not know. I am not perfect.'

'Keep telling us that. One day some of us might believe it.'

'Even if I had known I would not have been concerned. He was never man enough to deflect me from my chosen path. I proved that in the many times I resisted him at Uni.'

André relaxes back onto the sleeping bag, his arms unbinding from the fear he had felt upon broaching this subject, more afraid of her answer than he could have believed. 'So Henri went looking for help.'

Fabrienne watches his tension subside as he lays beside her. She reaches out a hand but doesn't need to touch him. She has already replaced all his old ghosts.

'He looked to the wrong people, it would seem. Are you now satisfied? Am I yet worthy of your approval?"

'I don't know. Tell me why you broke your promise to Raoul.'

'I didn't. It wasn't really a promise because Raoul always knew when I was lying.'

'And he didn't say anything? Didn't take the thing apart so that you…'

'It wouldn't let him. It deflected his thoughts away. It was only when I was around that he became entirely aware of it.'

'I thought you said he felt nothing. It had no effect…'

'That's true. But what Raoul felt was a negation of effect. He could never have recognised it as a withdrawal of his future. How do you detect an absence?'

'That's easy. Just try leaving me.'

'That's not an absence. I am ultimately replaceable. You of all people should know that. What the device showed me about Raoul was a *nothing*. And that was his future.'

André rolls over onto his side, away from the penetration of sun. He knows that his face will be in shadow and in that shade she may not find his age so readily apparent… this ridiculous thing that he feels separates them without ever breathing its name.

'Then why didn't you stay to protect him?'

'The device was showing me a bullet. In my ignorance I thought it was intended for him. I could not physically protect him from it and, no matter what I could have said, Raoul would never have left La Roque. In La Roque he was complete. He was the part of me that meant I could go out into the world without fear.'

'There are ways…'

She places her finger against his lips again. 'And I chose one. I chose to learn… to understand… I worked hard in the hope that I might find a knowledge solid enough that would stand in the way of what I had seen. Why do you think I came to your attention?'

He lifts her hand away, folding the fingers inside his own.

'And how did I come to yours?'

'You are the only man I have ever known who does not think in straight lines.' She lifts a finger to his cheek, tracing a crease that runs from the corner of his eye. 'So why do you worry about these?'

He tries to return the gesture but finds nowhere for his finger to begin. 'Then what a crime that Time is linear, for I find myself looking back at you.'

Fabrienne takes his hand and places it amongst the scar tissue of her back, sensing the warmth of his touch, even the moisture of his skin in a place where she has none.

'Never deny your experience. Time is the price it has to pay to find you. It also makes you more valuable.'

'To whom?'

'Stupid question… to which there can only be one answer.'

She draws him above her, fingertips stroking the birth mark she'd found at the nape of his neck while salving his back, her limbs accommodating him gently, opening a path through which the remains of his fear of age, time and consequence might disappear forever.

For a moment, he breaks free. 'You know my destiny?'

'Yes, but it's a two-millennia story. Have you got time to listen?'

He rolls onto his back, momentarily incapable of words, giving himself entirely into her hands.

She leans across and kisses him slowly, releasing only when she feels the last of the tension leave him.

'I'll make it quick, then. Your star arrives in only seven thousand, seven hundred years…'

'Wait…' He catches her shoulders in both hands and holds her above him. '…which hat did Minerva say should I be wearing now?'

'André… women have always slept with the enemy.'

TO BE CONTINUED

IN

MEKANISMO

JOURNAL
III

OPHIUCHUS RISING

INDICES

Roman Republican Calendar

86 B.C.

Martius: after Mars, the Roman god of war. It marked the beginning of the agricultural season.

Aprilis: possibly from 'aperire,' signifying the opening of flowers in spring.

Maius: after Maia, Roman goddess of growth and fertility.

Junius: after Juno, goddess of marriage and the well-being of women.

Quintilis (July): Meaning 'fifth.'

Sextilis (August): Originally the sixth month.

September: Derived from 'septem', meaning 'seven.'

October: Derived from 'octo,' meaning 'eight.'

November: Derived from 'novem,' meaning 'nine.'

December: Derived from 'decem,' meaning 'ten.'

Prior to the introduction of the Julian Calendar, the Roman Calendar had ten months as above. These totalled 304 days. In order to make the year work, an 'Intercalary Month' was added periodically to align the lunar calendar with the solar year.

This month, known as **'Mercedonius,'** had an uncertain length and was inserted by the Pontifex Maximus (high priest) as and when needed to bring the number of days into alignment with the solar year of 365.25 days.

Hours of the Roman Day

(Horae)

I	hora prima
II	hora secunda
III	hora tertia
IV	hora quarta
V	hora quinta
VI	hora sexta
VII	hora septima
VIII	hora octava
IX	hora nona
X	hora decima
XI	hora undecima
XII	hora duodecima

To distinguish between the day and night hours a preface of either *diei hora*, or *nocte hora* was applied.

Athenian Calendar

86 B.C.

There was no single Greek calendar in this time. All communities had their own, differing from others in the names of the months and the start of the New Year, though all were originally lunar. Months were named after festivals or deities specifically honoured in them. Dios and Artemisios, were named after Zeus and Artemis; Anthesterion at Athens from the festival Anthesteria.

In theory, the New Year began with the appearance of the first new moon after the summer solstice, and the months following that were;

Hekatombaion
Metageitnion
Boedromion
Pyanopsion
Maimakterion
Posideon
Gamelion
Anthesterion
Elaphebolion
Mounichion
Thar-gelion
Skirophorion.

All were named after festivals held in that month. Each month was in length 29 or 30 days; an ordinary year was 354 ± 1, a leap year 384 ± 1 days, inserting a 'second' or 'later' month.

The Athenians did not use any regular scheme such as the *'Metonic Cycle'* in determining leap years.

Athenian Hours

(Kóres tou Chrónou)

Daughters of Chronos

Auge	First light
Anatolê	Sunrise
Mousikê	Hour of music and study
Gymnastikê	Education, training, exercise
Nymphê	Ablutions (bathing, washing)
Mesembria	Noon
Sponde	Libations after lunch
Elete	First of afternoon work hours
Aktê	Eating and pleasure
Hesperis	Start of evening
Dysis	Sunset
Arktos	The night sky, a constellation

True North vs Magnetic North

True north is a fixed point on the globe. Magnetic north is quite different.

Magnetic north is the direction that a compass needle points in as it aligns with the Earth's magnetic field.

What is interesting is that the magnetic North Pole shifts and changes over time in response to changes in the Earth's magnetic core. It is not a fixed point.

At Greenwich, the magnetic North Pole has been positioned slightly to the west of true north for hundreds of years. However its position is constantly changing and soon magnetic north and true north will briefly align.

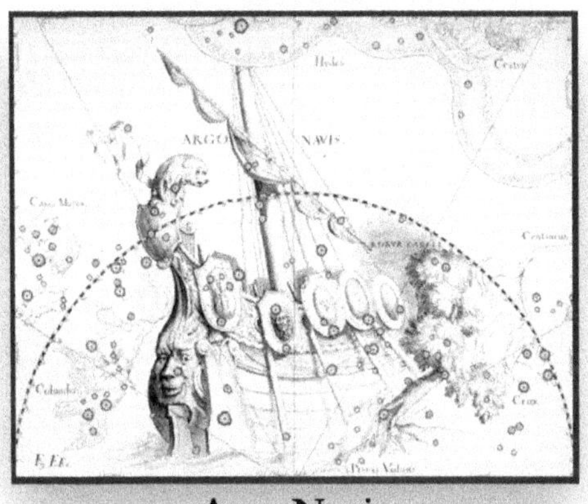

Argo Navis

is one of Ptolemy's 48 original constellations.

Formerly a single large constellation in the southern sky, its attributed origin is the Egyptian 'Boat of Osiris'. It comprised mainly of Carina, the keel, Malus, the mast, Vela, the sail and Puppis, the stern ornament.

Over time, Argo became identified exclusively with the Greek myth of Jason and the Argonauts. In Ptolemy's Almagest, Argo Navis occupies the portion of the Milky Way between Canis Major and Centaurus.

(Image by Johannes Hevelius, 1611-1687)

The Corona Borealis 'Blaze Star'

T Coronae Borealis has been dubbed the 'Blaze Star' but is known to astronomers more simply as 'T-CrB.'

It is a binary system in the Northern Crown constellation some 3,000 light-years from Earth.

The system is comprised of a white dwarf – an Earth-sized remnant of a dead star with a mass comparable to that of our Sun – and an ancient red giant. The red giant is slowly being stripped of hydrogen by the gravitational pull of its hungrier neighbour.

The stripped hydrogen accretes on the surface of the white dwarf until it creates a buildup of pressure and heat. Eventually, it triggers a thermonuclear explosion big enough to blast away that accreted material.

For T CrB, that event recurs, on average, every 78 to 80 years.

The next event is due on or around September 24th. 2024

(Thank you to NASA.)

Glossary:

In France

L'ATELIER	THE WORKSHOP OF…
LA MAISON	THE HOUSE OF…
CHAPELLE DE MAIRIE	CHAPEL OF ST. MARY
L'ANCIENNE CHIRURGIE	THE OLD DOCTOR'S HOUSE
PLACE DU MARCHÉ	THE MARKET PLACE
CENTRE HOSPITALIER	HOSPITAL

Greece & Antikythera

TO LIMANI TOU POTAMOS	POTAMOS HARBOUR
GALANIANA	VILLAGE ON ANTIKYTHERA
GALANIÁNA CAMP	CAMP NEAR RUINED TOWER
TO SKÁPSIMO	'THE DIG'
PERIPATOS AKRÓPOLI	ACROPOLIS PERIMETER PATH
NAÓ PLATEIA	TEMPLE SQUARE
NAÓS TIS ATHINÁS	TEMPLE OF ATHENE
LIMANI TOU ZEA, PEIRAIA	ZEA HARBOUR, PIRAEUS
SIMEIÓ GLYPHADIA	POINT OF GLYPHADIA
LOUTRÓ LEIPSÓ, AEDEPSUS	LEIPSÓ SPRINGS, AEDEPSUS
VRÁCHOS GALANIÁNA	GALANIANA ROCK
AEGILA	ABANDONED ISLAND CITY
TO SPÍTI TOU KYVERNÍTI	THE HOUSE OF THE GOVERNOR
I AGORÁ	THE MARKET PLACE
L'ANNEAU DE LA VÉRITÉ	THE RING OF TRUTH

Afterword:

In the museum at Athens are all the artefacts recovered from the Antikythera Shipwreck of 86 B.C., including the original Mechanism.

I can't really describe how it felt to finally see it.

In all its corroded beauty it hangs behind glass in a clear plastic framework and, for reasons I find impossible to explain, still holds me in thrall, even after so many years.

(I don't have blonde hair, although I do have grey-blue eyes, but without the split iris or green segment. I do, however, have the birth mark…(so read on…))

Getting to Antikythera was a story in itself. The ship from Piraeus to Kissamos on Crete has a scheduled stop at Kythera before sailing on to call at Antikythera.

When I enquired at Piraeus about a ticket to Antikythera, I was told categorically by a Greek with a foul-smelling cigarette hanging from his mouth that under no circumstances would that ship stop at Antikythera. So we booked passage to Kythera, in the hope of getting a small boat the next day to Antikythera.

When we arrived at Kythera it was midnight. That was when we found that the ferry port had recently been moved to a place half-way down the east coast of the island, miles from the town.

Disembarking there with cases, we were reassured to find there were taxis waiting all over the car park.

Gradually, one by one, they all left.

Alone and deserted on a vast new car park, we made our way across to the ticket office/cafe that was just closing and explained our circumstances to a lovely lady behind the counter.

Within fifteen minutes we had a hire car, a splendid apartment in Kythera town, and a man who arrived to hand it all over to us.

The Greeks can be efficient when they try.

We asked our saviour/benefactor why we were told the boat didn't stop at Antikythera. He shrugged and replied that it had always stopped there. What was the problem?

We left Kythera on the midnight ferry the next night. An hour or so later the ship began to slow.

Nerves completely on edge, we watched the hills of Antikythera slide eerily alongside us in the dark. The ship then turned abruptly into Potamos Bay and prepared to make fast in the tiny harbour. The planks clanked down and, as vehicles were being driven on and off, I asked the purser who was stood on the edge of the dock apron if I could at the very least step out onto Antikythera just so I could say I had been there.

I explained why as best I could but language got in the way. I was told strictly that if I set foot off the ship I would not be allowed back on again because my ticket did not include that stop.

The thing that stays with me the most from that night, after the frustration subsided, was the sight of the buildings behind the harbour, exactly as I have described them here in the book. They seemed positively biblical in the dark under sparse, hanging lights.

I took the picture on the rear inside cover.

I didn't set foot on Antikythera until a year or two later.

Our friends at the Hotel Kissamos on Crete made the bookings for us to take the early ship out towards Piraeus and to catch the next one coming back in. They also arranged for a friend of theirs to show us around the island in his car.

His name is Vasilis, which he assures me translates in English as William. So we had an immediate connection.

Vasilis was wonderful. He took us to all the places I had envisaged, even taking me up to the top of the island to his parent's abandoned house where we ended up firing his shotgun at old Feta tins perched on rocks. Another first for me.

Most revealing was the fact that every place I had imagined for this book was instantly recognisable. On my return I made no corrections to it.

Vasilis took us down to Glyphadia Point and showed me where the wreck had been found, just a short distance offshore.

He handed me a few small shards of ancient unglazed pottery which he suggested could be at least two thousand years old.

There were hundreds of them scattered about the small rocky inlet.

Two of them now live on my bookshelf.

As, now, does this book.

I hope it now lives happily on your bookshelf, too.

There is one more thing I might mention. My partner and I began to wonder if both the island and its history were trying to protect itself from us.

Whilst there I experienced an almost ethereal warmth of embrace, despite the harsh reality of the ochre, dusty soil and rocks and abandoned beacon towers, and I remain unconvinced by the argument that what I experienced was just the growth of the novel in my sub-conscious mind.

If it makes any sense at all, it was too 'surreal' to be 'surreal'.

What finally convinced me was that the copious amount of photographs I took while on the ferry and all across the island disappeared without trace in a camera memory card 'accident' after I arrived home.

I need to go back.

I hope you enjoy the story and the places and times it has taken you to.

Bill Allerton

Books in the Cybermouse range:

Bill Allerton;

Novels:

The Fox & The Fish	(ISBN 978-0-9548373-2-7)
Magpie	(ISBN 978-0-9930424-5-4)
Mekanismo Journal I:	(ISBN 978-1-0686097-0-1)
Mekanismo Journal II	(ISBN 978-1-0686097-1-8)

Short Fiction:

Firelight on Dark Water	(ISBN 978-0-9930424-4-7)
A Day for Tigers	(ISBN 978-0-9930424-3-0)
Watch & Wait	(ISBN 978-0-9548373-1-0)

Childrens Books:

Foxes, Frogs and Rice Pudding	(ISBN 978-0-9930424-6-1)
Sir Tingly & The Quest for The Dargon	(ISBN 978-0-9930424-8-5)
The Time Mouse	(He's running late!)

Bryony Doran;

The China Bird	(ISBN 978-1-7392643-2-1)
The Sand Eggs	(ISBN 978-1-7392643-0-7)

Sara Jane Harding

My Brilliant Boobs	(ISBN 978-1-7392643-7-6)

Sylvia Wright;

My Crazy Brain (A Life with M. S.)	(ISBN 978-0-9930424-7-8)

Audio: (Available free on Spotify and all podcast stations)

Urban Tiger Radio (Mature fiction, Song & Poetry)
Urban Tiger Radio Childrens Hour (5 to 12 yrs.)

www.ingramcontent.com/pod-product-compliance
Lightning Source LLC
Chambersburg PA
CBHW042031120726